# VENETIAN BIRD

This meticulously constructed, logical and credible plot is a classic example of the thriller. Edward Mercer, the ageing, self-questioning, unsuccessful English private eye searching Venice for the young Italian Gian Uccello. Adriana who is the wife of an Italian criminal; Rosa Melitus who has had a murky past and is now mistress of a 'House of Accommodation'. The colourful Venetian background is brilliantly drawn and the story unfolds with the speed, realism, excitement and suspense which one expects from such a magnificent story-teller.

# VENETIAN BIRD

# VENETIAN BIRD

*by*

Victor Canning

**Dales Large Print Books**
Long Preston, North Yorkshire,
BD23 4ND, England.

British Library Cataloguing in Publication Data.

Canning, Victor
     Venetian bird.

          A catalogue record of this book is
          available from the British Library

          ISBN    1-84262-165-3 pbk

First published in Great Britain in 1951
by Hodder & Stoughton Limited

Published in Large Print 2002 by arrangement with
The Estate of Victor Canning, care of Curtis Brown

Dales Large Print is an imprint of Library Magna Books Ltd.

Printed and bound in Great Britain by
T.J. (International) Ltd., Cornwall, PL28 8RW

# Chapter 1

As Carlo Boldesca moved across the Piazza San Marco a muzzled dog ran out from the shadow of a café table, barking at the pigeons which strutted about the great flag-stones that lay, lemon-coloured, under the pale April sunlight. The birds flighted upwards in a noisy rush of wings, swinging high above the square as though sucked skywards by some tremendous vortex of wind.

He passed under them, oblivious of the noise and movement, making for the far corner of the square. Hands in his shabby blue jacket pockets, his head thrust forward on his hunched shoulders, he walked with short, impatient steps, as though he were anxious to shake from him the open stretches of the great square.

Turning into the maze of streets and alley-ways north of the piazza, his steps slowly began to slacken. On the little bridge which crossed the canal at the head of the Calle San Giorgio, he stopped, leaning against the balustrade and looking down the street. The sunshine lay warm against the left-hand façade of shops and houses and the air was full of the sweet, thick smells of fresh bread and restaurant kitchens. He rested there, not with the idleness of a man enjoying the coloured and noisy delights of a Venetian morning, but with the uneasy, half-furtive, half-reluctant indecision of a man who, coming so far, wonders if he should go farther.

He turned his back on the crowd passing over the bridge and pulled a newspaper from his pocket. The movement brought the sunshine full on his left cheek which was marked by a deep, curved scar. The paper was the previous day's *Corriere della Sera*. It was folded to the advertisement page and one of the items in the miscellaneous column had been marked with a thick pencil line.

REWARD given for information leading to the present whereabouts of Gian Uccello, last heard of La Spezia area, June 1944, formerly resident in Venice.– Mercer, 13 Calle San Giorgio, Venice.

He nodded gently to himself as he read, and then abruptly slid the paper into his pocket. The reading brought back the resolution which had been dying in him.

A small bare-footed boy came running up the bridge steps, a long loaf under his arm, and calling over his shoulder to someone in the crowd. He collided with Boldesca. The man turned, startled, and with an angry movement seized the boy by the hair, shaking him roughly before releasing him. The boy gave him a cheerful obscenity and scuttled away.

Boldesca went down the steps to the street, threading through the crowd. Near the door of a bakery an old woman in a black dress and shawl, shapeless and tooth-less, held out her hand to him, begging. He frowned at her, but dipped his hand into the pocket of his patched waistcoat and gave her a tattered two-lire note. He passed on, his head turning nervously now and again to mark the street numbering.

Number Thirteen was on the shadowed side of the street, almost at the end. It was a bric-à-brac shop, its dusty windows crowded with loops of cheap beads and jewellery, little replicas of the Basilica of San Marco, postcards and plaster figures of madonnas and saints. Over the door in gold lettering was the name – Alfredo Gostini.

Boldesca stood outside, eyeing the window hesitantly. Somewhere behind him a woman began to quarrel happily with a fruit seller, their voices echoing richly in the narrow chasm of buildings. Boldesca turned quickly into the shop, giving his reluctance no time to form again. It was empty except for the proprietor who was sweeping the floor. The man straightened up and looked at him, leaning on his broom.

'Signore?'

The voice was husky, asthmatical.

Boldesca put his hand into his pocket and pulled out a cheap blue envelope. He held it before the man's face.

'You know about this?'

The proprietor nodded.

'Leave it with me.'

'Signore Mercer doesn't live here?'

'This is an accommodation address.' The proprietor took the envelope and moved around the counter with it. He slid it into a pigeon-hole among the shelves and then came back, holding his broom half-poised, ready to go on with his sweeping. Boldesca shifted uneasily.

'What kind of man is he? Italian?'

'I get paid for passing letters. I don't discuss my clients.'

Boldesca guessed that he would talk if he were paid, and considered venturing a hundred lire. Then he thought of the free day ahead of him, and the prospect of spending money on information when there would be other calls on his few hundreds seemed unrewarding. He turned and went out of the shop.

Gostini went on with his work. He swept methodically, coughing to himself now and again as the dust touched his throat. Finally, with stiff, brusque strokes, he shot the accumulation of dirt across the threshold into the cobbled street. He stood there leaning on his broom and looked casually up and down the street. Boldesca had disappeared. The lips of the man's plumpish face pursed gently and, as he turned back into the shop, he began to whistle softly. A fleshily-built man, the broad tub of his body insecurely perched on short, thin legs, he wore a green felt jerkin with black, full-length sleeves and about his waist was tied a grey apron. He passed behind the counter rubbing both hands over the top of his bald head, fingering the iron-grey tufts of hair above his ears. Reaching up to the pigeon-hole, he drew out the blue envelope. He turned it over curiously, crinkling it with his fat fingers. Then he went through the door at the back of his shop. The room was full of light and movement. Its one window gave on to a canal, and the sunlight on the water outside threw trembling reflections across the ceiling and walls, a series of vibrating patterns which had the effect of expanding the confines of the small, untidy room as though it were some underwater cavern, distorted and striated by jade and pearl shadows.

Gostini threw the letter on to a green-clothed table. Whistling quietly to himself, he set a kettle to boil. When the kettle was steaming strongly he took the letter to it and began to open it. He worked expertly, cocking his large head to one side to prevent the drift of steam and the thin line of his cigarette smoke from moving into his eyes. In a few moments he was reading the letter.

SIR,

Regarding your advertisement in the *Corriere*, I can give you some startling information of the present whereabouts of Gian Uccello which should be worth a lot of money, – say twenty thousand lire. Between eight and nine this evening I shall be on the steps of the church in Campo San Zaccaria.
CARLO BOLDESCA.

Gostini shook his head regretfully. There seemed to be nothing for him there. He took a little pot of gum from the table drawer and resealed the envelope. Then he made himself a drink from a bottle of meat extract and carried it, with the letter, into the shop. Sitting behind the counter, he sipped at the drink, coughing as the warmth touched his throat.

An hour later, Edward Mercer, an Englishman who was staying at the Albergo Adriatico on the Riva degli Schiavoni, came into Gostini's shop. He waited while Gostini served a tourist with a small glass globe which, when shaken, showed snowflakes drifting slowly over a little model of the Rialto. The tourist gone, Gostini nodded at Mercer and reached behind him into the pigeon-hole for Boldesca's letter.

'Is this all?' Mercer asked as he took it.

'That one only, signore.'

Mercer reached for a paper-knife from the counter and slit the litter open. As Mercer read, Gostini began to polish some brass ashtrays. He kept his head down and all he could see of the Englishman was his trouser bottoms and his shoes. The shoes were well polished, but he noticed that they were old and the edge of one of the trouser turn-ups was frayed. He heard the letter rustle as it was put into a pocket.

'Did you see the man who brought this?'

'Certainly, signore.' Gostini breathed heavily on an ashtray and stroked it gently with his rag.

'What was he like?'

Gostini shook his head sadly. 'In a business like mine, signore, it wouldn't be ethical to discuss my clients.'

Mercer smiled and took out his wallet. He dropped two one-hundred-lire notes before the man. 'That should take care of your ethics. Tell me about him.'

Gostini picked up the notes and let his eyes traverse the length of the figure before him.

'He was a working man, wearing a dark blue suit – a good suit once.' His eyes came up and met the other's frankly. 'He had a scar on his left cheek, and from his accent I should say he wasn't a Venetian.'

'I see.'

Mercer turned towards the door. There was a finality about each of his movements and a directness in his speech which gave the impression of a man who knew the exact moment when talk became a waste of time.

'A hundred lire would have been enough,' he said.

Gostini shrugged his shoulders, and when Mercer had gone he went across the shop and began to unpack a crate of plaster-of-Paris figures. Half an hour later the models of saints, madonnas and dancing girls were lined up on the counter and he was busy marking their prices. He had almost finished when two men came into the shop. As he looked up an expression of alarm passed quickly over his face.

''Morning, Gostini.'

''Morning, Gufo.'

The man called Gufo moved over to the counter and dropped a newspaper on it. He was of middle height, and with a strong muscular body shaping from its prime into fleshiness. His hair was darkish and a little thin, and he wore a neat, well-cut, dove-grey suit with a broken red line in it. A dark bow-tie was fastened to his throat like some wide-winged predatory insect. His companion, standing behind him, was an ungainly, under-sized man with a dark-skinned, dull face. His suit hung awkwardly on him, exposing bony wrists. He grimaced a little as he watched the proprietor, the movement showing his gold teeth. There was a gold band around his gaudy tie and a trio of rings bit deeply into the calloused fingers of his left hand.

'How's business?'

'Slow. The tourist season is only just beginning.'

'I mean business.' Gufo fiddled for a moment with the heavy horn-rimmed spectacles he wore and then nodded at the paper. It was open to an advertisement page and one of the items was heavily ringed. 'This kind of business.' Gufo smiled and there was a blandness about him of a man well pleased with his own strength and wisdom.

'What do you and Moretto want?' There was suspicion and nervousness in Gostini's voice as he drew back from the counter.

'We're interested in this Signore Mercer. How many letters have you passed to him?'

Moretto picked up a plaster figure of a Spanish dancer and began to scratch at the gold paint on her skirt with a dirty nail.

'Why should I tell you?' Over his nervousness now was a note of anger. Moretto looked up at him, grinned, and then let the plaster figure drop to the ground. It smashed into chalky pieces. Moretto rubbed his foot among them.

'We want to do business with you, Gostini. Don't make it difficult.' Gufo's voice was gentle, encouraging. Moretto picked up a large cast of the Madonna with a sheaf of lilies in her arms.

'He's had one letter which he picked up half an hour ago.' Gostini spoke hurriedly.

'Sure?'

'Of course. Why are you interested in Mercer?'

Gufo shook his head. 'It's going to be a race which kills you first – your cough or your curiosity. What did the letter say? Who was it from?'

'What do you think I am? I don't read the letters that come here!'

Gufo laughed and Moretto turned the statue upside down and blew smoke into the hole of the base.

'You read every letter that comes through here. Now and again you make something out of what you read. Tell us about the letter and you'll get a thousand lire.'

Gostini watched them. Gufo rubbed one cheek and pouted his lips. Moretto was absorbed in watching the smoke rise from the hole in the statue.

'Three thousand lire,' Gostini said suddenly.

Moretto tossed the madonna into the air. Gostini made an agonised movement forward. Moretto caught the figure as it fell and grinned. Gufo hit Moretto with a sudden viciousness, his fist thudding against the man's shoulder. 'Stop playing the ape,' he said. 'Gostini's going to be sensible. A thousand lire we said.'

Gostini gave in.

'It was from a man called Carlo Boldesca. No address. He's offered to meet this Signore Mercer tonight between eight and nine on the steps of San Zaccaria church. He says he's got some startling information of the present whereabouts of Gian Uccello, and wants twenty thousand lire for it.'

'Describe him.'

Gufo listened attentively as Gostini did so. Then he nodded, picking up the paper from the counter. 'Good. Don't pass any more letters until you've let us see them. Pay him, Moretto.' He moved towards the door.

Moretto dropped a thousand-lire note before Gostini and, as the man reached quickly for it, he hit him with the back of his hand across the flabby pad of his stomach. A wheeze of air retched from Gostini's open mouth and his face whitened with pain. Moretto went to the door, laughing to himself, and as he left he said:

'Keep your mouth shut.'

A few minutes later Gufo and Moretto entered a small bar near Saint Mark's square. Moretto sat down while Gufo went to the telephone. It was twenty minutes before he came back.

Moretto pushed him the drink he had ordered while Gufo was away. 'What did they say?'

'They know the name and the scar. It's his day off and they don't know where he's gone. It's going to be one of those complicated jobs.'

'Who are they?'

Gufo grinned and tossed off his drink. 'I wish we knew. I don't like these jobs at second-hand. Come on. We've got to go and pick up some stuff for tonight.'

## Chapter 2

A screen of potted shrubs, spotted with little red berries, masked the end of the café from the narrow, arch-slung alleyway that led into the *campo*. Edward Mercer reached out his hand and picked one of the berries. He slit it open idly with his thumb-nail and began to count the little seeds inside it. He sat there, slumped in his chair, his trousers rumpled above his ankles, his cigarette burning to waste in the ashtray on the table. He looked bored and indifferent, a man who had been swept through the long, turbulent channels of the day to end up in this quiet, dark-spread pool of night.

A burst of laughter from the regular customers inside the bar made him turn. The waiter at the door was craning his head sideways towards the laughter, a finger fretting at a grease-stain on his lapel. Mercer slumped deeper into his chair. For a moment he envied the laughing group inside the bar. Sitting alone here, watching the steps of the church of San Zaccaria across the square, was making him think about himself. It was a subject which gave him no pleasure, a subject from which at times it was not easy to escape. He sat there puzzling over it as a man caught in idleness sometimes puzzles over a bad joke...

He was a sandy-haired man with a broad, rather bony forehead. His face was long, not unpleasant, but there was nothing about it to attract immediate attention. His whole appearance was indefinite, one of the un-exceptional figures that crowd the streets and pass unnoticed; but isolated from the crowd the anonymity presented to a casual glance began to disappear. One saw that with the broadening of waist and the slight droop of shoulders, which marked approaching middle-age, there was still a prim muscularity, an economical compact of strength and hardness; that the mouth was thin with a faint twist that marked, not merely stubbornness, but a mild humour; that the eyes, the whole expression of the face, were less tired than speculative, and that, although he was not tall, he was by no means so short as one had first imagined. There are some men who, satisfied with their qualities, mark their characters openly by their behaviour, and others who give little since they are still unsure of what lies within them to offer to the world. Mercer was one of these last.

He flicked the mutilated berry from him, watching it drop on the cobbles washed a livid red and green from the coloured bulbs that were strung along the canvas awning of the café. He raised his eyes and picked out, against the lifeless indigo of the sky, the Renaissance curve of the church's pediment, the strong line of an antique bow. Above the main entrance a small light burned in a niche and he could make out the tarnished gleam of a cross and the faint edges of the shallow steps rising to the dark doorway. Third-class hotel and second-class travelling expenses ... he was thinking. It summarised his present position neatly. Placed him perfectly. But he had been in no position to argue. Ten thousand lire a week, and a bonus of twenty thousand if he succeeded – which seemed unlikely. If he made thirty pounds clear out of the whole thing he would be lucky... Something had happened to money since the war. It no longer flowed around tidily like the Gulf Stream so that a man could dip himself out a bucketful now and again. Tidiness and regularity seemed to have gone out of life...

From behind the great bulk of the church, a clock struck the half-hour. Idly, keeping time with the bell, Mercer tapped his spoon against the glass on the table.

The waiter came across to him.

'Signore?' He picked up the ashtray and tipped the litter of cigarette stubs on to the cobbles.

'Sorry, I didn't mean to call you.'

The waiter hung there, bored, hoping for talk to while away the long evening hours. Mercer smiled suddenly, a smile that gave the long features an unexpected alertness and grace.

'You can bring me a cognac. Have one yourself, too.'

'*Grazie, signore.*'

The waiter turned away, moving towards the door. As he did so, Mercer heard a sound from across the dark square – a dry, scraping sound and then a short exhalation of breath. He sat forward, looking across at the church steps curiously. In the shadows

23

he fancied he could see some movement. The noise came again – the unmistakable sound of men's feet scuffling on stone as they struggled. Mercer stood up, and he ran quickly, his body moving easily, a directness and vigour about him which banished completely the indifference of the man who had slumped wearily at the café table. There was a short, bubbling note, broken, desperate, and then cut short. The noise by the church fitted into a pattern of memory that raised an edge of excitement in Mercer as he ran.

The waiter called after him as he swung into the great scallop of darkness under the church doorway. A patch of shadow broke away from the gloom, and on the top step he saw three men struggling. He saw an arm lift and strike. One of the men dropped to the ground and the other two bent over him.

'What goes on here?'

The great volute of the doorway drew up the brief words and rolled them in a succession of echoes. The two men stood up hastily, and he heard one of them swear.

'Signore, signore – what is it?' The waiter came running towards them from the café.

Mercer jumped forward as the two men turned and ran towards the dark shadow of the church wall. His hand caught one of them by the shoulder, but the man spun sideways, striking at his arm and he was thrown against the wall.

'Are you all right, signore?' The waiter came up to him, panting, and reached out a hand to help him up where he had stumbled to the ground. From the far entrance to the square he heard the dying beat of running steps.

'I'm all right,' he said. 'But I don't know about this fellow.' He went over to the still figure that lay in the shadowed doorway. He knelt down at the man's side. 'Let's have some light.'

The waiter struck a match.

'Did you see them, signore?'

'No.'

The man was lying on his side, breathing heavily. Mercer rolled him over gently. Before the match died he had a glimpse of a dark, twisted face, a ragged blood contusion over the right eye, and a long scar on the left cheek. He stared at the still face and for a moment, woven into his surprise, there was an ancient bitterness. Here it is, he thought, the familiar, violent stupidity and sordidness amongst which he found his bread-and-butter. And this time he had imagined he had found a job clear of all that...

The match went out suddenly. The waiter at his side struck another and reached out for a newspaper that lay by the man. He twisted it into a loose flambeau and set light to it. The flames flared unsteadily.

Mercer reached into the man's inner jacket pocket and his fingers felt a wallet. He drew it out, opening it. Inside was an identity card with the name Carlo Boldesca. Mercer put the wallet back. It was what he had expected. He slipped his arm around the man, raising him from the stone slabs. The waiter took one of the man's arms and together they held him upright. He groaned, opened his eyes and made an impatient movement of protest.

'He's coming round, signore…'

They walked him slowly between them to the café and put him in a seat. The man sat there, his head swaying backwards and forward.

'Get him a drink, and don't say anything to the people inside. No need to make a fuss.'

The waiter gone, he leaned forward and spoke very deliberately to the man, emphasising his words as though to an inattentive child: 'We must get you home. Where do you live?'

Boldesca blinked at him and raised a dirty palm to his forehead. He winced with pain and lowered his arm quickly, holding it above the wrist with his right hand.

'Here–' Mercer took the glass from the returning waiter and forced cognac between the man's lips. He spluttered, then still holding his left arm raised it and took the glass, drinking greedily.

'Where do you live?'

The raw cognac sent a shiver through him and he swayed forward. They reached to hold him, but he pulled himself up and said heavily: 'Palazzo Boria ... I ... I'll be all right.' He closed his eyes and leaned back in his chair.

'How far is it?' Mercer spoke to the waiter but his eyes were on Boldesca.

'Some way. Beyond Piazza San Marco.'

'I'll take him.'

'He needs a doctor.'

'He'll be all right when the cognac works.'

'I could 'phone for a doctor...' The waiter hesitated. 'The police too...'

Mercer watched Boldesca's dark face stiffen, and he had the impression that behind the closed eyes the man had now become alert and conscious of them.

'Yes ... the police. They should know.'

Boldesca sat forward, shaking his head as he opened his eyes. He spoke coherently, his voice touching the edge of anger.

'No ... no! I don't want the police. It's a private affair...' The tip of his tongue moistened his lips and for a moment he smiled at them salaciously. 'You know what it is ... there's a woman...'

'How do you feel?'

'Head hurts, but I can manage.' He stood up, holding on to the edge of the table,

27

anxious to leave them.

'I'll go with you.' Mercer was at his side.

The waiter shrugged his shoulders. 'Maybe he's right about the police. But he needs a doctor.'

'I'll get fixed up at home.' Boldesca moved towards the square.

Mercer threw down some money for the waiter and went after Boldesca, holding the man's arm. Boldesca tried to shake him off.

'Don't be a damned fool! You need someone with you.'

The waiter watched them go. He was puzzled, not on account of the assault – it wouldn't be the first time a man was knocked on the head because of a woman – but by the behaviour of the Englishman. Somehow it seemed as though he half-expected the whole affair. Somewhere, the waiter felt, he had missed something. The charade had been played but the word escaped him. He turned back into the café, wondering.

Mercer and Boldesca went through the archway, but in the street beyond Mercer turned him to the left down a passageway that ran towards the Riva degli Schiavoni.

'Where are you taking me?'

'We can get a gondola from the quay. That'll take you up to the Palazzo Boria without walking.' He took a chance on the place fronting the Grand Canal.

'Who said anything about the Palazzo Boria?'

'You did.'

'Never ... not me.' Boldesca tried to break away but Mercer held him easily.

'What's your name?'

'I live up by the Rialto. When we get to the quay I can manage alone.'

'What's your name?'

Boldesca walked in silence for a moment. Once he half-stumbled and Mercer held him firmly. Then very slowly he said: 'Sandro ... Sandro Mercanti.'

In the darkness Mercer smiled without humour.

'You ought to leave the women alone. You were lucky they didn't take a knife to you.'

'One of them did.' Boldesca said it without emphasis. They were at the mouth of the passage now, and before them was the broad quayside bathed with light. A thin movement of strollers passed up and down. Boldesca raised his left arm and Mercer saw, between the fingers of his right hand clutching the sleeve, a slow trickle of blood.

The blood decided Mercer.

'You're coming with me.'

He turned to the left down the quay, taking the man with him. A few steps brought them to the narrow doorway of the Albergo Adriatico. Boldesca struggled but once inside his resistance went from him.

The hallway was empty and smelt of cooking and cheap cigars.

They went up two flights of stairs and along a narrow corridor to Mercer's room. He set Boldesca in a chair by the washstand and then drew the curtains.

'Take your jacket off.'

'Listen, I don't need–'

'Jacket.' Mercer stripped the jacket from him as he sat and then rolled up the left shirt sleeve. There was a wound about an inch long just below the elbow. He held the arm over the washbowl and bathed it. Boldesca watched him uncertainly. Mercer got a clean handkerchief from a drawer. Boldesca winced and swayed a little as the wound was bound, but he said nothing. When the job was done Mercer helped him on with the jacket.

'Here.' He gave Boldesca a cigarette and lit it for him. He went to the bed and sat down, watching Boldesca.

Boldesca watched him, too, sucking nervously at his cigarette, the end fraying into bitter shreds in his mouth. In the quiet of the shabby little room with its walnut furniture and green curtains, he slowly began to see the significance of the incidents of the last hour. The more he thought about it, the more his fear increased.

'You've been very kind, signore. I must go.' He made a movement to stand up, but

30

Mercer waved him down.

'Stay where you are.' He got up and walked to the window, his eye following the faint vine pattern that bordered its curtains.

Mercer turned.

'I want to get this clear. You're not Sandro Mercanti of some address near the Rialto–'

'Then I'd like to know who I am!'

'You're Carlo Boldesca of the Palazzo Boria.'

'You've got something wrong. I'm not well enough to argue. Good night, signore.'

Mercer stood over him and pushed him back gently into the chair.

'What's the matter with you? What are you afraid of?'

'Let me go. I never heard of anyone called Boldesca.'

'You'd do better to pretend you'd lost your memory.' Mercer dropped the letter Boldesca had written him into the man's hands. 'You wrote that to me. I'm Mercer – the man you were coming to meet.'

'I never saw this letter before, or heard of you.' Boldesca looked at him expressionless.

Mercer shrugged his shoulders. 'Let's pretend you *have* lost your memory. I advertised for information about a Gian Uccello. You answered that advertisement. You said you were in need of twenty thousand lire. Don't you still want it?'

Boldesca made no answer but Mercer saw

in the awkward set of his body and the furtive eyes the beginning of a stubbornness which was prompted by fear. Something had gone wrong. Boldesca had been coming to see him, and now he wanted to get away, covering himself with a cloud of denials. Boldesca handed the letter back to Mercer.

'I don't want to know anything about this.'

Mercer turned away. 'So you're not Carlo Boldesca, you're not the man who was meeting me tonight to tell me something about Gian Uccello?'

'No.'

Mercer stared at himself in the mirror of the wardrobe door and, although he never lost awareness of Boldesca behind him, he was absorbed by a passing, larger awareness of himself in a spreading relationship to the things in this room and far beyond it; himself, in a shabby hotel room, dealing with lies and suspicions, playing around the fringe of a man's fear and waiting for the moment to drive it to panic or pitiful confusion, holding down any sympathy or real kindness because they got in the way and would mislead him. How far back in experience had that lesson been learnt? There was this room, and a hundred others like it; this hour and the shadow of a thousand past hours, and the whole of memory framed in a shabby haze of moments he could never forget, with himself caught in the centre of the picture as the mirror now held him, growing older but never less uneasy, the constant distaste of his existence like bile at the back of his tongue. He turned, speaking evenly.

'There's nothing illegal about this. I want to find Uccello for good and innocent reasons. Why have you decided not to help me? Don't you still want that twenty thousand lire? Eh, Boldesca?'

'I'm not Boldesca.'

Mercer's anger showed then in action. He went quickly to the man and put his hand inside his jacket. He jerked the wallet from the pocket and moved back under the light.

'Like hell, you're not!' He opened the wallet and a photograph, loose in one of the pockets, fell to the floor, but he ignored it and pulled out the man's identity card. He held it up.

'Now tell me you're not Boldesca!'

Boldesca came at him, angry and frightened, snatching at wallet and card, struggling with him. Mercer held him off, putting his strength against the man's momentary panic and prolonging the clash with a deliberate callousness. All life was a struggle against the truth about oneself. Let this greasy-haired liar struggle for a while. But almost at once his disgust killed the need for cruelty and he pushed the man away, throwing wallet and card after him.

Boldesca collapsed across the bed, his face wincing with pain, his breath coming in hoarse waves of sound. He sat forward, pulling himself up and swaying. *'Per piacere, signore...'*

Mercer put out a hand to steady him.

'All right... But let's be sensible.'

Boldesca bent forward, elbows on his knees and holding his head.

'Get me something to drink and ... I'll talk.'

Mercer looked at him. The blow and the knife wound had taken more out of the man than he had realised.

'I'll get you some brandy.'

He went down into the hallway and through to the small bar at the back of the restaurant. The barman was leaning on the counter writing a letter. He pushed the paper away, glad to be interrupted.

''Evening, Tio. A large brandy.'

Tio reached up for the bottle of Sarti.

'Why don't they get the bells fixed in this place? No one likes walking from their room to the bar between drinks.'

*'Domani.'* Tio pushed the glass towards him. 'Shall I charge it?'

'Tomorrow, always tomorrow. No, I'll pay.' He handed over the money.

'Take a bottle, signore, and save yourself the walking.'

'It's an idea.' Mercer smiled.

34

He went up the stairs, carrying the glass carefully. As he turned down the corridor a doubt rose in him like a cold spasm, a sensation which had become too familiar in the past few years. He swore softly to himself and hurried forward. The door of his room was open and as he entered he saw that Boldesca had gone. He kicked the door shut behind him.

He walked across to the bed and sat down. Four years ago and he would never have left the room without locking the door, eight years ago and he would have made the man talk first and take a drink afterwards. He drained the brandy and lit himself a cigarette. Lying back on his bed, his feet on the low rail, he felt suddenly cold and very much alone in this small, shabby room. Each job he found seemed to bring rooms that grew smaller and shabbier. One day, in a room like this, he would quietly and, if he were lucky, with the warmth of a passing brandy still touching his throat, subtract from the great sum of shabbiness and shame his own little fraction of unpleasantness. He rolled over and with a casual accuracy pitched his cigarette into the dirty water of the washbowl. The movement released him and he sat up, annoyed and amused by his self-pity.

He slid off the bed and moving to the square of rug by the wardrobe picked up the photograph which had fallen from Boldesca's wallet. Back on the bed, he held it up to the small overhead light.

It was a woman, head and shoulders, dark-haired and smiling. He dropped the photograph to the bed and lay looking at the cracked ceiling and the opaque bowl of the light pendant, its curdled whiteness blotched with dark blurs of the dead flies and moths collected within in.

## Chapter 3

Towers and domes and the baroque lines of palaces traced a black and gold edge against the pale sky. Not a ripple touched the water of the great lagoon. Steamboats and launches slid away to the distant line of the Lido and against the warm, grey flank of the quay, the gondolas lifted their black necks and stared like grotesque sea monsters towards the space before San Marco where the pigeons paraded with a delicate, measured stiffness. The lion of Saint Mark on his pillar raised a pontifical paw towards the gilded horses above the far basilica and ignored the thin drift of people below.

A street photographer in a white beret, grey suit and flaming red tie, his Leica held before him like a prayer-book, half knelt to take a shot of a passing couple. He handed them a ticket and in a gay, rich voice made a comment to them that brought a blush to the girl and a laugh to the man with her. Waiters set out their tables, hopping about like restless magpies, office girls waggled their rumps and smiled as they crossed the piazzetta, and the balloon man at the corner of the Ducal Palace lost a red balloon. It sailed away across the mouth of the Grand Canal, above the steel-grey line of corvettes anchored off the Dogana, and Mercer, sitting on a stone bench under the Ducal Palace arcade, smiled as he listened to the balloon seller pour out a friendly profanity on his own clumsiness and the twenty-lire loss.

Mercer's self-anger at letting Boldesca get away from him had long gone. It was a mistake, but not an important one. If the man were still afraid, he would have to find means to overcome that and get him to talk.

The business of Gian Uccello, even though it represented his board and lodging and his cigarette and wine bill for the past three weeks, and may be for the next few weeks to come, raised no enthusiasm in him. Enthusiasm in his work came rarely and more often than not brought disappointment. Nevertheless he had his job to do. He was going to the Palazzo Boria to see if he could find Boldesca. The hotel porter had told him where it was.

But first he had called at the accommodation address on the chance of there being more replies to his advertisement. The three letters he had received there were in his hand now. One was ordinary, a letter from a Milan agency offering to trace Uccello for him, and quoting their fees. Professionally, he decided, they were high. The other two letters were mad. One, in purple ink, explained that the writer ten years ago had met a man named Urigo Uccellino who had served with him in the Abyssinian campaign, had been captured by the natives and mutilated by their women and, after rescue, had jumped overboard from a hospital ship to the sharks of the Red Sea. The writer had a photograph of him and, for a fee of eight thousand lire, was prepared to paint a portrait for Mercer. The fee included frame. Mercer's own portrait – on receipt of a photograph – he would do for ten thousand lire. The other letter was typewritten, contained three pages of lyrical nonsense, and ended with an indecent proposal couched in such delicate terms that Mercer had to read it several times before he was certain.

Both writers, Mercer felt sure, walked the streets of their town with every appearance of sanity. Most people had their madness.

They carried it close to them and, if you wanted a glimpse of it, you had to watch them, wait for the moment of privacy, the quick look through the keyhole… How well he knew it. The fantasy of their impossible prides and ambitions and a lust for things beyond them… Among these things he had spent so much of his life.

As he rose, the street photographer raised his camera invitingly, calling out to him, but Mercer shook his head pleasantly and passed on. Following the hotel porter's instructions he turned down a narrow passageway and soon found himself in the Campo Boria. On the far side of the square was the palace.

Mercer knew nothing of architecture but he liked the look of the palace. Its ground floor was of heavy masonry, cut by tall windows which were closely grilled. Above this was a narrow, pillared arcade forming a loggia along its front and supporting the top floor which was decorated with three-arched windows, heavy scroll work and a series of plaques framing painted sculptural work. The main door was a great arch, topped with a stone coat of arms. A dozen wide steps ran up to tall, double doors of heavy wood and glass, the glass covered with a thin tracery of iron work. He went up the steps and saw a small notice at the side in gold letters on a blackboard – *Galleria Boria*.

Inside, behind a small table at the foot of a broad flight of steps, sat an attendant. He got up as Mercer crossed to him and looped back part of thick scarlet rope which ran from one shining brass support to another across the bottom step.

'*Buon' giorno, signore.*'

Mercer nodded and was about to ask him whether he knew Boldesca when he changed his mind. It was not always wise to be too direct.

'What is this place?'

The man smiled. 'The Boria Gallery, signore. You would like to look around?' He held the loop back a littler farther.

'A museum?' Mercer put his hand in his pocket.

'There is nothing to pay. Everything here is for sale. Please go up and look around.'

He stood back as Mercer passed him and went up the stairs. He called after him: 'If you are interested in anything, please ring. There are bells in most of the rooms. Someone will come to you.'

At the top of the steps a long gallery ran through the building to a tall window which looked out on the Grand Canal. From the gallery pillared arches opened into a series of saloons, and gallery and saloons were furnished with pictures, carpets and china. Mercer walked through various rooms reading the little black and gold notices. At

40

first he was glad of them for they made him feel a little less lost. To some of the things which he liked it was pleasant to be able to put a name. *18th-Century Marqueterie Escritoire, inlaid foliage, rosewood bands. Ch'in Ling green jade Jardinière* ... and the water reflection on it from a far window set the intricate carving into motion. He moved on, now and again putting out his hand to touch a piece of furniture and watching the print of his fingers fade on the highly waxed surfaces. *16th-Century Tapestry – Loire atelier. 20th-Century – Aubusson, designed by Lurcat* ... the vivid reds and blues and the distorted muscles of a man wrestling with a bull held him with its raw colour and vicious pattern. He was aware of the silence in the palace, heavy and solid.

He went to a window and looked out at the canal. On the far bank a steamboat was just drawing away from the fare-stage at the Santa Maria della Salute. He lit a cigarette, surprised by the noise the match made scraping against the box. On his right was a large glass case full of tiny figures and he examined them closely, delighting in the colour and fineness of the moulding. There must be thousands of people who would need no telling that they were Russian porcelain. But he was not among them. Somewhere in the past this world and many others had been barred to him. Ask him to judge

41

when a man spoke whether he lied or not and he could give an opinion with the sureness of an expert, but ask him what this was, this piece of furniture which pleased him with its curves and its gilding, and he had to look at the label. Now he was getting touchy and stupid and dissatisfied with himself. He sat in a window-seat and stared at a row of African masks until his cigarette was done.

He went into the next room and found himself in the midst of an eighteenth-century reception. The room was crowded with full-size wax figures of men and women all dressed in the costume of their period – high, elaborate wigs, panniered skirts, rich velvet and brocade coats, and lace at throat and wrists. They sat and stood, staring at one another with glassy surprised looks, and under a green silk baldachino at the end of the room sat a man and a woman – some noble and his lady – she with a fan held to her high bosom, he with the great star of a foreign order on his breast. The stillness of the groups made Mercer imagine that his entry had surprised them, frozen their talk and movement into this elegant petrification. Then he heard the sound of voices. It came from beyond a half-open door at the side of the great throne. He crossed to it and went through, to find himself looking at the woman whose photograph he had taken from Boldesca.

She was carrying a pile of papers in her hand and coming towards the door. She stopped as she saw him, giving a slight, enquiring movement of her head. She was tall, and dark, and, he thought, much better looking than her photograph. Her face had a pale, ivory warmth, a delicacy of feature without weakness. He liked her at once. He liked the way she stood, the long, easy line of her body under the tight-belted, green working apron, and the slow, graceful movement of an arm as she raised the papers to her breast, holding them as though they were a sheaf of lilies.

'I'm sorry, this room is not open to the public. Can I help you?' Her voice was polite, but beneath there was a note of authority.

He hesitated for a moment. He wanted nothing to go wrong. 'I wonder if you could. I'm looking for someone who, I think, works here.' As he spoke, his eyes made a swift examination of the room.

It was some kind of work-room, littered with tools and pieces of material, lengths of wool and silk, and benches which were disorderly with papers and broken furniture. Standing at the far end of the room, under the light from a tall window which fronted the canal, was a wide, upright loom, a nearly-finished tapestry taking up two-thirds of the frame. Behind the loom, paused in their work, were two women, one young, the other much older.

'Who is it you want?'

'A man called Boldesca.'

He thought: 'You know him, he carries your photograph.' But if he hoped for anything exceptional from her he was disappointed. She merely nodded, and a hand went up to touch her hair, smoothing the dark line backwards.

'He works and lives here. But I'm sorry, he's not here today.' Her body swung slightly, preparing to move to the door.

'Will he be back tomorrow?' He stood firm, not wanting to leave the room yet. He was conscious of the stillness of the two women, watching him from behind the narrow grille of tapestry threads.

'We hope so.'

'I see. Maybe I could leave a message for him? If he lives here he may be back during the day.' His smile was an apology for bothering her, for keeping her here, but he knew what he wanted and waited now the moment for taking it if the chance came. He had the feeling, too, that she had become curious about him.

She turned from the door, and as she spoke he fancied that behind her words he could hear the faint ring of speculation.

'If you'd like to leave a message, I'll see that he gets it when he returns.'

'Thank you.'

She waited for him, and, in the moment before he went on, he was aware of a familiar tension and expectancy within him, an awareness of himself and the room and the people in it which imprinted the mind with sharp detail. Like all the rooms on this side of the palace, it was full of a soft, liquid play of water light. The two women behind the loom were strung into the fixity of a long pause, as though they waited impassively for his going in order to move into life. He saw the slight movement of this woman's fingers against the papers she held and a tiny patch on a thumb-nail where the varnish had broken away, and over her shoulder the colours of the tapestry on the loom.

'Perhaps you would tell him that I am still very anxious to hear about his friend...' As he spoke he glanced at the tapestry. He had an impression of birds, vivid-coloured creatures, of flowered shrubs and a rocky pool. The elder woman behind the loom frame was staring at him frowning. 'My name,' he said, and his eyes were on the girl now, 'is Mercer.'

He hadn't expected anything from her, but at the back of his mind there had been the familiar hope. Boldesca was away – perhaps for the reason that he wished to avoid him – and this girl might know what Boldesca could have told him.

'Mercer?' She repeated the name and, for

45

a moment, he wondered whether it was said, not to familiarise its strangeness to her but more as an echo of a name already in her mind.

'Yes, Mercer.' He smiled turning towards the door. 'English.'

She held the door for him, repeating the message now in unconcerned tones: 'Mr. Mercer would still like to hear about his friend?'

'That's it. Maybe you know this friend of his?' Here it was, he thought; a pleasant, nice-looking girl whom he had to treat covertly as an opponent since the possibility could not be overlooked that she might know something that would help him. As far as he was concerned the Gian Uccello business was entirely innocent but, remembering Boldesca and his fear, he had to watch her when he spoke as he had watched so many others, waiting for the scarcely perceptible sign that divided truth from falsehood. 'He's called Gian Uccello.'

She gave nothing to him. She merely shook her head and held the door a little wider. A noise behind him made him turn, and he saw that the two women behind the loom were working, ignoring him, their hands flickering across the weft and warp in quick archaic movements. As the door closed behind them it was this too-sudden resumption of work which convinced him that somewhere in the room he had for a moment come close to what he was seeking.

She walked silently before him to the long gallery. From behind her, watching the movement of her firm shoulders, he said:

'What is it they make in there? Tapestries?'

'Yes. The Boria tapestries.' She half-turned as she spoke. 'They're quite famous.'

'And expensive?'

They were at the head of the great stairway and she halted, one hand holding her papers to her breast.

'Everything is expensive here. Is there anything you would like me to show you... Some of the furniture, perhaps?'

'No, thank you. The only furniture I've ever owned is an American trunk. Now – I'm down to a couple of suitcases.'

She gave a little laugh that echoed dryly in the long gallery and with a shrug of her shoulders said quietly: *'Buon' giorno, signore.'*

He went down the staircase, feeling for his cigarettes. He knew she was watching. Whatever he had imagined about her – and in his work he knew the misleading potency of imagination – he liked her. He was about to turn and smile back at her when he heard the beat of her footsteps echo away down the gallery.

At the desk he stopped and talked to the attendant who had watched him come to the head of the stairs.

'Who is she?' He was blunt and direct.

'Signorina Adriana Medova. She's the director of the gallery and does the designs.'

'Designs?'

'For the tapestries.'

As the attendant spoke the door behind his desk opened and a small girl came through. Under the left arm she carried a wriggling brown puppy, which yelped to be set down. She was about eight, neatly dressed, and held an orange in her free hand. Without a word she gave it to the attendant who took out his penknife and began to peel it.

'What does Boldesca do here?'

'Carlo? He's the outside porter and odd-job man.'

Mercer frowned.

'I wanted to see him.'

The attendant looked up at him curiously. He split the peeled orange in half and gave it to the girl.

'You choose the wrong day, signore.'

'He's taking the day off?'

'A day ... two days ... maybe three. Every now and then Carlo goes off. He didn't sleep here last night. Maybe he'll be back tonight or tomorrow. But one never knows with Carlo.'

'Drink?'

The attendant grinned and shrugged his shoulders. 'I never enquire, signore. If you come back tomorrow…'

Mercer looked at the two, touched by the impression they gave of completeness and affection, the dark head of the man tilted towards the fair curls of the girl and the easy, trusting thrust of the little body against his bent knees. She was sucking at the orange now, ignoring Mercer.

'Thanks. I think I will.'

Mercer left them, pushing open the glass and going down the steps to the Campo Boria. As he stood on the pavement, wondering if he would cross the square to the little café and make a few more enquiries about Boldesca, a man came out of the shadowed alcove at the side of the steps and crossed to him. The sound of his footsteps made Mercer turn.

A captain of the *Polizia* was standing by him. He was a young, good-looking man with a tiny dark moustache, elegant in grey uniform with scarlet piping. He touched the peak of his cap in a polite salute and the movement made the sunlight glisten on his epaulette stars and ripple over the black leather of his belt and pistol holster.

'*Buon' giorno, signore.*'

'*Buon' giorno.*'

'You are Signore Eduardo Mercer of the Albergo Adriatico?'

'That's right.'

'I should be glad, signore, if you could

49

come with me to the Questura.'

'What do they want with me?'

The officer smiled, holding it a fraction longer than was necessary so that Mercer should have time to admire his fine teeth. 'I am not told that, signore.'

There was no apprehension in him, only a mild enquiry which rose from a calm sureness of his innocence. Nevertheless, the police were no friends of his and he felt the stir of a familiar antagonism.

'The porter at my hotel told you I was here?' They were strolling easily across the square now.

'*Si, signore.*'

'It must be important – to send a captain?'

'I am not told what it is, signore.' The teeth smiled again, but the man was looking away at a pretty girl who was passing. 'Maybe, because you are English, it is a compliment?'

'It'll be the first time the police ever wasted a compliment on me.'

In Adriana Medova the visit of Mercer to the palace had roused some anxiety. Ten minutes after Mercer had left the building she was talking to her employer, Count Boria. They stood on the small terrace which fronted the palace at water-level where she had found him sitting in the shade of a small awning taking his morning coffee.

He did not see her at once as she came on to the terrace and, for a moment, she watched him. Occasionally she had caught him before when he had thought himself unobserved and she was impressed again with the careless collapse of figure and spirit which seemed to mark him in such moments. He was slumped in his chair, a thin, tired old man, his chin resting on his clasped hands, staring across the canal and, because of her affection for him, her gratitude for all he had done for her, she felt a swift sympathy take her. But she knew there was nothing she could do for him. With most people the years marked a progress of friendship or dislike, but with the Count one went so far and then halted, all further intimacy or warmth blocked by his own patrician self-sufficiency.

She moved across to him and at the sound of her steps she saw the long body stir stiffly, take strength to itself and assume the elegant formalities of its public self.

'Signorina!' He stood up and moved a chair for her. He watched her sit down. He knew from the small frown over her brows that she was worried, but for the moment he was unconcerned, noting the composition of colour and mass made by her as she sat with the sunlight across part of her body. Then, an ancient weariness with no regret in it for him, he thought how, if he had been twenty years, ten maybe, younger he would have found means to have brought her to his bed ... but not now. He was old and had only one ambition ... and even that at some moments seemed worthless.

Adriana said quietly, 'The Englishman Mercer, whom you told me about, has been here this morning asking for Boldesca.'

He sat down and one hand slid upwards and rubbed the side of his face; an old face, but one which showed nothing of the strain within him. The lines there came from an ancestry of inbreeding and the strain of aristocratic responsibilities and the years of planning and vigilance which they forced on him.

'I'm not surprised that he should be enquiring for Boldesca, but I am curious to know how he comes to make his enquiries here.'

'But what has Boldesca got to do with it? This man says that Boldesca was going to give him some information about Gian Uccello.'

The Count was silent for a moment, watching the movement of the flies about the blood-red blossoms of the canna lilies which had been set out along the terrace edge. He said slowly:

'Yesterday, I learned that Mercer had advertised about Uccello, and that Boldesca had answered it, offering him some startling information about Uccello's present where-abouts...' He saw the surprise on her face, but was unconcerned with it. He was more concerned with his own weariness with the whole business, the strain which he had to accept because beyond it was a principle he could not deny without denying his own nature. There was a fiery particle in him which was his master. How much easier it would have been if he had been in time to stop Boldesca's letter from reaching Mercer ... but nothing came easily these days.

'But what could Boldesca know?'

'I suppose that living here he must have picked up some information. Whether "startling" would properly describe it, I doubt. However, until now I'd thought that I had prevented the two from meeting.'

'But his coming here? If he didn't meet Boldesca how did he know he lived here?'

'Exactly, signorina. I know Boldesca put no address on his letter, so it now seems to me that the people I had deal with Boldesca didn't do their job properly, and that there was some contact between the two. Even so the Englishman could have learned nothing vital, otherwise why should he come here asking for Boldesca and enquiring about Uccello still?' The real proof – that if Mercer had discovered anything like the truth then the police would already be in this palace – he could not give to her. She thought that he was only helping her, but beyond her and her narrow anxieties lay so much more which she must never suspect.

'That may be so. But what about Boldesca now? They may still meet?'

He shook his head. 'That can't happen. Boldesca has been sent away.'

'Sent away? Where?'

The tone of her voice irritated him, but he held his feeling down. Everything she felt and thought lay on the surface, and the necessity of having to hide so much from her induced in him now an arrogant impatience. He said quickly:

'A good friend of mine has taken him to Milan. There's no need for you to worry further about him. You can rest assured that he won't talk.' Or ever would be able to talk again... What a wealth of deceit could lie in a word, he mused. But there was virtue in deceit. He saw her relax before his assurance and knew that for her the promise of security was real.

'I shall be glad when all this is over.' Adriana bit at her lip gently, turning towards the canal, watching the frothy wake of a passing barge. He had calmed her anxiety, but with its going she found herself left with the traces of uneasiness which from time to time this man stirred in her. It was no good saying she understood him. They inhabited different worlds. For him, she was little more than any of his peasants. For her, he was an enigma, a man who followed his eclectic desires and loyalties from motives which were seldom simple. Even the help that he was giving her she could not place definitely as the outcome of past association, a regard for her and her family and the ability she brought to his service. What he said he would do, he did. But the reason why he did it was often obscured, and there were moments, like this, when she felt reluctant to attempt any search for his reasons, as though she feared what she might inadvertently find...

He stood up and put his hand on her shoulder, and the touch reassured her. He had helped her so much in the past, he was helping her now. Against his certainty she felt her own anxieties begin to fade.

'It can't be long now. Nearly all the arrangements are made. However...' He drew away from her, moving to the edge of the flight of steps that led down to the water. 'We can't afford to have anything go wrong. Tell me, what is your opinion of the Englishman?' He turned, and he stood there, framed within the canted lines of the black and red mooring posts that rose from the water at the lip of the canal. Tall, his thin shoulders stooped, the grey hair cropped closely to his skull, he was like a figure carved out of wood, ancient but hard, and no weariness in him now. She knew that his mind had gone ahead of her, planning, considering expedients.

'I wouldn't know what to say.'

'Oh, come, signorina – that's not what I expected from you. The world can be divided into tolerable and intolerable people. Where does Mr. Mercer stand?'

He came closer to her, but for a moment it was not his tight-lipped, old man's face she saw. She was seeing Mercer as he had faced her in the workroom. There had been nothing aristocratic about him, no dignity, no distinction of features, and the play of his hand with a loose waistcoat button had marked some strain in him which had matched her own wariness. Yet even so there had been something about the man...

'Tolerable, I should say.'

'In that case, I think we ought to help him. Otherwise he may help himself to too much. After all, he has nothing to do with the police and we know his enquiries are for an innocent end. I'd hoped that he would come up against a blank wall. Boldesca has spoiled that. It would be easier now to help him to finish his job and go away. We've always known we might have to do that.'

'But how is he to be told?'

'By you. He'll come here again to enquire for Boldesca.'

'But I've already told him I never heard of anyone called Gian Uccello.'

56

He laughed quietly. 'It's a lie so easily explained. He asks you the question in a workroom with other people about, you are unprepared for it, don't know him or his purpose … why should you give him details of an intimate character…? No, no, he will find that reasonable.' There was the faintest touch of authority in the voice now and she knew that he was no longer friend, but *padrone* giving an order. 'To him, the whole thing is straightforward. His profession is to make people give up their secrets. That he finds you ready to help, he will put down to his professional skill in handling you. Talk, and let him talk. Draw him out so that we can be sure Boldesca told him nothing of importance, and when you've done that – tell him what he wants to know.' He put his hand on her arm and moved with her towards the door.

'When the Englishman comes again, I'll talk to him.'

'Good – there is no need to worry, *cara signorina*.' His grip tightened on her arm, paternal and strengthening, and she was grateful to him for the help and loyalty he gave her.

'You've done so much for me–' she began, but he stopped her with a gesture, smiling.

'I need no thanks. Everything will soon be settled. In the meantime, if anyone enquires about Boldesca tell them he has gone off to

57

Milan to another job.'

When she had gone, Count Boria went slowly up to his room to telephone. Something had gone wrong with his arrangements for Boldesca not to meet Mercer and, although he was convinced that Mercer represented no danger to him, he meant to have the truth from his agents. Not all the wisdom and cunning in the world, he was thinking as he picked up the telephone, would ever give a man complete armour against the mistakes of other people. But that, after all, was one of the risks he had accepted. There was no virtue in being alarmed at a danger narrowly passed... As he gave the number he looked across his desk at a predella panel hung on the wall. The clear golds and blues brought a small smile to his lips. Time passed but did nothing to exorcise the dæmon from men like himself. The years merely made one more its creature...

## Chapter 4

The Questura di Venezia was a grey, severe building fronting the Rio di San Lorenzo. They went in, past the carbined guard at the door, to a large, barren hall that smelled unpleasantly of disinfectant, tobacco smoke and poverty. The place had the hostile, untidy air of all Italian public buildings. Mercer had enough experience of the Italian police to know that there was no doubt about the hostility, and that the untidiness was not to be taken as a sign of inefficiency. They climbed a flight of monastic stairs to the first floor and Mercer was left alone while the captain disappeared through a door marked – *Dirigente L'Ufficio Stranieri*. For a while he wondered if the call was to be merely something about his passport or certificate of sojourn in Italy. Most people visiting Italy never bothered to get a certificate. He had done so at Milan, knowing that he would want police help and that they would not listen to him until he had satisfied them with his papers.

He sat there, watching the little groups in the hall, people waiting, people moving in and out of the side doors, all of them with that subdued attitude with which the Italians approach the *Polizia* and the carabinieri. The captain came back, but instead of taking him to the office which dealt with foreigners, he led him down the hall. He was shown through an unmarked door into a small office which – after the bareness of the hall – seemed overfurnished. It had a large desk, a sofa, various chairs, a picture of Garibaldi on the wall over the electric fire, a large bookcase full of swollen files and fat legal books and, by the window which overlooked the canal, a tall Japanese screen which shaded the desk from the strong sunlight.

The man sitting at the desk had his hand over his mouth as though he suffered from toothache. He nodded to a chair before the desk and then signed to the captain to go. Mercer sat down and found himself staring at a folded cardboard slip on which was printed the name – Alcide Spadoni.

'Signore Eduardo Mercer?' It was greeting, question and caution.

Mercer nodded.

'*Il vostro passaporto.*'

Mercer handed over his passport. Signore Spadoni took it and went carefully through it, turning it sideways sometimes to decipher a stamp or visa marking. Then he closed it, gave its shabby, well-worn cover a reflective scrutiny and handed it back.

'*E vostro permesso di soggiorno in Italia?*'

Mercer handed over the form which he had been given at the Questura di Milano, entitling him to a five-month stay in Italy. As Spadoni looked at it he pushed an ashtray across the desk and said absently: 'I don't smoke – but if you wish.'

Mercer lit a cigarette and looked up at the portrait of Garibaldi who was wearing a woollen cap very much like an old-fashioned nightcap. At the same time he watched Spadoni from the corner of his eye. The man had the form on the desk, staring at it, and Mercer knew that he had exhausted it. Passport and form were both in order. Mercer waited silently. Experience had taught him that one offered the police nothing, answered their questions or avoided them and kept one's papers in order so that they were never given any excuse to restrict one's actions through quibbles about minor formalities.

'How long have you been in Venice?' The form was pushed back to him.

'Five days.'

Spadoni leaned back in his chair and there was the beginning of a smile on his face.

'You are used to dealing with the police, signore?'

'Why?'

'You do not ask why you have been sent for?'

'My curiosity can wait until you tell me.'

Spadoni smiled openly now. He looked, Mercer thought, rather like a sleepy, elegant spaniel. The face was large and long, tired skin folded about his mouth, and his eyes, brown and moist, were drawn back under heavy brows. He was running one hand through his loose brown hair which sprouted over his ears in untidy, but picturesque, wings. That part of his body which showed above the desk had a muscular heaviness which was emphasised by the jacket of his well-cut brown suit. He wore a thick, blue tie, twisted into a large knot and the points of his white collar rose above the lapels of his coat giving a careless artistry to his appearance. He leaned forward now, playing with a gold signet ring on his right hand and Mercer saw that the brown hair was touched with grey.

'How many times have you visited Italy, signore?' The smile was gone, but the large eyes were gentle, watching Mercer with a dolefulness which suggested that at any moment he might close them in sleep.

'Five. In nineteen twenty-four ... twenty-eight ... thirty-two ... thirty-eight ... and now.'

Spadoni nodded and stood up. He walked across the room and moved the Japanese screen so that the sunlight fell across the room in a great wedge. He was the kind of man, Mercer decided, who should always sit behind a desk. Seated, he was impressive, with a powerful, easy elegance which impelled respect and caution. Standing, he was a little absurd, for his legs were short, inadequate to the strong body, and he was paunchy, a round, low-slung pot of a belly which should have graced a butcher. He came back to his desk and sitting down wiped his mouth with a silk handkerchief.

Then very quietly he said:

'Tell me what you know about Valentino Grandini.'

'Nothing.'

'You're sure?'

'Yes.'

Sadoni began to tuck the silk handkerchief into his sleeve. He leaned forward, his elbows on the desk. The large face hanging before Mercer was wrapped in an expression of sad dejection.

'That's very strange, signore – for the body of Valentino Grandini was taken out of the Rio dei Greci, five hundred yards from here and not so much farther from your hotel, at six o'clock this morning. He had been stabbed several times, his face was battered, and around a wound in his left arm was bandaged a white linen handkerchief. The handkerchief was marked in black silk with your name.'

Oddly enough it was the man's last phrase which had touched his memory, taking him back fifteen years to a cold room in Paris. The handkerchiefs had been a present from his mother, the black silk lettering her own work. He could see again the pleasure on the thin face as he bent down to kiss her. The dry warmth of her hand as she had held his against her flesh again, and he fancied that he could smell the charcoal fumes from the tiny chafing pot she had carried in her lap for warmth against the iciness of the barely furnished room. She was gone now, and all of the handkerchiefs had gone … all except this last one which he had used to bandage Carlo Boldesca's arm. But if the memory held him, there was no pause in his answering. He heard himself, fifteen years away, saying:

'A handkerchief with my name?'

'Yes, signore.'

Mercer came back. The past was gone. There was only this room, unsteady with water reflections, and Spadoni leaning across the desk.

'How did you identify him?'

'He had his identity papers on him.'

The identity papers, still damp, were dropped on the desk before him.

Then, because between his kind and the police there was never any full frankness from fear of unwittingly conceding some advantage, he said easily: 'He told me he was called Sandro Mercanti. He answered an advertisement I put in the *Corriere della Sera* for information about a Gian Uccello. I met him last night for the first time. On his way to meet me he was attacked – he told me it was some affair of a woman – and I took him to my hotel. I bandaged his arm. He left while I was getting him a drink and he gave me no information about Gian Uccello.'

Spadoni said nothing for a moment, but he pulled a note-pad to him and made a memorandum in shorthand on it. Then holding the pencil before his face – and there was in the gesture something of a priest holding up a cross, impressive, demanding respect and solemnity – he asked gently:

'For this advertisement – you used an accommodation address?'

'Yes.'

'Why?'

'It's the only way to keep a safe distance between yourself and cranks.'

'Sandro Mercanti must have been a false name.'

'Why should it be?'

'Because an accommodation address usually encourages people to keep their real identity under cover, and because we have identified him as Grandini. For the last four years he has been wanted by us as politically undesirable. You may take my word for it that Grandini was his real name.'

Mercer shrugged his shoulders. When the police were definite only a fool argued with them. He wanted to be out of this room, to find himself a drink somewhere and sit alone. Somewhere behind Boldesca lay Gian Uccello. Into what he had considered an innocent affair, violence had obtruded itself. But why? Unexpectedly, Spadoni held a lighter out to him.

'Your cigarette's out.' Mercer leaned forward and then, through the haze of smoke, the man's voice came to him sardonically, the first open sign of antagonism. 'How would *you* describe yourself professionally, Signore Mercer?' The emphasis was intended to goad him and it did, but he refused the other the satisfaction of showing it.

'Variously,' he said shortly.

Spadoni nodded indulgently and leaning back recited, as though he were memorising a school lesson: 'I see ... confidential clerk, confidential agent, confidential enquirer? There isn't one dignified phrase which covers the whole range, is there? Though if we were vulgar the description would be easy.'

He had gone too far, overplayed his dislike so that it now left Mercer untouched and free to answer:

'This is your office. Let's stick to business, shall we? If you think I killed Grandini, arrest me.'

Spadoni laughed. 'I don't think you killed Grandini. Between ourselves I don't care who killed him, though I suppose we shall have to find out. The person I'm beginning to be very interested in is Gian Uccello. Perhaps you'd better tell me about him.'

'This place must be badly organised.' He

allowed himself a little irony now, wondering why – since they both did the same kind of work, one under a private and the other under a public aegis – there was always this discord.

'It's an impression strangers get.'

'I was here five days ago and told all I knew about Uccello and asked for help. I didn't get any help. Maybe that's why my visit has been forgotten. Signore Lisco can tell you all about it. I saw him.'

'Signore Lisco was transferred to Rome three days ago. I have taken his place. It would be a kindness to me if you repeated your information and saved me the trouble of ringing for a file.' Mercer looked across at the man and saw that he was regarding him with a quizzical lift of an eyebrow, a faint smile wreathing his lips. The flat, unemotional voice carried on: 'I was unforgivably rude to you just now. Let us forget it.'

'Certainly.' Mercer stood up. If he couldn't get away from the room, he could at least walk about. He went to the window. Outside, drawn up at the canal edge, was a long, crimson-painted launch with a canvas awning and the word *Polizia* on its stern. Boldesca's body had probably been brought from the Rio dei Greci in that.

'You came to Italy to look for Gian Uccello?' Spadoni was standing by him.

'Yes. A Paris firm of lawyers, Gevlin Frères, for whom I have worked before, employ me.' Behind that what a world of weariness and near despair ... the elder Gevlin like a vulture with his bald head, throwing the job at him, cutting him down on money and hinting that it was the last act of charity, that younger and better men waited to do the jobs of the future for half the old prices.

'And why do they want Uccello?'

'A client of theirs wants him. An American. His son was a flyer in the American Air Force. He was shot down in Italy during the war and found himself in the mountains with a broken leg in mid-winter. A man – whom he later knew as Gian Uccello – carried him for two days through the snow to a partisan head-quarters, an inn. Without Uccello he would have died in the snow. At the inn he was in a constant fever, not knowing where he was, and at the end of the second day the Germans raided the place and took him prisoner. The partisans escaped. This was in February, nineteen forty-four. My job was to trace the inn from the little information supplied to me and to find Uccello. Father and son owe him a debt of gratitude...'

'Do you believe this story?'

Mercer turned away from the window. Coming from Gevlin Frères it was unlikely.

His other work for them had been in a differing category, but a conviction had settled on him that for once the ostensible framework of a commission was true.

'Why not? Flyers did get shot down and rescued, and the Americans are a generous race. Besides, I found the inn.'

'Where?'

'In Montevasaga, in the hills east of La Spezia. The innkeeper remembered the incident and Uccello. But he could tell me nothing of him except that he thought he remembered Uccello saying sometime that he was from Venice. He had drifted there during the war and, four months after the German raid, disappeared. I came here, hoping there might be some police or commune record of him. But neither your people nor the city authorities have any record of him. So I advertised…' Behind that, three weeks of patient reconstruction from the tenuous details given him in Paris which had brought him to the inn, and then the sullen indifference of the innkeeper and the sergeant of the carabinieri at Montevasaga to whom Uccello had become a dim memory but the German raid a living wound since they both had lost their wives in the shooting.

'What would happen if you found him?'

'Dollars – enough to make him a rich man in Italy, anyway. Maybe an invitation to

America. He's a hero – an unusual one, for there's a reward waiting for him. He picked a man out of the snow and saved his life.'

Spadoni nodded. 'And this morning we picked a man out of the canal … much too late to save his life. Professionally' – and the friendliness had dropped now to a patient note of half-interest, as though the real attention of his thoughts were far away – 'what would your opinion be about the juxtaposition of these two events?'

'I deal in facts. My only interest is to supply the present address of Uccello to Gevlin Frères.'

Spadoni nodded, his eyes dropping from Mercer's face, taking in the tweed jacket with leather-bound cuffs, the neatly pressed grey trousers with the virtue long gone from the flannel and the well-worn, highly-polished shoes. He turned away and stared at the top panel of the Japanese screen, his eye following the delicate lines of a spray of peonies. Then he spoke absently, as though he intended his lack of emphasis to hold an ambiguous force, a talking out loud of private thoughts which he invited Mercer to share or disregard according to his inclination: 'Gian Uccello and Valentino Grandini … there may be no connection, but I lack the ingenuousness to believe that. I deal in facts, too. Now we know each other, signore, perhaps the next time we meet we shall find it easier to be a little franker. You'll find me most mornings taking a *cappuccina* at the Quadri … about eleven. You're welcome to share my coffee any time… At present, I think we've said all we can to each other. Thank you for coming.'

He held out his hand and the sunlight made a tiny blaze of fire on his signet ring. Mercer took his hand for a moment, then turned away to the door. He was being let out, on string, not – he was sure – because he was suspected of murder, but simply because in the very nature of his profession he was suspected, because he was to them a hyena who had the temerity to try and run with the wolves, and because at times the hyena had made a quiet killing while the wolves circled a trail which led back on itself to a neatly picked carcase. He stopped in the open door and said quietly:

'You're wrong, you know. This is one time when – professionally – I could describe myself as the representative of a private charity.'

Spadoni lowered himself into his desk chair and, without looking up, answered impatiently: 'Charity often covers a feeling of guilt. You should read the history of the Medici family. Good-bye.'

When Mercer had gone Spadoni pressed a bell-button on his desk. He waited, making shorthand notes on his pad. A tall man in waistcoat and shirt sleeves came in from the next room.

'Luigi – is Cassana in the building?'

'Yes.'

'Call him.'

Luigi went to the communicating door and shouted. He came back, scratching his forearms through his shirt and watching Spadoni expectantly. He waited while Spadoni finished his notes. As his chief looked up he asked:

'Well?'

Spadoni grunted, running his fingers through his hair. 'I don't trust him.'

'Put a collar and a tab round his neck and he'd be a police dog – like us,' Luigi laughed.

'Tell that to the Prefetto sometime.' Spadoni sounded a little angry.

'Sorry. Did he do it?'

'No. But he's lost the habit of frankness when he speaks to us. He didn't recognise me, either.'

'I didn't know you'd ever met?'

'Not face to face.' Spadoni leaned back, his large hand rubbing reflectively over his mouth. When he spoke again the irony in his voice was thick, unpalatable. 'In Rome, in nineteen thirty-eight, in the sixteenth year of Fascism, Senator Ravaggio of the Fascist Grand council, beloved friend and counsellor of Il Duce – and as unpleasant a man as

72

this country could produce – was assassinated as he drove down the Via Colonna. Between ourselves he was driving from one mistress to another. A Frenchman was executed for the crime, taken in *flagrante delicto*. Behind him, although we could never connect them with any proof which would stand, were two other people: a Rosa Melitus and an Englishman, Eduardo Mercer – both certainly working for the Deuxième Bureau. Interesting, isn't it? I was only a fourth-grade official then, so I doubt if he ever saw me, but I saw him. He's a very capable man, or was. Now what do we find...?' The pencil was raised before him, but this time it was the admonitory flourish of a lecturer, forcing the attention of bored pupils. 'In Venice at this moment is Eduardo Mercer – not so prosperous, probably long discarded by the Deuxième Bureau, looking for a man nobody has heard of and for a reason that only a fool would believe. Already a man connected with Mercer has been murdered, and – not even you know this Luigi – on the Via Garibaldi, not far from here, a woman called Rosa Melitus keeps a house of accommodation and has done for the last eight years. Do you care to give an opinion on all this, or shall we let the facts stand? I wasn't transferred from Rome to this place in a hurry just to check the hawkers' licences in the Piazzo San Marco.' He paused as though expecting Luigi to make some comment, but Luigi was silent, and at this moment Cassana came into the room.

He seemed out of place in this lofty, severe room. He wore a neat, grey flannel suit, rather flamboyantly cut, suède shoes, a blue silk shirt, red tie, and held a white beret in his hand. Looped from his neck on a leather strap was a camera in a case.

'Cassana.'

'Signore?' He came forward – a restless, graceful figure, bright-eyed, dark-haired, and he was smiling, his white teeth showing between his broad, soft lips.

'I've got a job for you.'

'At your service...' Cassana gave him a mock bow, and the weather-brown face, intelligent, creased with laughter, reminded Spadoni of a painting he had seen of Pan.

'I want you to watch someone.'

'A woman?' For a moment Cassana's hand went up to his tie.

'No, a man.' Spadoni smiled as he saw the disappointment in the lean face. Cassana shrugged his shoulders.

'Who, signore?'

'Eduardo Mercer, Englishman, Albergo Adriatico. I want you and your men to keep an eye on him, particularly in the evenings. He's no fool. If he spots you just carry on. A few photographs might be useful. Luigi will

74

give you all the information.' He dismissed them, but added, as Luigi held the door for Cassana to go out: 'I'd like the file with the record of Mercer's first visit of enquiry here about Gian Uccello, and I want a call through to the carabinieri post at Montevasaga – La Spezia district.'

## Chapter 5

That afternoon Mercer lay on his bed for a long time thinking over the Boldesca episode. Why had he been killed? His story about an affair with a woman might have been true after all, and he had been killed out of jealousy or revenge. But it seemed more likely that Boldesca had picked up some information about Gian Uccello which it was to someone's advantage to suppress. An attempt had been made to prevent their meeting and had failed. When Boldesca had left the hotel whoever had made the first attempt had got at him again, and this time there had been no mistake. But, for all the killers knew, Boldesca might have passed on his information. That being so, it would be assumed that he, Mercer, was now holding facts which made him dangerous and – the thought was unpleasant in the shuttered confines of his room – he might be marked down for the same treatment. But why should there be all this mystery, and danger, in the simple matter of tracing a man who had disappeared during the war?

He lay there smoking. The strangeness which now appeared in this innocent mission troubled him. There was the apprehension which he had known before, and with which it was so difficult to live, that some inimical force was now opposed to him. The only real answer was to leave Venice and that was impossible. A man had to live. If it were ever known back in Paris that he had left for reasons of personal safety he would never live it down.

He lay there until it grew dark, trying to make some sense out of the situation, but very little comfort emerged for him. He went out eventually, driven from the room by the dark fancies which the close walls gradually inspired in his active mind. He sat in the Piazza San Marco taking a glass of Marsala and, surrounded by the brittle talk, the idle passage of strollers and the coloured lights, a meagre optimism slowly formed in him. The longer he stayed in Venice, the more people he let know that he was still enquiring for Uccello and so far knew nothing about him, the safer he became. However, he had to go on with his job, and at some point he might learn something which would mark him as dangerous. There was nothing he could do about that until the time came... He sat there by himself in the evening brilliance of the great square and found, after a while, that his own anxiety had gone and that he was thinking about the girl in the palace. He'd liked her and, even though he knew he could take no one connected with Boldesca at face value, he found himself hoping that she had nothing to do with his death. Liking her, aware of the great body of decent, ordinary people outside the narrow circle of his own professional interests, he wished that he was anything but what he was.

He got up and strolled out of the square. It would have been good, he thought, to have someone to talk to now, someone whose only claim was friendship or affection. With her, for instance, he could have spent a careless, happy evening... He stopped at a bookshop window, staring at a volume which was open at a reproduction of Botticelli's head of Venus. The young Venus stared at him with eyes which were stupid with innocence and freshness, reminding him of a girl who had been in the same company with his mother, so beautiful that there had been no sex in her, a girl whose lips had been marbled into coldness, whose body could be touched but not moved into passion. The lips of the girl in the palace would have been warm, and her body... He passed on, hating this moment of loneliness, this moment which occurred so often. You could drive it away by taking someone to bed with you, by drink which forced back the contracting horizons, by telling yourself that a million other people were in the same boat... But all the time it was something which sat deep inside you, like a warty toad at the bottom of a green well.

He went past the Post Office and turned down the Calle Vallarezza. At the bottom of the street was the Grand Canal and the steamboat station. He wanted another drink and, for a moment, contemplated turning into Harry's Bar. But he wanted also someone to talk with. In both places he knew he would only have the barmen for company and this was one of those evenings when the agile flow of counter talk would merely be an obligatory noise passed over with the drinks as part of the service. He went out on to the little pier and bought himself a ticket for the Veneta Marina station.

On the boat he perched himself on the handrail amidships and smoked, watching the Venice waterfront. He liked Venice at this time of the year for there were few tourists about and it belonged to itself. Now, watching it slide by, hazily touched by the lights and bar signs, it had the look of a puppet city presenting a flimsy façade of cardboard shapes which the touch of a finger could disrupt. The ragged cross-hatching of lights over the water seemed less reflection than the swift brush marks of an impatient painter delighted by a palette of ochres and lemon. He remembered his mother, who had played here at the Fenice, saying that it was a city to be seen when one was in love for the first time. Poised between air and water, its unreality had a poignancy and ecstasy which matched the grace and sadness of youth awakening…

The boat bumped against the piers of the Veneta Marina station and he went ashore. The Via Garibaldi lay before him, one of the few really wide streets in Venice, running at an obtuse angle from the lagoon front. It was lined with hawkers' stalls, crowded with an idle, evening mob of sailors and girls, workmen and their wives. For all its open-ness it was a slum. Unkempt women stood in the doorways, calling to one another, children swarmed over the littered pave-ment, youths gathered around the stalls, hunching their padded shoulders and flicking their dark eyes over the crowd speculatively. The houses were mean and shabby. Dark little under-passages ran from it into courts which were noisome with the effluvia of a warren of families crowed into the decrepit tenements. It was a street where poverty did its marketing and found its pleasures; slack-bosomed women leaning from a window above a dingy oil-shop, a bar with pin-tables throwing its light over the kerb-side vegetable and meat stalls ... and a restaurant encased in a barricade of weary pot shrubs facing a cinema huddled into the ugly shell of an old chapel.

Half-way down the street, Mercer turned off to the left along a passageway. The passageway ended abruptly on the edge of a canal and across the water rose a square block of factory buildings. Above him a narrow line of sky was picked out carelessly with an untidy sprinkling of stars. He went up the steps of the house which formed an angle with the canal and rang the bell. The wooden door swung open automatically and the light from the hall gave sudden life to its faded green paint. From a half-open doorway to his right a voice called throatily:

'*Chi è?*'

'Edward Mercer.'

He stood, examining a viciously coloured print of the bath of Psyche above the hall table. Someone had stuck the business card of a dentist in one corner and the glass had a faint patina of damp. The throaty voice laughed.

'Well...' There was a richness in the word which bubbled and played like water in a bucket under a pump. 'You've been five days in Venice and at last you come…'

He stood there. The house welcomed him with a leering, impatient friendliness, shabby and full of whispers. And it was a welcome he didn't want. This was what Rosa Melitus had come to and, unless he was lucky, this – materially different but in spirit the same – was what was waiting for him … somewhere.

'I 'phoned you when I arrived.' He sounded and felt like a small boy excusing a rudeness.

'Yes … dear boy. To ask the name of a cheap hotel.'

From the darkness at the head of the stairway a man and woman appeared. Mercer stood aside in the narrow hall to let them pass. The girl looked at him curiously and moved her handbag from one armpit to the other. The movement stirred a draft of scent and a bracelet slid down her arm like a hoop-la ring settling awkwardly over a peg.

'Is that you, Renata?' The throaty sound sang about the hall brassily. 'Tell your friend from Chioggia that the next time he comes over I'd like some more medicine.'

'Okay, Rosa.'

The man buttoned his overcoat and went out impatiently and the girl, after an impudent wink at Mercer, followed him.

81

'Don't stand out there. Come and have some of the medicine. He's the storekeeper of an American relief organisation.'

Mercer went into the room.

Rosa was lying on a chaise-longue, half her body covered by a green eiderdown, a silk scarf tied tightly around her thick white neck. She leaned forward to look at him and the long corkscrew curls above the absurd pink and white face shook like faded laburnum racemes. The stir of her large body under the eiderdown was fleshy and vigorous.

'You don't change,' she said happily, and a book slid off her lap to the floor. She reached down for it and he saw the pallid expanse of her bosom press heavily upwards above her low blouse. She grew fatter each time he saw her, but her friendliness remained unaltered.

'You still look the same,' he lied gently.

She laughed and shook her head. 'No – my bank balance gets bigger and so do I. What's a woman supposed to do with all this?' She slapped her breast with a white paddle of a hand. 'Help yourself. There's a glass on the side.'

He sat down at a large, round table at the foot of the long chair and reached for the bottle of Four Roses. He drank quickly and filled his glass again. Rosa lit a cigarette and watched him, and he knew she would miss nothing. She might be letting herself go, settling down into an obese and careless comfort, but there would be no lessening of her shrewdness.

'You still have throat trouble?'

'Yes, dear boy. What do you have?'

'Just trouble.' He grinned.

'You ought to retire.'

'What do you suggest?'

'I could find something for you. I've got a lot of friends.'

'I'm too fond of my work.'

'You never did like it, dear boy... Maybe for the first few years, yes. But not after. That's why I could never do anything with you. You could never forget I was the one who brought you into it. That's why you take five days to come and see me.'

'What would you have made out of me?'

'I could have given you two things in those days, but you only ever wanted one.' She threw her book into a corner and reached out a hand for her glass. 'Loyalty and love. The two "l's".' The large throat pulsed as she drank. 'Sometimes I console myself with the thought that you just don't like blondes. In those days the ten years between us didn't show... However ... here you are. And you haven't decided to retire?'

'Gevlin Frères. A cut-rate job.'

'You swore you'd never touch them after that Rome business.'

'This is fair enough.'

'They're double-crossing bastards.'

'I still hate their guts. But a man must eat.'

'There's plenty of food in this house, dear boy…' She shook her curls coquettishly and the thick column of her neck was horrible, fascinating. He shut his eyes momentarily so that he might know only the strength and loyalty in her and his affection for her.

'What do you know of a girl called Adriana Medova who works at the Palazza Boria?'

'Nothing. Do you want me to know anything?'

He hesitated, and she knew why. He didn't want there to be anything to know about Adriana Medova.

'Yes. I have to eat.'

'I'll find out.'

'Thanks.'

'Anything else, or shall I get out the cards?'

'That's all – except that it's nice being with you again.' He raised his glass to her.

'Dear boy … but it could have been nice being with me all the time.' She pulled a pack of cards from under the eiderdown. As she shuffled he said quickly:

'There is something else.'

'I'm not surprised.'

'If you wanted a couple of thugs to go to the limit for you, who would you pick?'

84

She stopped shuffling and looked across at him sharply. 'You said this job was fair enough?'

'So it is – treat the question as an academic one.'

'This is Venice. It wouldn't be difficult to make a list of a dozen with sixteenth-century instincts... I'd have to ask Bernardo.'

'Who's he?'

'An honest advocate with a poor clientele. He drinks a little too much. He's the man I've finally unloaded my two "l's" on. He'll be here soon.'

'Reliable?'

'If I told him to stand on his head on top of San Marco he'd do it.' She began to deal the cards.

As they played he was remembering all the other occasions when they had sat together like this, filling up time with the same game. He had met her first when he was a youth of sixteen travelling with his mother. They had been in the same company. In those days she had been a tall, vigorous woman, who had loved to catch him in a darkened coulisse, rumple his hair, caress him and then abandon him with a rich slide of laughter. Four years later, when because of his fluency with languages he had been a courier for a travel agency in Paris, she had found him and shown him a new profession, but from that moment she had been the one who waited for caresses. They knew each other so well, had worked together so often … and they had both waited, playing cards when the drag of time became too severe. Soon after the Rome business she had retired and here she was, a large, plump woman who made him feel like a schoolboy, a woman whose good-humoured obesity and sighs over the past would have embarrassed him if that past had not taught him so much about her true qualities…

She looked across at him affectionately as she picked up a hand.

'Your mother should never have married an Englishman. Then I might have had a chance.'

A bell rang in the hall.

'That's Bernardo – push the door switch.'

Avvocato Bernardo came in, bent over Rosa and kissed her hand with a mumbled speech of greeting. He was a little old jackdaw of a man, greying, his shoulders hunched under a black coat, his manner mild but capable of perkiness and his eyes, in the drink-veined face, bright and restless. Turning enquiringly towards Mercer, he dropped a paper-wrapped salami on to the floor. Mercer picked it up and Rosa introduced them, finishing:

'I've told you all about him before, Bernardo. His mother was a French actress and his father an English corn-chandler.

What does that make him?'

'You're the oracle. You should answer your own riddles, *cara*.'

He sat down and helped himself to a generous whisky. Mercer remained standing, conscious that the bright eyes were sharp and intelligent and that he was being examined.

'How long have you been in this house?' The question was put idly but there was no doubt of its pertinent undertone.

'About twenty minutes.'

Rosa laughed. 'He's jealous, my dear boy.' But she too was aware that the question had nothing to do with jealousy.

'Here on business – or what?'

Mercer stirred uneasily. The advocate was smiling, friendly, but he saw now that there was a hardness under the ancient shabbiness.

'Business.'

Bernardo leaned forward and gathered up the loose cards, tidying them. Then he stretched out a hand and patted Rosa's thigh under the eiderdown. 'I brought the salami. Is there anyone else in the house?'

Rosa shook her head. 'Light me a cigarette and say whatever you've got to say.'

Bernardo lit a cigarette and handed it to her. Then, with a sudden bob of his head towards Mercer, he said cheerfully, 'The police are interested in someone in this house. It's not Rosa. She pays all her dues and sails with a clean ticket. It's not me because I'm too full of law, and anyway they'd know I'd have to be handled differently. So it must be you.'

'I'm in Venice on business, just that.'

Rosa watched them mischievously now.

'He won't tell you anything he won't tell me, Bernardo. Just business – but he wants a list of the local *bravi*.'

'I'll leave it with Rosa for you sometime. You'll find them expensive. I think they over-insure themselves or maybe it just is that everything is dearer these days.'

'I'm not hiring.' Mercer ran his finger along the dusty mantelshelf. 'How do you know the police are interested in me?'

Bernard nodded towards the shuttered window.

'Outside now. When I came in he was standing in the shadow by the canal edge pretending to admire the furniture factory opposite.' He drained his glass and tilted the bottle to see what was left before pouring another. 'I've been in this town too long. I know them all. They change from time to time naturally. This one is a pavement photographer ... you know, candid photographs when your mouth is full of sundae. He's been with them sometime now, so they'll soon be paying him off or moving him to another district. Have a look at him as you go out. A good-looking fellow with a moustache. His name's Cassana...'

'Thanks for the tip.'

'You're welcome. You will be going now?'

Mercer came and sat down. 'No. Waiting is part of his job. I'm here on straight business no matter what the police think. At the moment I'm relaxing ... cards, then salami and Orvieto.'

Rosa stirred happily. 'I'm so glad. I thought you might make it an excuse to go.'

'I was sure he would go. But I see I overlooked the corn-chandler element... How did you get on with your father?'

'I didn't. He died when I was three.'

'I wish mine had. He lived to be eighty and was a constant source of indiscretion and expense. You cut, *cara* – and keep the stakes low, eh?'

A guide with a party of French tourists fired a blank cartridge and the pigeons rose from the square in a sudden susurration of wings and swept around in a great circle. It was a familiar performance and Mercer stopped, watching the wheeling mass of birds that swung past and over the heads of the crowd. Momentarily, he was encompassed by the flashing of grey and white wings. Then the birds rose clear and began to settle on the cornices of the buildings. As a boy he had kept pigeons and he watched them now with a professional eye. They were a mixed lot.

'The pigeons of San Marco,' a voice said from his left. 'No tourist leaves without being photographed feeding them.'

Spadoni was sitting at one of Quadri's tables taking his morning coffee. He tapped the chair at his side.

'Come and join me. Perhaps you were looking for me?'

'I'm sorry, I have an appointment.'

'With Gian Uccello?'

'Unfortunately, no.'

'A pity. A hero should get his reward. I'm sorry the police couldn't help you.'

'Perhaps they spend too much time drinking coffee.'

Spadoni smiled, and brushed a large paddle of a hand over his untidy hair.

'How much longer are you giving yourself?'

'A week.'

'Come and see me before you go.'

'I won't forget.'

As he moved away Mercer was thinking of the week which lay before him. Late the previous night he had written his report for Gevlin Frères and it was in his pocket now to be posted. To keep the job going he had to feed them with facts, and the prospect of more facts. At the moment he was lost, and he was worried about it. Too many other jobs had run into dead ends before.

He turned into the Calle San Giorgio. The front part of Gostini's novelty shop was empty. He stood there for a while and then, impatient, rapped on the counter. He heard someone coughing in the room at the back of the shop. When Gostini still did not come he walked over to the half-glass door of the room. A small curtain covered the glass. He pushed the door open.

Gostini, in his green waistcoat and apron, was leaning over the table, his back to the window. His head was lowered over a bowl of hot water and a dirty towel was draped over his shoulders and forehead to trap the steam that rose from the water. He was sucking in the steam with great, hungry gasps and a pungent odour of friar's balsam filled the room. The man's head came up, the towel slipping away from him. He blinked, his eyelashes fogged with vapour, his plump face red and shining. If he were surprised he made no sign of it. He nodded, recognising Mercer, and said:

'Asthma.'

'I came to see if there were any more letters.'

'None.' The large head drooped forward and he gulped at the rising vapours.

'I see.'

Mercer went into the room. A gondola swung down the canal outside the window, the shadow of the rower dark across the untidy room, and the hoarse cry of *'Premi*!' echoed between the buildings.

Gostini wiped his face slowly with the greasy towel.

'Is there anything else, signore?'

The morning light, frayed by the water reflections, gave the room a melancholy air. Mercer pulled four broken envelopes from his pocket and dropped them on the table before him. There was no great hope in him, but he knew the value of neglecting nothing. 'Remember these?' he asked.

Gostini shuffled forward. He nodded, one hand scratching at the iron-grey tufts of hair above his ear.

'All addressed to me. You passed them on. Take a look at them – at the way the flaps have been sealed down.'

Gostini coughed, his broad neck muscles tightening against the spasm. 'I don't know what you mean, signore.'

'The flap of an envelope which has been steamed open always shrinks a little. It shows when you seal it up again.'

'You mean someone has been opening your letters, signore?' The tones were threaded with a faint indignation as though the old man brought him his active sympathy.

Mercer smiled. 'Don't play-act, Gostini. You're the only one who could have opened my letters.'

'But, signore, how can you suggest–'

Mercer stood up. 'Save it, Gostini.' He went slowly to the window, turning his back on the man. What could you do, he thought? There was no way open to him to get the man to talk. He'd known other men in a similar position rely on force. The idea of hitting Gostini made him feel a little sick...

He turned round suddenly and said swiftly: 'I'd pay you, you know. Pay you well. All you have to do is to tell me why you did it, or who you did it for. I'd keep my mouth shut.'

And then he saw it: the old, familiar struggle with deceit and avarice, marking a man's face, stilling his body, and the whole battle traced in the slow, appraising purse of the mouth, the quiet, abstracted look in the eyes. Gostini stood there, silent, thinking. Mercer said nothing, made no move, knowing that in this pause there was nothing he could do. He watched the faint steam, curling off the surface of the murky liquid in the bowl.

Gostini shrugged his shoulders suddenly.

'I don't know what you're talking about, signore. I didn't open your letters.'

That was it. He wasn't going to get anything. He'd felt that when he had started, but one had to try, trying at least made the bread-and-butter one ate honestly earned. But he was angry now and saw no need to conceal it in this shabby room, in front of this shabby creature.

'I offered to pay you, Gostini, because I'm a reasonable man. I might try other ways to make you talk.' He went towards him. He saw the fear move into the man, saw the puffed bloodlines in the blue-stained eyes, but Gostini held his ground and cried with a kind of choked desperation:

'I swear I never opened the letters. You can't come in here and treat me like this–' He made a movement to pass, but Mercer put out his hand and held him back.

'You're an old liar. You did open them. Why are you interested in Gian Uccello?'

Gostini dropped back towards the wall, his eyes flicking nervously.

'I don't know what you're talking about... *Dio mio*! Believe me, signore, I know nothing about your letters.'

Mercer stood there, knowing he would get no farther. Any fear he could induce in the man, any bribe he could offer, would be matched, were already matched by more potent ones from another side. He heard the door swing behind him and, as he turned, a voice said:

'He's lying, of course. But then you can't blame him.'

Two men were standing just inside the door. The taller of the two was regarding him with placid interest through his horn-rimmed glasses and fingering his red and white spotted bow-tie. The other stood at his side, his mouth open in a canine grin showing a row of gold teeth, his large red hands kneading one another gently. The taller of the two moved across the room to the table and sat down.

'Who the hell are you?'

The man reached out for the letters on the table. 'Gufo's my name. The ape at the door is Moretto.'

'And how do you know he's lying?' He heard Gostini move away from the wall behind him, and then the draw of water through the tap as the old man filled a glass for himself. Gufo sat watching him through his glasses like the owl after which he was called. The calmness of the man made him cautious. Behind the quietness of manner there was power which wanted only the right spur for action. He had met the kind before, knew that there never could be any certainty of what provocation would set them off.

Gostini moved forward anxiously:

'Gufo, I didn't–'

'Shut your mouth!'

Gostini drew back. Gufo turned the letters over in his hand curiously.

'Are these the letters?'

Mercer moved across to him and took the

letters from his hand. 'Yes,' he said, putting them in his pocket.

Moretto edged forward, but the other waved him back.

'The letters belong to him.'

'I'm still waiting to know why they were opened.'

'So you shall, Signore Mercer. *Inglese, eh?*'

'Yes.' He had the feeling that Gufo had decided nothing was going to touch him off this morning.

'This is an accommodation address, signore. People who use it generally have something to hide. Gostini's a bundle of curiosity. Now and again he opens a letter. If he's lucky – then maybe he makes a little money from it.'

'Blackmail?'

Gufo shrugged his shoulders. 'It's a harsh word to use for such a miserable old man. I've known him for years. You can see he hasn't grown rich on it.' He waved a hand round the shabby room.

For all he knew, Mercer decided, Gufo might be telling the truth. An accommodation address gave plenty of scope for blackmail. But he was too aware of the contrary currents which disturbed the sluggish depths of human behaviour to accept what he saw on the surface without question. Gufo had given a straightforward explanation, but with the air of a man who hugs a malicious and private joke to himself. Then, too, Gostini had been about to say something to Gufo and had been shut up. It was more than likely that Gufo shared in the blackmailing activities. With this Mercer set other facts. Boldesca had been killed on his way to an appointment which more than likely he would not have mentioned to anyone. Gufo – assuming he worked with Gostini – had known about that appointment. Was it coincidence that Gufo had walked into this room so appositely? Or was he being watched by others than the photographer he had seen outside Rosa's house? Mercer found himself wondering if Gufo knew anything about Uccello. He said slowly:

'You overheard what I was saying to Gostini? About this Gian Uccello?'

'Certainly, signore.'

Someone came into the outer shop and rapped hard on the counter. Gostini, with a glance at Gufo, went out, glad to leave them.

Mercer moved to the window, leaning his elbows on the broad stone sill. The water under the sun had the fine steel polish of a worn blade. Against the steps of the building opposite a tall mooring post, striped in blue and yellow, reared drunkenly from the canal. A woman ditched a can of rubbish through one of the windows and shattered the burnish on the water.

'I'm trying to find him. It's not being very easy.'

Gufo came and stood close to him, blowing the smoke from his cigarette at the window so that it flattened against the small panes and crept viscously over the glass. 'Moretto and I always have a drink at this time of morning. Why don't you join us? We might be able to help.'

He wasn't looking at the man, he only had his voice, and he was thinking how little the voice gave. It might be that Gufo knew something... He turned. Gufo had his arms crossed over the front of his grey, red-striped suit and was examining the burning end of his cigarette. Moretto was standing behind him, his head jutting forward, his tongue pushing gently at his loose lower lip and his great hands rubbing at the thighs of his tight suit.

Mercer nodded. 'All right. I will.'

Five minutes later they were sitting at one of the outside tables of a café in one of the small squares behind San Marco. When the waiter had brought their drinks, Gufo said:

'Why are you looking for this Gian Uccello?'

'He did a great service for an American during the war. The American wants to reward him.'

'Generously?'

'He's an American.'

'But you can't find him?'

'No. And it doesn't seem likely that I shall.'

'What happens then?'

'I begin to look for another job.'

Gufo was silent for a while. Then he said slowly: 'We might do business – to save you looking for another job just yet. Listen, signore' – he leaned forward, rubbing his glass between his palms – 'I could find a girl who would play the part of his widow. We could say he was dead, arrange the papers, have everything in order, and then collect. The girl wouldn't want much. The rest we could share.'

Mercer laughed. The proposition was entirely unexpected, but there was no doubting the sincerity behind it. 'No, thanks,' he said.

'Why not?' Gufo persisted. 'Have you got so much money that you can afford to miss a chance like this?'

'I should have to have a great deal less than I have to do what you want.'

Gufo shook his head sadly. 'If you don't find him, the American will be disappointed. This way, we shall all be happy. It's common sense.'

Mercer looked across at him. The antagonism which he had felt in Gostini's room had dropped away. It could be revived, he had no doubt, but at the moment it was unimportant in the prospect of making easy money.

'I'd rather you told me what you really know about Uccello,' he said.

'Nothing. He's just a name to me.'

'It's a name I'd like to find an address for. If you can ever help me I'll see you get paid.' Mercer finished his drink and would have stood up to go, but a voice broke in from the pavement:

'*Momento, signori... Ah, va bene! Benissimo*!'

A pavement photographer was half-crouched before them, holding his Leica to his eye. The man nodded genially to them and dropped a small card on the table. 'Any time between ten and four – at the address on the card. A distinguished group, signori. Thank you!'

'Take your arse out of here! Those things make me jumpy.' Moretto flicked the card off the table and made a half-move at Cassana who grinned at them, made an ironical bow, and slid away to the other tables.

Gufo chuckled. 'Moretto can't even bear to see himself in the mirror when he shaves.' Then, as Mercer stood up, he went on seriously: 'Think it over, signore. It's sound business.'

'But not my kind of business.'

As Mercer turned and threaded his way

across the crowded square, Gufo watched him. Moretto licked the sticky edge of his *cinzano* glass and muttered impatiently:

'I don't like him. Why'd you talk that way with him?'

'Because business is business, you ape, whichever side it comes from. And maybe because I don't care to be treated like a dog for a mistake anyone could have made. When people don't tell you things, when you don't even know for who or why you kill a man, it doesn't do any harm to keep a business eye on the other side.'

## Chapter 6

There was no one at the reception desk. The hallway was lit by a few yellow bulbs in the high chandelier. In contrast to the blaze of light coming from the gallery at the head of the stairs the place was a quiet tarn of shadows.

For the price of a drink at a café in the *campo* opposite the palace, Mercer had learned that the name of the gallery attendant was Minelli and that the small girl – Ninetta – was his orphaned niece. He waited now, hoping that Minelli would appear. Ever since he had learned of the

101

death of Boldesca he had known that he must come back to the palace. There might not be a great deal to be gained here but he was curious to know how the absence of Boldesca would be explained, and – since his mention of Uccello's name in the workshop had brought a tenuous response – he felt he had to try Minelli with it. He had a growing conviction that somewhere in this palace lay the core of his problem. A patient gathering of small detail ... he had to commit himself to this. It was his job.

He moved behind the desk and pushed open the small doorway. A narrow flight of steps led down into the basement of the palace. He went slowly down and along a short corridor. An open door was ahead of him and a flood of light from it threw long, rough shadows across the edges and worn surfaces of the wide stones that paved the corridor.

He stood in the doorway. The room was large and tidy: a table with a green cloth, a leather couch, hardwood chairs and a cane armchair before a dead stove, family groups on the walls and, above the lintel of the far door, a blue and white plaster madonna, set back in a recess with a jampot of fresh dwarf irises before her, flanked with votive cards. The little girl, Ninetta, was sitting on the edge of the cane-armchair undressing a doll. The puppy was curled up in a basket beside the chair. She looked at Mercer without surprise, her eyes round and solemn, and said gravely:

'*Buona sera, signore.*'

He nodded, smiling.

She lowered her head over the doll, picking with her thin fingers at the tapes of a small vest. He liked children and wanted to be accepted by them yet, for him, it was always difficult to find a way into their world.

'I've brought something for you,' he said. He went over to her and held out a cellophane packet of pink and blue sugared almonds.

She reached up and took the packet, placing it carefully on her lap with the doll.

'*Grazie.* Did you buy them for me?'

'Of course,' he said firmly. 'Don't you like sweets?'

'Very much. But I would rather have chocolate…'

He laughed. 'Next time, perhaps.' He knelt down beside her, watching the undressing operation. She turned her head to him and the solemn face flowered into a smile, tolerant, undeceived, saying: 'I like you to watch me, but you're not really interested.' In a woman he could have countered it, from her it made him awkward.

'What do you call her?'

She lifted the doll slightly so that he could see the face and corrected him:

'Him.'

'And his name?'

Childishness flowed back now. 'He's Beppo and he's been very naughty. He fell in the canal and was nearly eaten by a fish. Now he's going to have a chill and die…'

There was a stir from the far doorway.

'Ninetta – your stories.' Minelli was standing there. 'Don't take her too seriously, signore. Tonight he dies, maybe, but tomorrow he will be alive again and I shall be tripping over him on the stairs.' He took his presence evenly, the poise of a servant who never questions his superiors and the friendliness of a man who likes the company of his fellows.

'My name's Mercer. I was here yesterday–'

'I remember, signore.'

'I couldn't find you upstairs. I came to ask if Boldesca was back?'

'I was in the courtyard feeding the pigeons and rabbits. From the amount they eat you would think all rabbits had been born in Naples.' He laughed and went to a cupboard and drew out a bottle and two glasses. He held the bottle up. 'It would give me pleasure…'

'Thank you.'

Minelli put the bottle on the table. 'It's Buton cognac from Bologna. My sister and her husband live just outside. When they visit me they always bring three bottles, never more, never less.'

'When I was a boy I kept pigeons, mostly tumblers and red checkers.'

'You must come sometime when it is light and see mine. One has difficulty keeping a pure strain here. I give them a little lecture on eugenics and the dangers of San Marco before I let them out, but many of them are still indiscreet.' There was a gleam of white teeth as he grinned.

They drank. As he put his glass down Mercer asked:

'And Boldesca?'

'Not back. Maybe this time he has gone for good. If he has I shall have to find another lodger.'

'You keep lodgers?'

'Certainly, signore. This whole basement is mine and there are more rooms than I can use. It is an understood thing.'

'It's a pity Boldesca isn't here. I wanted very much to get in touch with a friend of his, but I don't know his address.' He was watching Minelli. The man was picking with one finger at the loose edge of the label on the cognac bottle.

'Perhaps I could help, signore? I know some of his friends.'

'Maybe you could. This one is called Gian Uccello.'

'Gian Uccello?' Minelli repeated the name thoughtfully, then shook his head. 'No – I've never heard of him.'

Mercer knew there was nothing for him there. The man could as well be lying as telling the truth.

'A pity. I must wait until he returns.'

'I'm sorry I cannot help you, signore.'

While they talked, Ninetta, a quiet figure absorbed in her doll, paid no attention to them. From Minelli, Mercer learned something of the three women he had seen in the palace. They were all sisters; Adriana Medova and the youngest girl, Maria Pia Medova, were unmarried, but the eldest was married and called Luisa Orlino. She and her crippled husband and Maria Pia lived together. Adriana lived in a flat on her own. They were all skilled loom workers and Adriana – of whom Minelli spoke with respect – a designer who was largely responsible for the growing fame of the Boria tapestries. They weren't Venetians but from somewhere in the South. They had settled in Venice just before the war. The palace and the business belonged to Count Alessandro Boria whose family had been in Venice before San Marco had been built.

As they talked a man came into the room through the little door which Minelli had used. He was dressed in the uniform of a *tenente di vascello* in the navy – a tallish, stiff figure with a grim, arrogant expression. He nodded to Minelli, gave Mercer a quick, curious glance, and passed through into the corridor.

'That's Lieutenant Longo,' Minelli explained. 'One of my lodgers.'

When Mercer rose to leave, Minelli came with him. 'It's nearly seven,' he said. 'Everyone will be leaving and I must do my rounds before locking up.'

As they went into the hallway there was the sound of footsteps from the great stairs. Adriana and Maria Pia Medova were coming down. The younger girl carried a cloth bundle under one arm and a straw shopping-bag hung from her right hand. She was looking back at her sister and talking.

'Good evening.' The words from Mercer brought the girl's head round and a look of surprise flashed across her face. One of the handles of the shopping-bag slipped from her hand and the bag gaped open, spilling a riot of vegetables and small parcels down the stairs.

'Leave it to me.' Mercer went forward and began to collect the onions and paper bags. The girl crouched on the steps with him, her face hidden as he helped.

He took the bag from her when it was full and stood up.

'Thank you, signore.' She reached out her

107

hand for the bag, but he shook her head, smiling.

'May I help you? You both seem loaded.' He was looking at Adriana who stood watching him. She had a pile of books under one arm.

'No, no – I can manage...' The girl's voice was fresh and a little hurried.

'That's all right, Maria. We shall be glad of Mr. Mercer's help.' She came down the stairs until she was level with him. 'An Italian wouldn't dream of carrying a shopping basket, but if Mr. Mercer doesn't mind...'

'I'll walk between you and then no one will see it. That should save my face.'

He crossed the hall and Minelli, holding the door, called a good night.

'It's not very far.' The young girl spoke without looking at him as they crossed the square, but he could sense the excitement in her; no surprise now, but a pleasure in finding herself involved in a situation which was so unexpected.

'I should warn you,' Adriana said as they turned into the lighted Calle Larga, 'that in a moment Maria is going to ask you if you know anyone called Brown who lives at Burton-on-Trent. He was a sergeant who was billeted with them during the war. He gave her his chocolate ration because she reminded him of his daughter.'

'I've never been to Burton-on-Trent. I'm seldom in England, anyway.'

'He writes to me,' said Maria. 'Next year he is bringing his family for a visit to Italy. Someday I'd like to go to England. Is it so cold and foggy there, signore?'

Maria Pia bombarded him with questions which he did his best to answer. Now and again he turned to find Adriana, her face smiling and friendly, watching him. He would like to have talked to her, but Maria Pia demanded his attention... Young, all quicksilver, turning on him the new weapons of her armoury of youth. But all the time he was aware of Adriana on the other side of him, and he was wondering what it was about her that claimed his interest and then roused a slow excitement in him.

They went to the home of the eldest sister, Signora Orlino, a bottom flat of a house near the Campo San Angelo. Outside Mercer hesitated and would have handed the bag over, but Adriana said quietly:

'Carrying that has earned you a glass of wine. If you care to...'

He went in gladly. In the living-room he was introduced to Signore Orlino – Adriana's brother-in-law, a middle-aged man who sat in a wheeled chair by the window. He accepted Mercer as though he had known him for years and felt no need to stand on ceremony with him. He waved Maria and her chatter into the kitchen to help his wife, who did not appear, and ordered Adriana to get wine and glasses. She dropped the books she had brought for him in his lap. He gave them a glance and then added them to the pile on the window-seat. He had a brusque manner which seemed to cover an irrepressible good temper. His voice had a compelling strength and charm. He swung his chair round and wheeled it over to the table to take his wine.

'If you ever get paralysis of the legs – and there are worse things, signore, for most people suffer from paralysis of the mind and don't know it – see that you don't get it in Venice. They give you a wheeled chair, but what good is that in this town? Every yard a flight of steps, or a bridge. Useless! Unless I get them to put me in a gondola, I'm confined to the Campo San Angelo, or to a house of women. Adriana, *cara*, what are you doing serving this stuff? Get the other bottle. What are your political views, signore?'

'I don't know that I have any.'

Adriana was filling a fresh glass for him.

'Then at your age you should have. Not that I can give you many years, but a man without legs is an old man–'

'You'll frighten Mr. Mercer away if you talk like that,' Adriana scolded him.

'Nonsense. He knows an honest man and a good wine when he meets them.' He turned to Mercer. 'You English never have any political faith, just political excitement which crops up at election time. Now in Italy we're all serious politicians, certain of the truth of our own faith. That's why there's always chaos here. Sometimes when there aren't any women about to bother us you must come along and I'll explain it all to you. Stop laughing at me, Adriana, and tell me how you met this man?'

'He came to the gallery to look at some things and kindly offered to help us home with our shopping.'

'Gallantry! And of no more account than a peacock's feathers or the courting antics of a monkey. Which one was it that attracted you, signore? Adriana or Maria Pia?' He dropped his hand over Adriana's as she stood close to him and squeezed it affectionately, and Mercer saw her raise her free hand and touch the back of his neck.

Mercer smiled, and before he could answer Orlino ran on:

'Have some more wine and tell me what piece of faked furniture you're going to buy from that swindler Count Boria.'

'I'm not buying anything. It was just curiosity took me there.'

'Good.'

He talked on with a fierce, good-natured

111

impetuosity, swinging his chair in the little space of the room, dropping his head and looking across at Mercer under his eyebrows from time to time as though he wanted to study with particular care the effect of his more impertinent remarks. Mercer had the impression of a restless spirit, seeking always for some fresh outlet of talk or thought – a blackbird, caged and unreconciled to its prison.

As they spoke Signora Orlino, a tall, gaunt woman whom Mercer had seen before behind the tapestry loom, came into the room to set the table for the evening meal. He rose to go, but Orlino held him with an absolute demand that he should stay and share their meal. Momentarily he hesitated. Then, glancing across at Adriana, he caught a small movement of her head, a gesture so slight that it became pleasantly conspiratorial between them.

Orlino was in high spirits all through the meal. He made everyone drink a little more wine than they should have done, and it was obvious that Mercer's presence had excited him, relieved the heavy monotony of his day tied to a chair. Mercer had little idea of what he ate, nor could he remember later the cause of their laughter – they were small, formless family jokes, the incidentia of this comfortable circle. Signora Orlino said little, watched his plate and glass, and shook her head now and then as her husband risked some small lewdness of speech, Maria Pia chattered away and Adriana sat next to him, laughing with Orlino. It was of her that Mercer was most conscious. Her body, so close to him, a movement now and again bringing her arm against him, stirred him so much that he could not keep his eyes from her ... the way her hair curled over the nape of her neck, the loose fold of her dress above her breasts and the long, lovely line of a partly bare arm... He knew what was happening to him. This room, these people, represented what he had so long missed, a place to which he belonged, a group in which he was no stranger... And here, too, he had found a woman who awakened an old dream in him and – he had no power to deny himself the hope – might open to him the prospect of a closer, intimate relationship. His hopes raced ahead of this moment and he had no control over them. And because of this, he was drawn back to her, found himself watching her as she spoke to him, finding in her smile, in the movement of a hand as she helped him to the things on the table, small significant tokens of some possible response in her to the emotions which it was useless to call himself fool for entertaining. A man has no defence against the hunger in his own imagination.

Before Mercer left, Orlino made him

promise to come again.

'One afternoon when the women are working,' Orlino wheeled his chair to the door, opening it with an awkward gesture that was a mark of honour.

'I'm leaving, too.' Adriana picked up her coat.

She went out with Mercer. They moved down the street in the direction of the Fenice Theatre.

'How did it happen?' he asked.

'During the war. A piece of shrapnel in his back.' She stopped at the edge of a shallow flight of canal steps. It was dark now and he could not see her face. 'It was nice of you to stay and let him talk. He loves meeting new people.'

'It's a rotten life, tied to a chair.' He looked across at the black bulk of the theatre. 'That's the Fenice, isn't it?'

'Yes.'

'My mother played there once.'

She liked him, felt a warmth for him which contrasted strongly with the anxiety in her to be cleared of the things she must tell him.

'I have to see a client on the other side of the town. Perhaps you'd like to share a gondola as far as the Grand Canal?'

'I'd like to.'

Since he had walked out of the palace with her, he had realised that a part of himself – the professional, probing element – had been dormant, lulled by his own desire to be free of it. He had walked and laughed with her and her sister as though he had been a long accepted companion, had gone into the house and left outside so much of himself that he disliked, and for a while he had been part of a family group which offered him a comfortable relaxation from the strangers amongst whom he lived. Now, despite himself, it awakened into an alert and cautious readiness. As he handed her down into the gondola he cursed himself silently for wondering why she should be so friendly.

'What were you doing at the palace this evening?'

'Enquiring for Boldesca.' He sat down at her side, the black canopy hiding them from the gondolier. He lit a cigarette as the gondola was pushed off. In the darkness her face and body stirred amorphously, and into the silence between them he knew had been written a question which she was too polite to ask. 'Do you know what I am?' he asked.

'What are you?'

'I'm a private enquiry agent. I came to Italy to trace a man called Gian Uccello. I advertised for information and Boldesca came to see me. But he told me nothing. He had been beaten up on his way to me, and he got away from me while I was fetching him a drink. He acted like a very frightened man. All this makes me very curious. You see, the reason I want to find Gian Uccello is quite straightforward.' As he talked the long prow of the gondola sheered into the darkness. Above them the tall buildings leaned forward, crowding over the dark waters so that there seemed to be neither water nor air, only a dark medium which isolated them, drawing them together against the surrounding gloom.

'Is that how you earn your living? Doing this kind of thing?'

'Yes. That's how I live.'

'It sounds romantic.'

He laughed. 'Maybe. But it isn't. It's just a job, and it isn't always pleasant or praiseworthy. But for once this business is. I only want to find Uccello to tell him that an American father would like to make him a handsome present for having saved the life of his son during the war.'

In the darkness he heard her laugh gently, and she said: 'You sound almost indignant.'

'Why shouldn't I be? I don't understand why Boldesca ran away from me.'

'Boldesca's an odd, uncertain man. I've never liked him, but I think I can tell you as much about Gian Uccello as he can.'

'You?'

'Yes.'

She moved slightly in the shadows and his hand touched her, a fold of her linen dress

116

coarse under his fingers for a moment. Her offer to help was unexpected and he found himself wondering whether the darkness which hid her face now, hid innocence or subtlety. He hated the thought but habit forced it on him, just as professional caution made him keep back from her the knowledge that he knew Boldesca was dead. In his job a man had to hang on to this advantages until he was certain of people.

'If you can help me at all, I shall be very grateful,' he said.

'I can help you,' she said, and then was silent for a while, her eyes on the little lantern at the prow of the boat. The gondola passed under a low bridge and she heard the clatter of wooden soles above her. The gleam from a cornice lamp lit up the grey, rustic-stoned side of a house in a moving cloth of elephantine grey, patched and stained with the weird outlines of damp. Another gondola passed them, the lapping water racing between the boats in low, confident chuckles. This man, she thought, was straightforward and it was hard now to recall the keen anxiety which had settled upon her after his first visit to the palace. She went on evenly, watching the spasmodic illumination of his long face as he drew at his cigarette: 'If I'd known what you were when you first came to the palace I would have helped you then.'

'You said you didn't know Gian Uccello.'

'I knew him, but he's not someone I find it easy to talk about to a stranger. Even now, if isn't very easy.'

In the gloom in the canopy, he was glad that there was only her voice. If he could have seen her face he would have watched it, watched it with the eyes of a man who had studied so many faces, waiting for the sign which flickered over the flesh when deceit or fear stirred. With her voice alone he was content because there was nothing he wanted to discover... Nothing, perhaps, to discover.

'You didn't know it, of course ... but when you mentioned his name to me yesterday morning, you were bringing back memories...' She hesitated for a moment. 'The kind of memories which one doesn't lay bare without–'

He broke in quickly: 'The man I'm looking for was a partisan near La Spezia in nineteen forty-four.'

'That was he.'

'Tall, dark ... about my age?'

'Yes.'

'Do you know where he is now?' He heard the rub of the oar against the crotched post by the gondolier. From the grilled garden of a small restaurant a soft blaze of coloured lights turned water and houses into a grotto of reds and blues through which they floated, and fleetingly he saw her face, pale, untroubled and with a quiet beauty which touched him strangely. No woman had ever moved him like this before. As darkness came back, she said:

'He was in Venice during the last part of the war. It was here that I met him and we were together—'

'There's no need to tell me any more than where he is now.' He spoke softly, covering some jealous turbulence in himself. He could not hold down the thoughts which strung themselves on that word 'together.'

'He's dead. He's buried at Mirave, where he was killed in an air raid. It's not far from Venice and he'd gone there on business.'

The calmness with which she spoke stilled his jealousy. The man – whatever he had been to her – was dead, and when she talked of him her voice was untroubled by any emotion.

'Has he any relatives?'

'None.'

'Or friends?'

'I am the only one who remembers him.'

The gondola grounded against a dark flight of steps where the small rio they had been following debouched into the Grand Canal. There was more light here, and he could see her face, white and drawn back into the shadow of the canopy, like a flat stone shining in the darkness, and momentarily her lips softened into a hesitant smile for him. He took it with gratitude.

'You understand that I shall go to Mirave tomorrow?'

'Yes.'

'And thank you for helping me.'

'I should have told you when you first came to the palace. Only at that moment–'

'I understand. I'm grateful to you now, anyway.' He put out his hand and rested it on hers. She made no move to avoid it, but she turned her head from him slightly.

'Does this mean that after you've been to Mirave, you'll be leaving Venice?' She spoke very quietly.

He felt the warmth of her hand against his palm, and her words echoed in his mind raising hope, pushing his impatience for her until he felt his body tremble. He drew his hand away, and as he rose, said:

'After Mirave I shall be my own master.'

He watched the gondola dip out into the main stream and slide caterways across the broad waters, the gondolier's body swaying and arching in an ungainly rhythm, flexing and contorting itself in a silent ritual. He stood there, knowing that the caution with which he had approached her was now gone. This was all that Boldesca could have told him, the story of a man and a woman and the place of the man's burial. Then the death of Boldesca must lie entirely outside all this, an odd coincidence of events obtruding into a simple affair… Anyway, he wasn't concerned with Boldesca now. He was aware only of his own hopes – what had she meant when she asked him if he would be staying? Surely on that something of the feeling he had for her had been recognised and had drawn this response from her. He turned away, whistling happily to himself.

## Chapter 7

Mirave was fifty miles to the south-west of Venice and reached by a branch railway from the main Milan-Venice line. A diesel-engined coach, looking like a battered cigar-container, took Mercer the last part of the journey across a flat stretch of reclaimed marshland, furrowed with sluggish, gravelly streams, and fat with newly turned earth and fruit trees just breaking blossom. He watched the country rumble by without curiosity. The Italian countryside, any countryside, had little interest for him. He belonged to the towns, to the crowded places and the dark anonymity of back streets. That day, too, he felt a relaxing absence of any kind of curiosity. He could only think of Adriana. He couldn't even bother to speculate which of the few other travellers who had left the Milan train with him might be one of Spadoni's men. Whoever it was, it wasn't the photographer.

A slatternly woman at a crossing held back the red and white bar for them. A line of geese waddled in a pompous frieze across a gravel spit and the bamboos at the side of the track changed colour as the wind slid along them; olive trees were contorted in that silent agony which time and the rich earth inflict on them, and the sky was stretched as thin and taut as a balloon on the point of bursting. They rattled into Mirave station and he got out with three other people who immediately disappeared into the early afternoon silence with an adroitness which seemed natural in the face of the unwelcoming barrenness of the station. The coach hissed and then lumbered away into the long distance of sky and fields.

Mercer went down the station approach into the town. Mirave was a shabby huddle of buildings, gathered about a large main square. Plaster peeled from its walls, a litter of papers and dust moved uneasily along the gutters in the warm wind, and the blistered window shutters gazed blankly at a new, unpainted *pissoir* that stood in the centre of the square. A row of young acacia trees threw meagre shadows over the cobbles.

Their thick supporting posts, attached to them by broad ligatures of felt, seemed to have sapped all the strength from the thin limbs.

Mercer walked across the cobbles, wondering if he had entered a town emptied by plague until he remembered that it was afternoon and, although not hot, the siesta hour. If ever, he thought, he wanted to cut his own throat and doubted his courage, he would come back to this place, at this hour, and it would be easy.

Across the face of the largest building one of Mussolini's slogans had been so imperfectly scrubbed out that the old lettering still showed – *Noi, Italini, siamo pronti.* It was one thing they had never been in their lives, of course. In smaller letters over the door at the head of the shallow steps leading up from the pavement was written – *Commune di Mirave.* Across the shield of the remaining one of a pair of supporting heraldic beasts which had graced the sides of the door was an old army sign in blue and white paint, reading – 293 Signal Section – Officers Only. Mercer stood for a moment at the bottom of the steps wishing he had chosen a more fitting hour to make a call at a public office. Somewhere behind him came the desultory tapping of a small hammer and he remembered that he had passed a stone-mason's yard at the entrance to the square.

The public urinal flushed itself noisily.

He stepped over a man sleeping on the bottom step and went into the building. It was dark inside and it took him some little time to find the door which he knew would open to him the information he wanted. It told him in handsome gold letters that it was the office of the mayor.

He had to knock three times before there was the sound of movement within and a sleepy voice called out to him to enter. The mayor was seated at his desk, frowning at a mess of papers before him. He looked like a man caught in a frenzy of trying to decide which, out of so many things, to do next. Underneath the desk his feet showed in socks and from an ashtray by the side of a leather couch on the other side of the room a cigarette stub sent up a thinning tail of smoke.

'I'm sorry but I couldn't make anyone hear down below.'

'Sleeping probably.' The mayor yawned, and waved to a chair in front of the desk and then buttoned the top of his waistcoat. He was a largish, hairy man with the resigned expression of one who is so used to being provoked that it no longer put him out of temper.

'I've disturbed you?'

'Probably, but it doesn't matter. If it isn't one thing it's another – and there's never any end to this.' He patted a pile of grey documents with the pride of an owner smacking the rump of one of his hunters. 'Who are you?'

'Mercer's my name.' He handed him his passport. 'I've come to you for some information.'

'Well, we've got plenty of that here.' The mayor smacked another pile of papers. 'I thought you might be from Padua. They worry me all the time down there. Of course, I know they've only got their job to do.' He was looking at the outside of the British passport. 'Your government make a better job of these than we do. The only time I ever had one was the year I married. Honeymoon in Austria. Only went to Klagenfurt, not more than fifty miles over the border, but I had to have one.' He handed it back.

'I'm making some enquiries – for legal purposes – about a man who was killed in an air raid on this town during the war.'

'Would have had to be during the war – no air raid otherwise. And there was only one air raid that killed anyone. Awful affair, though I wasn't here myself. I was in Ancona. But I can tell you anything. Got all the records. There's nothing wrong with our records, except for the years forty-one to forty-three. The British officers burned those to keep themselves warm. New Zea-

125

landers – that's the same as British?'

'Yes. But don't quote me on it. The man I'm interested in was called Gian Uccello. Are you sure there was only one air raid?'

'My family and I have been in this town for longer than anyone. Maybe I wasn't here all the war but I'd certainly know how many raids there were. Let's look at the records.' He got up and walked across the room in his stockinged feet and opened a cupboard at the foot of the couch. Mercer heard him muttering to himself as he went through the loaded shelves.

He came back and stood at the window overlooking the square, ruffling the pages of an untidy file.

'That's it. At half-past eleven on the night of January the third, nineteen forty-five. This place was in German hands then, but we never knew whether it was an Allied or a German plane. Killed everyone in the hotel.'

'It fell on a hotel?'

'Yes. Albergo Risorgimento – across the square there. No point in getting up – there's nothing but an open space now.'

'Was there a man called Gian Uccello among the dead?'

The mayor turned a few pages of the file, then nodded.

'That's right. There were eight killed, five of them were local people and the other three from outside. A man and two women. But they were all identified.' The mayor sat down at his desk.

'And the man was Gian Uccello?'

'That's the name it gives here and on the plaque outside.'

'Plaque?'

'You can see it as you go out. The town raised a subscription for a memorial right away. The Germans didn't object. They always said it was an Allied plane.'

'How was Gian Uccello identified?'

'I don't know. There's nothing about that in the file.'

'Who would know?'

The mayor leaned back considering this for a moment. Then he said:

'Crespi would be the best man for you. He was mayor at the time. He was first on the spot. Pulled most of them out, too, and arranged the whole lot for the funeral. Must have made fifteen thousand lire out of the whole business.'

'As mayor he doesn't seem to have missed any opportunities. Where will I find him?'

'Sinobaldi Crespi? He's the stone-mason here. Carved all the headstones. You'll find him near the station.'

'I must see him...' He was silent for a moment. This looked like the end of the trail for him. 'So Gian Uccello is buried out in the cemetery...'

'Yes, with all the others.'

'Could you give me a statement, signed by you as mayor, confirming this?'

The mayor nodded. 'You'll have to pay two hundred lire for it, and the cost of the stamp.'

'Certainly.' Mercer smiled as the mayor began to make out the certificate. As the man wrote, he went on: 'Is there a photographer in the town? I'd like photographs of the grave and the plaque.'

'Filippo over at the café would do it for you. It's a hobby of his. Tell him from me not to charge you more than five hundred lire.' He pushed the signed statement across to mercer. *'Due cento dieci lire. Grazie, signore.'*

Outside, Mercer found the plaque. It was set just above head height at the corner of the building; a long, rather narrow panel of marble. Running along the bottom of the panel was an inscription recording that it had been set up as a memorial to those whose lives had been lost in the air raid. Then followed a list of names and amongst them the name of Gian Uccello. The greater part of the panel was given over to a very fine carving in relief showing eight people, each one symbolising some different trade or profession, walking along a cypress-bordered road. At the end of the road lay a little town over which hovered an angel of death. Mercer realised at once that it was far from being a conventional, five-hundred-lire-a-figure carving. The people stood out of the marble with a vigour which was grim, the whole feeling that of a sacrificial procession which nothing would interrupt. The hares and birds of the roadside, the turn of a goat's neck all marked a sense of sad wonder as the little group moved forward, a soldier with his carbine, a woman with a basket, a peasant with a flagon of wine and a reaping hook, a man in city dress with a suitcase ... all moving towards the high-poised angel who waited for them. If Crespi had done this, he thought, he was a genius who should not hide himself in Mirave.

In a café across the square, he found Filippo. He arranged for the man to take photographs and forward them to him at Venice. Then, as he sat over his beer, he reviewed his own position. There seemed no doubt about it that Gian Uccello was dead. That being so he had only to turn in his report to Gevlin Frères, substantiating it with the mayor's certificate and the photographs, and his job was finished. From what Adriana had told him he had no doubt that the Gian Uccello she had known and who had come here was the same man who had been at Montevasaga. Her description of Uccello was the same one he had been given in Paris and which he had checked at Montevasaga. The man was dead and his job was at an end.

He sat there tracing his finger against the glass fog of his iced beer and wondered what the next job would be – if he got one. From this one and with the little he had in his Paris account he could live for a couple of months. There were other people than Gevlin Frères he could go to, but it would be the same everywhere... The scarcely veiled suggestion that he was not as good as he had been, that he was getting on, surprise that he hadn't cut himself out a safe niche somewhere like so many of the others. What was it Gevlin had said, too? 'A man's face wears out after ten years. Lisbon, Tangier, Rome, Ankara... They know you. Get yourself a new face and it would be different.' Gevlin's face would never wear out because he never showed it. So what was there?

Divorce work, watching fat industrialists and infatuated elderly women making fools of themselves in back rooms, keyholes and rumpled blankets, hotel servants with itchy palms and all the sad evil of faded lust and jealousy... And, before he knew it, he would be over the edge he had so long avoided; black-market stuff and petty crime, into blackmail and fraud, and finally... God, what a smelly mess the whole thing was!

No, whatever happened, he was not going

to have any of that. He would have to find something else... Now, there was Adriana and a new courage and determination on his part to break clean away from this life. There must be that. There had to be that – but the very exhilaration of the thought made him cautious. He would be a fool to build too highly on a woman's smile, a few enigmatic words... If she meant nothing but kindness...? He couldn't believe that. He gave himself up frankly to day-dreams, sprawled in his chair, a no longer young man in a shabby tweed suit, dusty shoes, the sole of one worn thin... Then, into his abstraction came the sound of a stone-mason's hammer, tapping away, marking an irregular tattoo which broke up the line of his thoughts.

He finished his beer and looked at his watch. He had nearly an hour before the train went. He still had to question the stone-mason about the identification of Uccello's body.

The mason's yard was on the corner of the square, a little open triangle of ground fenced in by a low wall and a wide gateway. At the back of the yard was a run of sheds with a wooden notice board above them – Sinobaldi Crespi, Undertaker and Monumental Mason.

Mercer leaned over the gate. There was a man in the yard, bent over a marble slab supported on a pair of thick trestles, cutting some lettering. He was an oldish man in dusty grey overalls and wearing a brown paper cap to keep his hair clear of marble powder. He stopped work after a while and looked at Mercer. His eyes flickered weakly and he rubbed at an untidy moustache. Mercer had the impression of an under-nourished seal.

'*Buona sera, signore.*'

Mercer nodded and his eyes went from the man to the litter of devout statuary, angels and urns and vault panels carved with doves and flowers. You could walk into any Italian cemetery, he was thinking, and find the same kind of thing, the sexless angel face, a little bored with the effort of holding out a wreath and maintaining wings half-furled, the doves that looked too heavy to fly... The hand which had carved these had never, he was sure, worked the panel across the square. He said suddenly:

'Did you carve the air-raid panel across there?' His head tipped towards the Commune building.

Crespi looked up from his work, then dismounted from the trestle and came slowly across to him.

'You're not Italian, signore?'

'No – English.'

'I see.' He went up to a carved panel which showed a kneeling group of women before a

132

cross. 'You've seen the panel over there? Now look at this.' He slapped the stone as though he would push it away and forget it.

'There's a difference.'

'Difference! Signore – this is bread-and-butter, the work of a labourer. Over there – genius. My stuff they can do better in a factory.'

'Who did it?'

'My assistant, Paolo Cerva.' The pride in the man's voice was unmistakable. 'A genius, signore, if ever there was one. If you're interested I'll show you some more of his work. Come over to the hut.' He opened the gate for Mercer. 'Poor Paolo...'

'Why "poor"?' Mercer threaded his way over the yard.

'The Germans took him when they left here. They rounded up every man they could find and carted them off. Paolo was taken just after he'd finished that panel, two months before the war ended. To see him take the bare marble and bring it alive, laughing and singing there, and always full of jokes and fun ... and then the damned *tedeschi* took him just as though he were the same as other men. It broke my heart.'

Mercer could see that left to himself the old man would talk of his assistant for hours. He cut across his talk now with the question he had come to ask.

'You helped rescue the victims of the air

raid here, didn't you?'

'Yes. I was mayor at the time. What a night that was and all the business afterwards! Come in, signore.' He opened the door of the hut.

'This air raid. Do you remember a man called Gian Uccello who was one of the victims?'

'Perfectly, signore. Paolo and I carried him out. Now look at this panel. What a way he had with animals... There's a donkey for you, a real donkey, like all our donkeys, broken-backed and with a belly full of wind and sour hay.'

'What was he like?'

'Who?'

'This Uccello man.'

'Oh – smashed to pieces. They all were.'

'But can you remember what sort of man, his build, how he was dressed?'

'Why not, I buried him? Buried all the others, too. He was dark, well-built and... Oh, I don't know, your height, maybe less. Wore a blue suit, what was left of it. Now look at these...' He had lifted down a folder of drawings and was laying them on the rough bench.

'But how was he identified as Gian Uccello? Do you remember that?'

Crespi paused, his hands on the folder. 'Now let me see ... there were three from outside – two were women. Ha, yes, I remember – the other was a man and he had his identity card in his wallet. But why do you wish to know this?'

'I'm making enquiries for a firm of lawyers.'

'Oh. Well, there was his card, and… Yes, of course … a letter from a woman in Venice. We wrote to her.'

'Who was she?'

'That I can't remember. But she wrote back saying he was only a friend, had no relatives, and she enclosed money for his funeral expenses.'

'Where would the identity card and letters be now?'

'The good Lord might know. They were all packed up and sent to Padua after the Allies reached here. He's dead, all right. And so, probably, is Paolo who did the memorial for them all. The war robbed us of a lot of good men… Look at these drawings. If Paolo had lived he would have been famous…'

Mercer scarcely heard him. He was thinking of the woman in Venice. Adriana. Yes, it would be her. And this garrulous little mason had buried Uccello.

'Look at them. Sometimes he worked straight on the stone, but sometimes he drew first, chiefly the panels.'

Crespi turned them over, a jealous movement as though he wanted no one else to touch them, laying each one before

135

Mercer. They were mostly decorative arrangements of figures like the town hall panel, but there were some single figures and one or two faces. 'What a tragedy it was. He never came back, probably died in Germany or somewhere. You know how they treated them. Such a fine spirit, too... Look how he handles animals and children. He had a way with them in life, too. Children loved him and birds – he used to keep pigeons in the yard, knew them all by name and they'd come to him when he was sitting in the café over there if he whistled. Paolo and his birds. Just like Saint Francis. Here's one now, I always wanted him to do, but we never had a big enough piece of marble.'

He dropped in front of Mercer a large sheet of cartridge paper covered with the design for a panel. For a moment Mercer stared at it with the same half-attention which he had given the others. The stone-mason lifted another sheet, but as the man moved, Mercer put out his hand swiftly and stopped him.

'Did Paolo Cerva do this?'

'But of course.'

He picked up the design and stepped away from the bench.

'You like that drawing, eh? You're a discriminating man. It was Paolo's favourite. Ha, signore, it's nice to talk to someone who appreciates these things. Here in Mirave they have minds, or what they call minds, which would disgrace a congregation of frogs. It's good to talk to someone about him. Only I know what Mirave has lost, what Italy, maybe the world, has lost…' The weak eyes blinked and an engrained hand teased at the straggly moustache.

Mercer heard the old man talking, but his mind was far away. The drawing reminded him of something. He stood there, searching for it, tracing memory back from the moment when Crespi had dropped it before him. Then it came. Birds and shrubs and a rocky pool. Unless he was mistaken it was very like the tapestry in the Boria Gallery. He couldn't remember the tapestry clearly…

'Could I have this drawing. I'd pay you for it.' He'd like to show it to Adriana. If there was a similarity she'd be interested. For a moment it crossed his mind that she might have met Cerva and had one of his designs.

Crespi looked at him, and he saw the struggle going on in the old man. Then Crespi nodded:

'Take it, signore. I have the others and it will be good to know that someone else appreciates Paolo…'

It took Mercer another twenty minutes to get away from him and he almost missed his train.

He sat at the back of the diesel-coach, a few other passengers sitting ahead of him, and he unrolled the design. It was a pencil drawing, done with a faultless exactness of line, showing a forest pool fringed with fantastic shrubs and trees which were studded with heavy, ornate tropical blossoms. Around the pool and on the shrubs were birds, vivid, elaborate creatures. Others hung in the air or waded in the water, and on a low rock beyond the pool stood a bird of paradise, wings half-spread, its plumage in full display with delicate sprays of thin feathers cresting from its head and shoulders.

## Chapter 8

At ten-twenty in the morning the sun was off Florian's side of the piazza and shining on the tables of Quadri and Laverna. So Florian's was empty and the other full. Later in the year, when there was real heat in the sun, the rule would be reversed – hide from the sun not follow it. The front of San Marco was in shadow but the slender flagpoles, tipped with their golden eagles, glowed a warm rust in the light, and the shadow of the Campanile was a dark pathway across the worn flagstones. Post-cards, papers, balloons, beads and cheap metal figures, their sellers were all back again after the cramped night, not a wrinkle out of place on their clothes, nothing changed ... toy figures packed away in the nursery cupboard and brought out each day. The younger waiter who brought him his coffee had the face of a Pan, and wore his little silver badge with the number nine-teen as though it were a medal for valour in the face of overwhelming customers.

A man a few tables from him was tossing crumbs to a group of pigeons. Someone fired a pistol shot and the pigeons flapped away like leaves before a wind.

A hawker sold Mercer a map of Venice and went away surprised. The vultures gathered and his coffee grew cold as he beat off leather albums, a lightning sketch of himself in charcoal and a bunch of camellias. The woman with the camellias went to the man who had been tossing crumbs to the birds and got short shrift from him. He turned his head and Mercer saw that it was Lieutenant Longo. He called good morning to him pleasantly. The man returned the greeting stiffly and after a moment went away across the square.

Mercer sat there, relaxed and happy. That evening he would go and see Adriana. He had an excuse. She would be interested in

139

the design from Mirave ... and after that there would be no need of excuses for seeing her. There had been other women before who had excited his hopes ... but this girl was different. There was something there which he knew was for him. He sat there, knowing he was dreaming, but, for all that he could smile at himself, warn himself not to build too highly, convinced that beyond the dream was an equally pleasant reality.

A heavy body dropped into the chair beside him, and a signet ring tapped on the metal table top to call the waiter.

'Good morning, Mr. Mercer.'

Spadoni's large face was marked with a solemn, dog-like intelligence, knowing something was coming its way, ready to be walked or fed or disappointed.

'Good morning.' He wasn't pleased to see Spadoni. He would rather have been alone with his own lazy thoughts.

'You're taking it easy this morning?'

'I've joined the unemployed.'

The waiter brought Spadoni coffee and a glass of water, and Mercer watched him peel the paper from his sugar lumps. He put one in his mouth and dropped the other in his coffee.

'You've found Gian Uccello?'

The man's question gave him no surprise. 'In a way. He's dead.'

'A hero's death?'

Out in the square before them a mother and her daughter were being posed in a circle of strutting pigeons and Cassana the photographer was shaking a tin of peas and encouraging the pigeons to perch on the girl's arm. The man said something to the girl, and Mercer heard her high, delighted laughter and saw a quick, indulgent smile pass over the man's face as he snapped his fingers, enticing the pigeons. It would make a nice picture and the photographer was taking great trouble to get his effect.

'Suppose you tell me? It wasn't your photographer out there who followed me to Mirave, but one of your men must have done.'

Spadoni sighed and nodded his head. 'It was a woman actually. I'm not apologising for you must have expected it ... treated it as a formality. She got the same information from the mayor as you did. If we'd known about it before we should have told you...'

'Would you? Everywhere I've been I've noticed a reluctance on the part of the police to tell me anything.'

'Perhaps I can explain that.'

'Perhaps I can, too. In Rome in nineteen thirty-eight, because I put too much faith in my employers – I've learned better since – I came within an inch of being arrested for assassinating one of Mussolini's senators.

The police have long memories. The moment I crossed the border on a perfectly innocent mission the word must have gone round. Tell him nothing of importance – just in case. However, my job's finished now and I bear no ill-will.'

'That's very good of you. But it's not quite true. Until you came to Venice the police didn't know a thing about you. Many of the *Ovra* records were destroyed you know and twelve years is a long time.'

'And when I came to Venice?'

Spadoni drained his coffee and stood up. 'I recognised you. I was in Rome in thirty-eight. Come back with me to the office and I'll show you something.'

Back in the office, Spadoni dropped a slim folder into Mercer's hand.

'I had this sent up from Rome after your visit to me. It's been brought up to date and now a red line can be drawn under the last page. What gaps there are need not worry us.'

Mercer read the dossier through. Spadoni's frankness in showing it to him might be genuine, but he couldn't be sure. The police usually kept something back from men like him, even if it were an unimportant something. That had to be done out of pride, cautiousness ... to mark, not peace, but a truce.

Gian Uccello's early years had never been

fully documented. He had been born somewhere near Naples and probably in the year 1910. His real name was believed to be Lucio Gianbaptista Martellore. Until he was twenty-six – in 1936 – there was nothing against him. Then he had robbed and killed a man in Naples and had disappeared. Until the end of 1938 had followed various other crimes, robbery with violence and fraud and with the police always picking up his trail too late. In 1939 he had gone to South America, but within a year was back again. In 1943 he had turned up at La Spezia as a partisan. Then, for a price, he had betrayed his companions and had left that area in June 1944 just in time to avoid the justice handed out to those partisans found working for the Germans. After June 1944 there had been no trace of him until the proof of his death in Mirave in January 1945.

'He was a nice fellow, wasn't he?' Spadoni's voice came to him from the window where he was standing.

'Yes.' He dropped the folder back on the desk, showing none of his surprise, and his mind was on certain facts in the dossier which, he was sure, meant more to him than they could to Spadoni. 'A murderer, a thief... Everything, in fact. Even a hero. And always taking off before anyone could put a hand on him.'

'Yes. That's why we, and the people he worked with, called him "Uccello". And a very smart "bird", too. Using the name Gian Uccello with the partisans was sheer bravado – even though there were the Allied and German lines between him and his dossier at Rome.'

'Why did you never get your hands on him – before the war, I mean.'

Spadoni turned from the window.

'Because of the man himself. He wasn't an ordinary crook. He seemed to inspire some odd loyalty in the people he worked with. Hero-worship, perhaps. Whatever it was they never betrayed him. We've never even had a photograph of him.'

'It's not going to be easy to tell the truth to our American clients.'

'Decent people are entitled to their illusions. Let it stay that way, Mr. Mercer. With us it's different. Go back to Paris and tell them he's dead, killed as a hero should be.'

He came across as Mercer rose and held out his hand. 'I'm a policeman. But whichever way it was I've forgotten the Rome business. I hope something turns up for you in Paris.'

Mercer thanked him as they shook hands. As the door was held open for him, Spadoni said casually:

'I suppose you wouldn't tell me how you got a lead to Mirave?'

144

Mercer shook his head. 'I'm sorry.'

'I don't insist. After all it's nice to have a little loose change to jingle in one's pocket. Keeps one happy.'

Mercer walked back to his hotel for lunch. The pages of the dossier were clear in his mind and two items stood out from all the others. As a young man, before his first crime, Uccello had been working for a stone-mason in Naples, and in 1938 he had been one of a forgery gang – hundred-lire notes so near perfection that for six months they had been unsuspected – and Uccello, so convicted members of the gang had testified, had been the draughtsman.

The thin line of light at the bottom of the door disappeared. Footsteps died away down the great stairs and the echoes they made faded lingeringly into silence.

Getting into the palace, avoiding Minelli, had been easy. Getting out might not be so easy, but at the worst he could go down and brazen it out, say that he had lost his way in the maze of rooms and corridors or had gone to sleep in a window embrasure to wake and find himself locked in. A window embrasure, he thought, would have been more comfortable than this broom cupboard under the stairway which led to the top floor of the palace.

He looked at the luminous dial of his

watch. It was nearly eight, and he decided to give himself fifteen minutes before going out. Since his meeting with Spadoni that morning he had known that he must come to the palace and find out whether there was any similarity between the Cerva design and the tapestry. Until he had read Uccello's dossier the likeness had seemed only a matter of strange interest … something to take up pleasantly with Adriana. Now there was no escape for him. A man could deceive himself easily out of his own desire not to uncover unpleasantness where he wished none to be. That's what he'd done over Boldesca's death. And simply because a dark-eyed Italian woman, whose body and affection he would like to possess, had been kind to him and had made him eager from some damnable ache in himself to believe her untouched by the kind of muck in which he usually dabbled. So he'd pretended that there wasn't any muck, pretended – no, believed – that Boldesca's death after meeting him was some coincidental overlap from another affair.

Like hell it was all coincidence! Uccello's dossier had shown him how far and how easily he had let himself be turned aside from the truth. Boldesca undoubtedly murdered, Gufo and Moretto and Spadoni's men watching him, and Gian Uccello tucked nicely away in Mirave cemetery …

and somewhere a man called Paolo Cerva. Cerva and Uccello. Both had been stone-masons, both skilled draughtsmen and designers. Cerva had pulled a mutilated body from a bombed hotel at Mirave and helped bury it. If Cerva and Uccello were the same, then the body of an unidentifiable stranger would have been a godsend to a man with a criminal record who wanted to disappear for good... Boldesca who had worked here, and Cerva who, maybe, had one of his designs being made into a tapestry here... All this and innocence too? He'd been stupid all right.

And now? He knew where he was going. He was going to get to the bottom of this Uccello business. There might be danger in it for himself, but self-anger, which had grown since that morning, made him brush that thought aside. He could look after himself and he held some advantages which he had no intention of giving away. Nobody knew what he suspected. An open request to go into the workroom might have raised suspicions. Also, until he knew where Adriana stood in all this, he had no intention of saying anything to her. For the moment he held her apart, refusing to question her position out of his own uncertainty. All he knew was that he wanted to compare the two designs. Somewhere, here in this palace, lay the answer to the mystery of Gian Uccello and the reason for Boldesca's death.

When he left the cupboard it was to find that he was not in complete darkness. A pale light came through the windows from the buildings on the far side of the canal above him, at the head of the stone stairs which ran up to the top floor of the palace, a single electric light burned dimly. He moved forward cautiously across the gallery. He stopped.

From the great stairway leading down into the main hall he heard the sound of feet. At the end of the gallery he saw the glow of an electric torch begin to rise in a tiny dawn above the top stair. Turning he slipped quietly up to the top floor.

He was on a wide landing, a window to his left, a large door before him and a dark corridor running off to his right. He waited for a moment. The gleam of the torch came across the gallery below towards the foot of the stairs. He moved to the window and drew back into the cover of the long curtains which had been half-drawn. He felt the stir of the night air on his neck and saw that the window was open behind him. On the canal a water-bus fussed along – an illuminated insect. The tap of feet came up the stairs towards him. Someone passed the window. The footsteps stopped and he heard a throat-clearing grunt which told him that it was a man. A door handle turned. He heard a voice say, surprised, the beginning of irritation in it:

'What on earth's he doing here?'

From within the room someone answered, a tired, cultured voice:

'One might ask the same question of you. Come in and shut the door.'

The door was closed and the light filtering through the curtains was gone. Curiosity rose in Mercer. He would like to have heard the rest of the conversation. Curiosity with him was a professional habit. There was no need to be ashamed of it.

Outside was a narrow balcony, more ornamental than useful, and just wide enough to take a man. He dropped down to it and moved along. Five paces from him was another window. A crack of light came from the drawn curtains, too high up for him to look through, but one of the middle casements was partly open and he could hear the voices from the room. They came and went, sometimes clear, sometimes blurred as though the speakers were moving about.

He listened; a dark figure lost against the shadowed façade of the palace, the reflection-scored waters of the canal far below him, a warm evening breeze pulsing down the wide gulf of houses and buildings.

'I don't know who it will be. I've just had the message that he'll be at Orfeo's next

Saturday about six. We can see him there, but I've got to confirm it right away.' To Mercer it sounded like the man who had stood in the doorway.

'All right. Help yourself to sherry and stop frowning.' It was the tired voice, but authoritative now. There was a low murmur of sound and the sudden high note of a glass touching glass and then the first voice came clearly. The man must have moved to within a few feet of the window.

'But what's he doing here?' The irritation was back.

'I was just about to ask him that when you came in.' The tired voice answered, and then went on, changing tone and pitch as though its owner had turned to someone else. 'Why have you come?'

'Why shouldn't I come?' The speaker laughed as though at the concern of the other two. 'In a little while now I shall be gone for good. You understand how it is with men like myself, signore. We like to see our work when it is finished. All I need is a few minutes.'

As the man spoke Mercer was puzzled by something in his voice which was familiar. Somewhere he had heard it before, but not so often that it had become a firm part of his memory. Rich, attractive and somehow forceful – a voice to make you curious about its owner.

'Did Adriana tell you it was finished?'

'Who else, signore? She tells me everything.'

'I can only hope that you don't tell her everything.' Irritation had passed to scarcely veiled bad-temper in the first voice.

The tired voice came in quickly: 'That's enough.' Then, after a pause, it went on: 'Well, I suppose it's reasonable. It's your design, and there's no real risk. You can have five minutes. I shall wait for you here.'

There was the stir of feet inside the room. Mercer drew away from the window and moved along the balcony. By the time he had climbed back behind the curtains it was to find that the two men who had left the room were at the bottom of the stairway. He held the curtain aside, watching them, but they were no more than dark shadows. He saw the beam of a torch flicker over the still shapes of furniture. The men parted and the light swung away down the great stretch of gallery towards the main stairway. For a moment he fancied he saw a dark form standing at the foot of the stairs. Then it disappeared and he was left with only the sound of footsteps dropping down the stairs and the glow of the torch fading. He stood there, uncertain, listening.

The palace was still, the only noises the faint stir of night sounds coming in through the open window behind him, and he recognised in himself a flatness of spirit which he knew was the beginning of excitement, the deliberate forcing back of thought and tension which had to be practised if the mind were to be clear to work. On his way to the workroom now was the man who had designed the tapestry. Mercer knew that he must have a look at the man. All other thoughts he kept from his mind.

He went quietly and swiftly down the stairs and through the first of the great saloons, keeping close to the windows, hands outstretched to save him from bumping into furniture. He paused at the door of the large chamber which was arranged to represent an eighteenth-century levee.

A pale light from the windows struggled against the darkness of the crowded room. He could fancy that these were living figures, stilled by the surprise of his entry. A fan half-closed in an arrested hand, a pale butterfly at rest; cold fingers resting with a momentary wonder at the jewelled pendant, flat and precise, on the waxen swell of a bare breast; the crook of an arm, half-raised to the thin elegance of a dress sword, the fall of lace from the wrist stirring with tiny whispers in the draught from an open window... He smiled to himself at the fancy.

He went forward, threading through them and had almost reached the great throne at the end of the room when the light under the door of the workroom which he had been watching as a guide went out. The door handle rattled. He stopped and drew a step towards the shadows of the throne. The edge of the dais touched the back of his legs and he swayed. He threw out an arm to preserve his balance and, as the door opened, he felt his hands slide down the bare arm of a wax figure and for a moment the imperious, painted face of a dowager was close to him. The figure rocked gently, the wide sweeps of brocaded dress rustling noisily. He held on to the woman, steadying himself and her, but the noise must have been heard by whoever stood in the darkened doorway.

Mercer stood there, his body stiff and tight-held, his breathing muted, and he was one of the still company, lost like them in the shadows. In the silence, the sounds of the city outside lapped weakly into the room; a gondolier's cry came wailing to him like the lonely call of a sea-bird, the screw of a motor-boat thrashed in acceleration against the water close to the palace terrace. The steady pulse of the engine as it drew away seemed to match the pump of his own heart. He heard a noise from the door, the dry, crisp sound of cautious feet and he thought he saw the movement of a shape across the darkness.

Mercer released the dowager and moved forward, spacing his steps carefully. From his left, near the middle of the room, he heard the sudden stir of clothes and then something dropped lightly to the floor. He swung round silently. In a patch of grey light from the middle window he saw a young girl, her waxen face fixed in a coquetry beyond her years, nod gently to him as she teetered on her stand, and the bright eyes invited him to run and restore the fan which had been knocked from her hand. His attention was taken from her to the figure at her side. As he looked, he saw it melt into the abyss of shadow under the wall window.

Mercer, anxious to get a glimpse of the man's face, slid around to the throne and began to edge his way along the wall, working towards the dark mass of shadows, and now the light began to play tricks. A gallant stepped in his way and frowned at him. An old man, loose-lipped, a hundred dead lusts in his eyes, held out a snuff-box to him, and a party looked up from their card table watching him move through the shadows. Then, from the door at the far end of the room someone spoke, a clear, friendly voice with a tremble of excitement in it:

'*Buona sera a tutti. Son venuta solo per cinque minuti. Cosa volete fare stasera? Giocare, ballare o cantare?*'

For a moment Mercer thought that not only his eyes but his ears were playing him false. Who was this who could only stay for five minutes and wanted to know whether they would sing, dance or play games?

'*La contessa preferisce ballare? Ebbene...*"

There was the sound of light footsteps and then into a grey patch of light from the middle window stepped the figure of Ninetta. She made a small curtsey to the contessa who had dropped her fan and picked it up. With the fan in her hand she began to dance, childishly but with a certain formal grace, moving to and fro in the patch of light and singing gently to herself.

Mercer knew that any sudden noise or movement might terrify her.

Somewhere else in the room, he thought, was another person. A child's five minutes when the world is all fantasy might easily be fifteen. Until she was gone there was a truce between them. Whoever was in the room wanted to get away without being seen. But for himself, he now decided, there was no need of secrecy. Even if he had trouble explaining his presence here, he had every-thing to gain by seeing the man. He decided, while Ninetta danced, to work towards the door and be near the switch. When she was gone he would turn the lights on and take a chance.

He drew back silently to the wall and began to move along it. In his way were groups of figures, furniture and now and again a tall pedestal with, he guessed, vases or busts on top of them. He went carefully, the slight noise he made covered by the sound of Ninetta singing to herself.

He was in the far angle of the room when his way was blocked by a shadowed group of figures. Vaguely he could make out courtiers and the high, powdered wigs of women. He began to skirt around the inner side of the group, hands outstretched, feeling his way. His right hand touched cloth and he ran his fingers upwards, seeking to determine the position of the figure. Suddenly his hands were on a neck, then the bone line of a chin and in that moment he stood there shocked into a stupidity which left him without defence. The skin was warm and his fingers were pressed lightly against the gentle stubble of a man's cheek. Too late, he swung his free arm forward, seeking a hold. The man turned and his face, unseen in the gloom, was so close that the swift impulse of breath as he struck was warm on Mercer's face and sour with the smell of garlic. Something heavy hit Mercer on the side of the temple and he dropped, crashing backwards into a group of courtiers. As he went down and into darkness he heard Ninetta scream.

He was lying on an elegant sofa of rosewood with ebony insets, and the cushions under his head were stiff and uncomfortable with

gold thread. He sat up, rubbing the b.
his neck, his eyes going to the three
who stood before him. Two of them, M
and Longo, his lodger, he recognised.
little girl, Ninetta, was drawn close
Minelli's side, his arm holding her tigh
She was sobbing and watching Mercer w
dark, frightened eyes. He half smiled at h
but her expression remained unchange
The lights in the chamber were all on, th
wax figures once more stiff groups, all magi
lost.

The third man stepped forward and
handed him a glass of water. He drank it,
watching him. The man was old, the lean
face pouched and marked. But in his movements as he handed the glass over there was
a dignified elegance. He was wearing
evening clothes and the diamond studs on
the shirt front caught the light like snow
crystals. He took the glass from Mercer and
said in a cultured, commanding voice which
Mercer recognised at once:

'Perhaps you would explain yourself to us?
I suggest, too, that you hold your handkerchief to the cut on your forehead. I
should not want my cushions spoiled.'

Mercer pulled out his handkerchief.

'You're Count Boria?'

'I am.'

'My name's Mercer. Your man there,
Minelli, knows me.'

'So much I'd gathered already, Mr. Mercer. But that doesn't explain your presence here tonight or what happened.'

'It would be better if he did his explaining to the police,' Longo said curtly.

'If necessary Mr. Mercer can explain to them as well. At the moment I want to hear his story.'

Mercer felt in his pocket for his cigarettes. They watched him; Minelli, suspicious; Longo, intolerant and accusing; and Count Boria, smiling, patiently attending an explanation which, Mercer felt, he probably would not believe.

'I came in here late this afternoon to have a look around. I was tired and I must have gone to sleep in one of the window embrasures. When I woke up the place was in darkness. There was a light under the workroom door. I went across to get some-one to show me out, but before I reached the door the light went off and someone came out. Whoever it was must have heard me, but instead of calling out the person acted very suspiciously, trying to creep away. I thought it might be a burglar and went after him. In fact, we played hide and seek. In the middle of all this Ninetta came in and began to dance and sing. I didn't want to frighten her, but I tried to get up to the light switch so that I could put it on when she had gone. On the way I ran into

the man who knocked me out.'

'A likely story,' Longo sneered.

'Quiet, lieutenant.' The Count turned back to Mercer. 'You're sure there was another man here? You know at night one can get a very odd feeling in this room. And when one has just awakened the mind isn't entirely alert.'

'There was the light in the workroom and this...' Mercer touched the cut on his forehead.

The Count smiled and shook his head. 'That's what hit you, Mr. Mercer.' He pointed behind Mercer to a tall pedestal which had been overturned. On the ground by it lay a heavy bronze bust. The Count picked it up. 'Goldini, one of our play-wrights. One might call him the Noel Coward of his age. We heard Ninetta scream and when Longo and I got here you were lying by the pedestal. Minelli' – he turned to the man behind him – 'you'd better take that child down to your quarters, and in future see that you keep her down there. I've had to complain before about her habit of wandering in this part of the gallery. Then you'd better go over the whole premises. Longo will perhaps help you.'

'We shan't find anybody, or anything missing. I don't believe this man's story.' Longo nodded towards Mercer. 'He should be searched.'

Mercer smiled. 'You won't find my pockets stuffed with china and I didn't knock myself out with a bust of Goldini. However, if it'll do anybody any good please call the police. I've no objection at all.'

Mercer saw the edge of a smile touch Minelli's face as he turned away with the girl. Longo scowled and stood his ground.

The Count touched him gently on the arm and nodded after Minelli.

'Don't worry, Longo. I'm a fair judge of character and I think we can trust Mr. Mercer.'

Longo shrugged his shoulders and after a moment's hesitation followed Minelli.

Mercer stood up. 'I think that's very nice of you.' Over the Count's shoulder he saw the partly open door of the workroom. He had lost his chance of seeing Paolo Cerva, but at least he meant to see the tapestry. 'All the same I did see a man in that doorway.' He moved towards the workroom. 'Perhaps we ought to look in there.'

The Count followed him. 'As I said before, it's easy to imagine things in this room. However...'

They were at the workroom door and the Count, standing aside for him to enter, inclined his head with a tired smile. 'I find it as difficult to believe there was a man as you do to believe that you knocked yourself out with a bust of Goldini.' He switched on the

160

room lights.

Mercer saw that the tapestry was indeed finished. Under the hard lights the colours were vivid. The room smelt of some chemical and a tap dripped into a wash-basin in one corner of the room.

'There's no one here, you see.' The Count paused before the tapestry, speaking absently, his eyes moving across it.

'So it seems.' Mercer stood behind him. There was no doubt in his mind now. The design of the tapestry was the same. A detail here and there might be different, the arrangement of a sinewy liana, the poise of a bird, but this was the same cartoon which had come from the hand of Paolo Cerva, from the hand which he was sure had struck him in the darkness.

Even in tapestry work the distinction of the original design was preserved, the same sharp line, the clarity of vision, the work of an edged mind delighting in fantasy, absorbed for the while in the lush pulse of tropical life and the heraldic beauty of these exotic birds, a joyless, cold beauty caught perfectly in the central bird of paradise.

'This light spoils the colours. One should see it in daytime. However, as you see, there's no one here.'

They walked slowly back through the salons, the Count switching off the lights as they went. When they reached the foot of the stairway leading up to the top floor the Count said:

'Would you mind going out through my private entrance, Mr. Mercer? Minelli has the keys of the main door and he will be busy for a while. He has a great many rooms to look through...' He studied Mercer as he walked up the stairs behind him. The man was intelligent, confident of himself... A man, he thought, whom one could like, despite the slight roughness of an occasional vulgarity and the obvious lack of culture... He began to follow a line of thought which observation of the well-worn tweed suit aroused.

In his room the Count paused by a small table and lifted a decanter.

'You look pale, Mr. Mercer. Won't you have a glass of wine?'

They drank, standing, and the Count watched Mercer, recalling the information he had used his influence to discover. A private agent, shabby, unsuccessful; a man whom the police had known long ago in Rome ... a tool for other people, someone to be used, to be bought and sold, a man with little conscience or he would never have been in this sort of work ... a man whose loyalty and ability could be promoted or destroyed by money. There should never be any real trouble in handling him if he became a nuisance.

'Who did the design for the tapestry?' Mercer was deliberately blunt.

'I got it from a Signorina Medova who works here. Interesting, isn't it? It reminds me of a painting by Roelandt Savery, *Landscape with Birds*, which, as far as I can remember used to be in the Kunsthistorisches Museum in Vienna.'

The house telephone on the desk rang. When the Count had answered it, he said:

'That was Minelli. They've been through the palace, but there's no one here who shouldn't be.'

'Maybe I dreamt it all.'

The Count smiled and picked up his coat from a chair.

'Will you be in Venice long?' He moved across the room to the far wall which was panelled in dark walnut wainscoting.

'Another week, maybe longer.'

Mercer watched him curiously. He went up to the wall and pressed one of the rosettes of carved wood and a door opened in the panelling. The Count smiled at his look.

'It used to be a secret exit but now, since the whole top floor is my living quarter, I use it to save Minelli the trouble with the main door at night.'

The Count switched on the stair light, then turned and bolted the door behind him. They went down a twisting series of narrow stone steps. At the bottom of the steps was a pointed-arch doorway that took them out to a narrow walled garden, and then to a small quay at the angle of the palace. The Grand Canal was before them and a narrow rio ran sharply back to their right. A slim wooden bridge spanned the rio and gave access to a broad run of quay along the canal side. A gondola was moored waiting for the Count.

'Can I take you anywhere? I'm going to the other side.'

Mercer shook his head. 'I've been enough trouble already.'

He leaned on the bridge for a while, watching the gondola crab its way across the water. The Count must know that he had been attacked by Cerva. He must have a good reason for covering it up. What reason? Because Cerva was Uccello? But beyond that? Was Uccello working for him? Counterfeiting, or faking pictures... No, that didn't seem likely. Then what? He spat over the balustrade, suddenly angrier than he had been all day. The whole affair was running away from him.

He walked back through the Piazza San Marco on his way to Rosa. They were trying out the floodlighting in the square, in preparation for the high summer season. It was nearly nine and the square was crowded, a great human exchange where

Venice came to market gossip, bare the heart of love affairs and business worries, to watch the smooth rumps and provocative bosoms of the women, to catch the whisper of scandal from neighbouring tables ... people walking lazily up and down or perched in convocations around the shiny tables, hands fingering glasses and coffee cups. Children laughed and ran about. The Lord knew what time they went to bed in Venice, Mercer thought ... they were like all continental children, curious little adults whose animal movements seemed unnatural as though they knew they had to play the part of children but were impatient of the years that lay between them and long trousers and nylons. San Marco itself seemed cut out of metallic paper, livid golds and greens under the powerful lights, and the Campanile was a great raw finger scratching at the dark sky with its sharp nail.

Rosa was lying back in her chaise-longue listening to the radio when he arrived. She held up a hand to stop him from talking, nodded at the bottle on the low table and went on listening. Someone was reading poetry – a resonant, compelling voice. Mercer poured himself a drink, half-listening...

*'Sperai che il tempo, e i duri casi, e queste*
*Rupi ch'io varco anelando...'*

Rosa had always had a weakness for poetry. He lit a cigarette and watched her. Her eyes were shut and the large face was stupid in its contented collapse. Ten years ago and few men would have turned away from her bed if invited. Now ... her feet stuck out from the bottom of the wrap and he saw the pink bulge of flesh over the curve of her slippers like over-stuffed sausages.

'...*Amor fra l'ombre inferne*
*Seguirammi immortale, onnipotente.*'

The voice stopped and she switched the radio off.

'Ugo Foscolo – one of my favourites.'

'I like his voice.'

'You're a barbarian, dear boy. Foscolo's dead. It was being read by another poet – Madeo Nervi. He's coming to Venice soon for some Arts Festival. I shall go and listen to him. You can take me – if you're here.'

'I will – if I'm here.'

She said: 'Within the last hour someone's cracked you on the forehead. The blood's scarcely dry.'

'I ran into a wall.'

'In your job that happens sometimes.'

He got up and walked around the room with his glass in his hand. He stopped by the window, running one finger gently along the

166

slats of the blind.

'Did you find anything about the girl Medova?'

'Not much.' She knew he wasn't going to talk. She didn't want to know anything for herself, but talking might help him. She'd made it her business to have a look at the girl and had been jealous – pleased in fact by her jealousy like someone coming into a cold room and finding a red ember waiting to be blown to warmth under the grey ashes.

'Go on.'

'She's twenty-nine. Born in Potenza – that's in Lucania in the South. She came to Venice in thirty-nine, brought here with her two sisters by Count Boria who has estates around Potenza. Do you know about the sisters?'

'Yes. Why should the Count bring them here?'

'For the tapestry work, I suppose. He's famous for his tapestries and they design and work on them.'

'Married or…'

'It's the first thing you pick up usually, isn't it? But not with this girl. No men at all.'

'She had an affair with a man called Gian Uccello here, during the war. You should have got that.' It gave him a vicious pleasure to say it, a self-flagellation.

'But I didn't. I'd like to know how she did

it in this town without leaving a trace? Dear boy, I think you're dealing with one of the night-flying birds, heard but never seen. If you are dealing?'

'What's Potenza like?' He didn't want to discuss Adriana with her.

'Turks and Arabs and they live on vegetable soup. Have you found Gian Uccello?'

'I've been told he's dead. I suppose I could draw my cheque tomorrow.'

She watched the long face, the one eyebrow half lifted as he faced her, the humour in the twist of his lips a challenge.

'Dead but won't lie down – not unless you want him to?'

'Did Bernardo leave that list for me?'

She felt under her cushion and handed him a sheet of paper, typewritten. Half-way down the list of names were two which would have meant nothing to him had it not been for the bracketed nicknames which followed them.

'Gufo and Moretto.'

'The owl and the darky, dear boy. The only romantic things about such types are the trade names they dream up. Personally I'd leave them alone. Leave them all alone, draw your cheque and stay here until I find you something.'

'I can find something for myself.'

'Maybe ... but I hope it isn't at the bottom of a canal. No matter what you expected from her there's no sense in having your disappointment drowned while it's still inside you.'

He looked at her suddenly.

'You made a few other enquiries?'

'One picks things up. I know the police questioned you about a body ... Valentino Grandini. He finished up in a canal, too.'

'Don't worry about me. I can look after myself. You taught me how.'

'I never succeeded in teaching you anything.'

He laughed then. Crossing to her he held out a hand, saying: 'I came to take you out to dinner. Now stop worrying about me and dress yourself up.'

## Chapter 9

In the centre of the Campo Boria was one of those wellheads with an iron lid which are found all over Venice. A group of children were playing around it, leaping up and down the shallow surround of steps. Behind Mercer the café radio was muttering to itself about Marshall aid to Italy. To his right three business men had their heads over a glass-studded table discussing discounts on silk lengths with the air of conspirators. One of the children in the group by the well was Ninetta. The children scattered, like wind-sprung leaves, and drifted away to a chorus of *'Ciao, Mario! Ciao Ninetta! Ciao!... Ciao!'*

Mercer watched the girl go up the steps to the lighted palace. He sat there, waiting. He had found no way out of his doubts about Adriana. Uccello was alive, he was con-vinced, and it seemed clear from what he had overheard in the palace that she knew it. There was no escape from the fact that she had lied to him in the gondola. For the moment he was not holding that against her. She might have a good reason for not telling him the truth. Uccello might have some hold over her. It was this view which he favoured, linking it with his knowledge that whatever was going on was not fully known to her. That way ... there was hope left to him. Because she loved Uccello once, there was no reason to assume she still did. But he had to know. He acknowledged now that his interest was solely in her. The Uccello business he could write off, if he wished, since he had enough information to satisfy Gevlin Frères. The happiness and hope he had known in the gondola with her had diminished, but it was far from dead. Only by talking to her and confirming in her a parallel feeling to his own could it be revived.

Adriana came down the steps of the Boria

Gallery and moved obliquely across the square. Mercer called the waiter, paid his bill and began to follow her.

He turned after her into the Calle Larga 22 Marzo, moving towards San Marco, but at the colonnaded archway leading into the square she swung left past the Post Office and then right again. As he came round the corner he saw her turn into a doorway four yards from him. He paused, deciding to give her a little time. There was a curve of narrow canal before him, the floodlit face of an *albergo* leaning across the dark waters. Lighting a cigarette he drew back against the stone balustrade at the waterside to avoid the stream of evening passers-by. From an open window of the hotel room came the sound of a gramophone, a lazy, disinterested voice enquiring if someone was lonely, if someone was blue...? The question seemed directed at him. His impatience was too much for him. He jerked his cigarette into the canal, hearing it hiss on the dark scum, and went over to the door.

Inside there was a smell of garlic and cat. He went up the narrow staircase, reading the names on the doors, and with each floor the smell changed ... boiling *finocchi* and cheap scent, a cold mist of *pasta* steam and the sweet-sour odour of babies' napkins. Threading through them all was the bad breath of old tobacco smoke. On the blank wall at a landing turn were defaced posters, words still surviving... *Democrazia Cristiana... Uomini!... Partito Comunista ... lavoratori Italiani...*

He found her name on a green door on the topmost floor. There was no other door on the landing. Signorina Adriana Medova. It had been typewritten on a card which was slipped into a brass-framed holder. He pressed the bell and waited.

She came to the door, frowning, a woman interrupted when she had been about to settle into the privacy of her own home. Over one arm, pressed against the waist of her green dress, she held a bath towel. Her legs were bare and slippered with soft green leather mules.

'Good evening.' As he spoke he saw the frown go and she smiled slightly.

'Oh, hello!'

He saw the soft red lips, half-parted and, in the fraction of time before she spoke again, he created for himself a whole new life in which he had come running up the stairs to press the bell impatiently, to find her swinging open the door to him and her face coming up to offer the warmth of her lips.

'How did you know I lived here?' She held the door back for him to enter.

'I followed you from the palace. I wondered if I could talk to you for a while?'

'Why, of course.' She closed the door behind him and then nodded to a chair. 'Excuse me a moment.' She crossed quickly to a divan and picked from it a pair of silk stockings. She went out and he had a glimpse of a bathroom, heard the faint hiss of a geyser before the door closed and knew that he had interrupted her preparations for a bath. He could imagine her, coming home, dropping on the divan, kicking off her shoes – one of them showed under the edge of the pleated valance now – and rolling off her stockings. The intimate details which belonged to others and which only in imagination he could make his own...

He looked around as he waited for her to come back. It was a long, rather narrow room, comfortably furnished with easy chairs and the divan. A run of full-length french windows took up the whole of one wall. One of the windows was open, the curtains undrawn, giving access to a small loggia flanked by an iron balustrade. Through the canopy of creepers growing over it on a trellis of thin wires, he could see a patch of the darkening sky and the haze of light wreathing the city. Three doors opened from the room, one to the bathroom and the other two, he guessed, to bedroom and kitchen. On a small table at the side of the divan was a pile of books. She came back as he was about to lean over and read the titles. She offered him a cigarette and, when they were both smoking, she sat down in an armchair.

'I went to Mirave,' he said. 'It's not the most beautiful town in Italy.'

She smiled at that and said: 'But you found what you wanted there?'

'In a way, yes. But it wasn't what I expected.' He watched her, but there was no movement on her face, the light from a heavily-shaped lamp engrossing it with dark, upcast shadows.

'I don't understand you?' She wasn't surprised that he was here. Count Boria had told her that he had been found in the palace, but had been able to offer no explanation for it, advising her to be cautious what she said if he came to her again.

'That's why I'm here. You see, I don't understand you. Perhaps we should be frank with each other?'

'But I've told you all I can...' He could hear it then, the nervousness in her which she was schooling, and it made him worry for her, stirred strongly a desire to protect her and made him want to reach out and touch her. He could sense the tautness of her body as she sat there.

'Why are you – and maybe other people –

so anxious for me to believe that Gian Uccello is dead?'

'He is dead!'

He shook his head. 'In the gondola I was ready to believe that. But not now. I know he's not dead. I know he's in Venice and I know that you know it.'

'Gian Uccello is dead.' It was the voice of a child, stubborn, insistent and he knew that he wasn't going to get beyond her denial. He stood up.

'I'm not interested in Gian Uccello. I'm interested in you, that's why I'm being frank with you. You know I'm telling the truth, otherwise you would have asked me why I'm so certain about Uccello. What I want to know is what hold he, and maybe others, have over you? I get the feeling that there's a lot you don't know still... Boldesca for instance. What was Boldesca to you?'

'Nothing.'

He pulled a wallet from his pocket and dropped a photograph into her lap. 'I took this from his wallet the night he visited.'

She picked up the photograph, gave it a quick glance and handed it back to him. 'Boldesca lives for two things – drink and women. There are a lot of men who carry photographs of women beyond their reach. He must have stolen this, and anyway I don't understand why you should show it to me.'

'Because I've a feeling you're in trouble

175

and I'd like to help you. I know Uccello has a criminal record. Why should you help him unless he has some hold over you? But you're in to something deeper than you realise… I'm sure of that, otherwise I wouldn't be here, wanting to help you. Do you know that Boldesca's dead?' He threw it at her bluntly.

'That's nonsense! Count Boria has received a letter from him. He's in Milan.'

There wasn't any doubt about it then. The way she spoke, the incredulity in her voice, the look she gave him as her eyes came up from watching the loose slipper swinging on the end of a bare foot, all told him that she believed Boldesca to be alive. He turned away from her to hide his own relief. He went on evenly:

'I'm afraid he's dead.'

'You must be wrong.' She got up from her chair and walked across the room and he saw that now, isolated by some concern of her own, abstracted from his presence, her body had been taken by a slow grace, shedding the discipline and consciousness of herself which had marked her a moment ago.

'No. His body was pulled out of the Rio dei Greci the morning after he visited me. The police have already questioned me about him. They say his name was Valentino Grandini.'

'There's some mistake, I'm sure.'

'No.'

'Then why haven't the police been to the Gallery?'

'Because I didn't tell them that I knew where he lived or that he was known as Boldesca.'

'But why not?' She was staring at him in surprise and he could feel that whatever headway he had made with her was dwindling.

'The police and I seldom swap confidences. I earn my living in much the same way as they do. I suppose it's professional jealousy.'

She shook her head at that. 'I'm sorry I don't believe what you say about Boldesca.'

He was angry then because he realised her disbelief was his own fault. 'All right, don't believe me. I'm not here to make you talk, to worm some secret out of you. The only reason I'm here is because I want to help you.'

It was odd how the vehemence behind his words made her angry, angry because she could have wished this position had never arisen between them, and because she could see no reason why she should find herself concerned with the degrees of their relationship. He was nothing to her and she nothing to him... She wanted him to go and leave her alone.

177

'I'm in no need of your help. Uccello is dead and that's all I know.'

He stood in the darkened space near the window and there was a confusion in him. He felt as though between her and himself was a dark, clinging web of misunderstanding and disbelief which he had to fight his way through, as though everything in his life depended on reaching her, but the more he struggled the tighter became the vicious filaments about him. He jerked his cigarette on to the loggia and turned towards her. She was smoothing the material of her dress over one thigh and his eyes followed the slow movement of her hand. Suddenly it was as if his hand were there and to his confusion was added a desire which thrust him completely into the darkness so that when he began to speak he hardly knew what he was saying, wanting only to make clear to her the need which she had roused in him and which he felt she understood and might answer. He cried out fiercely:

'Don't you see, I'm not interested in Gian Uccello and all the mystery behind him? All my life I've poked about in dark little corners and there's no longer any surprise in me at the things which come to light. A thousand Boldescas could be murdered and I wouldn't turn a hair. Lies slide off my back like water from a duck... Evil, suspicion and fear ... that's my profession. But now and

178

again, in the midst of all the muck, you hit
somebody who makes you realise that a
man is more than a mouth and a belly, more
than a body he wants to keep warm, that the
world isn't just darkness, that there is
something worth having... A woman can do
that to you. You've done that to me...' And
all the time he was talking, he was watching
her, longing for her to cry out and deny the
character he was giving himself. But she
stood without movement, her face white
and still, offering him nothing, and the
thought went through him that she was
stepping back in fright from the lip of a
black abyss towards whose edge she had
been drawn in ignorance. 'Damn it!' he
cried suddenly. 'Don't look so scared. You
must understand what I'm saying...'

She did understand. She looked at him
now with a new curiosity, for deep under
her self-control she knew herself woman
enough to be unable to deny the warmth of
pride which comes from being loved. Every
detail of him leapt fresh to the eye; the crisp,
sandy hair, the long, deeply marked face,
the feeling of cleanliness about him, the
healthy warmth of skin, and the neatness
and easy personality of his shabby clothes,
the frayed point of a collar... Her eyes
dropped to the hand which played now with
a waistcoat button and she saw that the
fingers were long, flattened at their tips and

the nails well-kept, clean, nervous hands.

'I understand,' she said suddenly. 'But you're wasting your time. I wish you hadn't come here.'

For a moment she thought he was going to be angry. Then he laughed quietly and said: 'Time is the only thing I have to waste.'

He came across to her and put his hands on her arms, holding her for a while and looking at her, at the fine line of eyebrow, the stubborn beauty of her face, feeling the warmth of her skin run through his hands. Whatever she said, he thought, the last answer, the final anguish or betrayal lay in their flesh. He pulled her towards him and kissed her... But her mouth was like marble, like the mouth of the girl with the Botticelli face years back in his memory, and her body under his hands, forced against his own, insulted him with its passivity. If she'd stiffened against him, twisted from him, he could have saved some self-respect, but all he held was flesh without spirit or personality to deny or encourage him. He let her go. He went to the door and, his back to her, his fingers on the handle, he said: 'When you asked me if after Mirave I would be leaving Venice, it was because you wanted me to go?'

From behind him, her voice untouched by emotion answered: 'There's nothing for you in Venice.'

When he had gone, she stood for a while in thought. Then she went towards the bedroom. She paused on the dark threshold, her hand going slowly up for the light switch. A man's voice said lazily:

'Don't bother. I'll put this one on.'

A lamp on the low bedside table was switched on and a truncated cone of light picked out the thick carpet, the silver travelling clock on the table, and edged the tiny white flowers on the sprigged silk bed hangings with a sharp radiance. A hand and part of an arm still rested on the table, long dark fingers playing with the light switch. The silk canopy cast a dark shadow over the bed hiding the rest of the body.

'Gian – what are you doing here?' she spoke almost sharply.

'Waiting for you. What else?' He laughed quietly and there was a teasing note in his voice.

She went over to the bed and stood looking down at him, his face and the shape of his body no more than a blur in the shadows. He raised his hand and caught one of hers, moulding it tenderly and she smiled.

'You shouldn't have come here so early. It's not wise.'

'A man in love can't always be thinking about being wise, *cara mia*. Don't look so worried. You weren't likely to bring our friend Mercer in here. And if you had – which would have meant I should have cut your throat afterwards – there's always the window.'

'You heard him?'

'Yes.'

'He worries me. Why should he say a thing like that about Boldesca?'

He was silent for a moment. Then he laughed. 'His kind will try anything. He wanted to get you mixed up, shock you into talking.'

'Boldesca isn't dead, is he?'

'Adriana – what's the matter with you? You aren't falling for his lies, are you? Oh, come on' – his voice was low, cajoling – 'who on earth would want to kill Boldesca? He's in Milan. Don't worry about this man.'

'It's not only him. It's us. Gian, how much longer is this all going on?'

'Patience, *cara*. In another week I shall be safely away, and then it won't be long before you can follow and we shall have finished with this kind of life.' He laughed slowly. 'There's a certain excitement in coming here like this, but one can have too much of it.' He paused, and she was silent, playing with his fingers. They were long, thin, restless fingers, but they were stained with nicotine and the nails were bitten down and lined with dirt. The comparison with

Mercer's hands struck swiftly at a fierce loyalty in her and she pressed his hand against her own, warming it and sheltering it.

'Are you surprised he's fallen in love with you?' he asked idly and the question stirred her, making her wish he had said anything but that.

'I don't understand him. Every time I see him he gives the feeling of searching for something which even I don't know about.'

'Forget him. Boria knows how to handle him. He can't touch us. I'm a dead man, dead long ago in Mirave... Forget him.' He stirred suddenly when she was silent and his voice went on, hard now and with a bitter trace in it: 'What did he do out there? I heard but I couldn't see and you were silent before he went. Did he touch you?'

She answered him at once, heard her own voice, calm and assuring: 'Don't be a fool, Gian.'

He pulled her down to the bed with a hungry impetuosity and as his arms went round her and his hands moved in the licensed freedom which brought the first movement of her own hunger, she was hardly aware that for the first time in her life she had lied to him. She felt the close-grain of his stubble against her warm cheek and the little cry which was the abandonment of her fears in the solace of passion was cut

183

short as his lips took hers avidly. Her hands went up to him, and her fingers twined themselves through his thick, dark hair.

## Chapter 10

There was nothing to keep him in Venice. That morning he had telephoned Rosa and told her he was going. Apart from her there were only two other people to whom he wanted to say good-bye: Minelli and Ninetta. To both of them he felt he owed some gesture, Minelli because the incident in the palace might have caused him some trouble, and Ninetta because she had been frightened by him.

In his pocket now, as he sat in the sunshine on one of the long stone benches that marked the edge of the Riva degli Schiavoni, were a box of chocolates and a snow scene for the girl. He took the glass ball out of his pocket and shook it, watching the white flakes whirl against the painted representation of the Piazza San Marco. The snow drifted down, a startling whiteness against the false blue sky and the soft melon-coloured buildings. Across the quay a bill-sticker was pasting a poster on the dingy grey boards of a steamer station.

Mercer lit a cigarette and watched the busy waters of the lagoon.

A magnificent white-painted liner was lying in the channel opposite the Danielli hotel, a great white beauty that somehow put the houses and palaces and the domed churches out of proportion so that the whole scene had the appearance of a child's creation made from models badly matched for size. A red and yellow Coca-Cola barge fussed past the island church of San Giorgio on its way to the Lido, and off the Dogana – where the high-pooped argosies of Ragusa had once anchored – four slim Italian corvettes nosed at their moorings. The bone-bleached canvas of their gun covers and awnings hurt the eye. It was a city, he thought, in which life had made an uncertain compact with time. A waiter brought you a *cinzanino* from a café cellar where once the Greek wines and oils that filled a Doge's ampulla had been stored, the grime of five centuries mingling still with the thin layer of dust on the new bottle stopper, and when it was opened you peeled away the cork inset to see if it luck had brought you a ticket which would win you a Fiat car or a Vespa motor-cycle... If you were lucky. He never was. He went on hoping, fancying sometimes that he was within hand's reach of it... But always the things he really wanted were snatched away from him. He

185

had wanted Adriana. The memory of yesterday was a bitterness in him which he knew
would be long in passing. *There's nothing for
you in Venice.* He could hear her voice saying
it. And she was right. Not a thing for him,
not a damned thing. It wasn't any good
telling himself that he had had no reason for
hoping for anything from her. He had
hoped, and that was the end of it. The
disappointment was a hard core of dejection
in him for which the only relief was the
repetition of the thought that he didn't care
a damn. He was going. There was nothing
for him here. So far as Uccello was concerned – and the affair seemed unimportant
when he thought of Adriana – he was going
to be dishonest. Not that this would trouble
his conscience. The man was better thought
dead, anyway. Whatever heroic qualities he
had were discounted by the rest of his life,
and ignorance of the truth would serve the
client of Gevlin Frères more kindly than
truth would. He tossed his cigarette butt
away and watched the wind tease the smoke
into fine trails over the grey quay-stones.

At this moment, from behind him, two
men settled on the bench. They sat one on
either side of him and close enough to give
him the feeling of being hemmed in. Gufo
was on his right and Moretto on his left.
Moretto stared at the bill which had been
freshly pasted on the shed at the quayside,

ignoring him. Gufo leaned forward, his elbows on his knees, and cocked his head towards Mercer.

'Congratulations, signore,' he said pleasantly.

'Why?'

'Because I've got a present for you.'

'It's not my birthday.'

Gufo laughed and straightened up. 'People get presents for other reasons. You know' – he paused raising his horn-rimmed glasses a little from his nose for relief – 'I thought you were wrong to refuse to do business with me. But I take that back. You've done very well. I couldn't have done better myself.'

'Let's cut out the praise and come to the present. I suspect them both.'

'There's no need to talk like that, signore.' As he spoke he put his hand into his pocket and pulled out a long envelope, the flap heavily sealed, and passed it to Mercer.

'Is this from you?' Mercer turned it over. It was thick and heavy.

Gufo sighed a little. 'No, signore. Unfortunately I don't know who it's from originally. But I am sure you do, or will when you open it.'

Mercer opened the envelope and pulled out its contents. In his hands he held a thick wad of new one-thousand-lire notes. He'd met this situation before, but never with the same absence of feeling. He heard Gufo suck at his teeth and then his voice, a little thick with envy held down, say:

'How many, signore?'

Mercer counted them, turning their edges over slowly. As he did so he was wondering what it was about new notes that gave so much pleasure, for as his fingers went over them the feeling had taken him swiftly. There was no denying it. They were good to feel, their crispness holding a promise... For a moment he was inclined to be annoyed with his pleasure, but the anger was suddenly spent. Damn it, why shouldn't he be pleased? Money was money and with money one lived. Each sibilant as he counted was a promise and, rarest of promises, one which would be fulfilled.

'A hundred.'

'Have they underestimated your nuisance value?'

'My nuisance value is something I never quote in public. But I'm surprised they trusted you with the delivery.'

'You're not an easy man to get on with, signore.' There was a note of genuine sadness in Gufo's voice. 'I'm a business man like yourself. You and I should understand each other. When we have an advantage we turn it into cash. But plain robbery is another thing. You disappoint me, signore.'

Mercer slipped the notes into his inside

pocket. 'You'll get over it,' he said, but it was odd how he felt that he been unnecessarily outspoken and he quickly realised why. Even in Gufo – a man to whom murder meant nothing – there was a shadowy form of conscience, a standard of his own which he had set up to maintain a rudimentary element of self-respect. He said sharply, wanting to escape from the line of thought which threatened to rise, 'Was there no message with this?'

'Yes.' Gufo held out his hand to him. 'This, and the instruction that you must use it. It's a ticket for a first-class, reserved seat, on the Paris train which leaves Venice at six o'clock tonight.' He handed over a small agency folder with the ticket and reservation in it. 'In my opinion, and if you want my advice, you'll use it. In fact, signore, I suggested that there was no need to waste so much on you to make you leave Venice. Moretto and I would have been prepared to persuade you for a quarter of the money. But you can't make people see things like that unless you deal with the principal, and unfortunately we don't. I suppose it's too much to hope that you won't be leaving Venice?'

'You'd like to set Moretto on me?'

'Moretto or myself. Both of us need the exercise, and I'm curious to know how you would stand up to it.'

'I'd be a fool to satisfy your curiosity.'

Gufo stood up and Moretto rose too.

'You would, signore.'

'Don't worry. I'm leaving Venice.'

'I never doubted it. It's exactly what I would do.' He tipped his glasses up a little, smiled broadly, and moved away, Moretto ambling behind him.

He watched them out of sight and then rose and made his way towards the Palazzo Boria.

It was from the palace, he was sure, that the money had come. His original enquiries there after Boldesca, his talks with Adriana which she had probably recounted to her employer, the attempt to satisfy and get rid of him by sending him to Mirave, and then his being discovered in the palace at night... He could imagine the Count working it out, considering him and his character. He was being paid off because he was obviously the kind of man one could pay off. That was what Adriana must think, too. Maybe she'd even suggested it. Perhaps, even, she had wanted him to be paid off, some twisted kindness in her insisting on it as a compensation for his other disappointment. He'd made no more impression on her than that! He laughed to himself bitterly. The irony was – his fingers felt the outside of his jacket, crinkling the notes against his breast – that he had meant to leave Venice anyway.

If they had waited another day they could have saved themselves one hundred thousand lire. He was glad they hadn't waited. The money pushed farther into the future the moment when he would have to find another job. Anything which did that was welcome, and now – since there was the slight professional distaste of turning in a report to Gevlin Frères which he knew to be false – the money more than laid balm to that wound.

In the palace he found a strange attendant at the desk. It was Minelli's day off and there was some doubt whether he was in the palace. Eventually, however, he found him and Ninetta sitting in a small courtyard walled off from the narrow strip of garden into which the Count's private door opened. Minelli was sitting on a bench, smoking and feeding his pigeons. Ninetta was tunnelling into a pile of building sand which she had studded with her collection of sea-shells and sprigged with tiny mimosa slips from the wall creeper.

It was an awkward interview, despite the good will on his side. Minelli was disinclined to say much, as though he bore him a grudge for the palace incident. Mercer guessed that he had been in trouble for missing him on his locking-up round. The man tossed corn to his birds, stroked the metallic neck sheen of one which settled on his hand and kept his eyes from Mercer. He took the news that Mercer was leaving with a short nod. With Ninetta there was no awkwardness, only a lack of interest. She took the presents, thanked him, and as soon as she could escaped back again to her tunnelling, forgetting him within a few seconds as she began to chatter to herself, scooping at the soft sand. It was this which, for a moment, lifted Minelli from his reserve, and even then Mercer realised that it was more in defence of the girl whom he loved like a father than to make him easier.

'You must not mind, signore, if she seems ungrateful. She lives in her head the whole time. Tonight, maybe, she will refuse to sleep unless she has the snow-scene under her pillow. But now ... she is a dwarf, mining a hill for fairy gold.' He smiled and tossed the bird on his hand into the air. It went upwards in easy, widening spirals.

'When I was a boy hawks used to take so many of my best birds. That doesn't happen here?'

'Rarely, signore...'

And after that it became so clear that the man wanted him to go, that he went, disappointed.

He spent an hour in the bar of the Albergo Adriatico before his lunch and drank more than he usually did. To celebrate, he told himself cynically. But afterwards, as he lay on his bed heavy with lunch and drink, preparing to sleep the few hours that remained before he should catch the train, he was uneasy. He had the curious sensation that since lunch something had happened which was important, something which escaped him still ... and then as sleep gathered itself around him in the shuttered coolness of the room, he remembered. He had paid his bill at the desk before coming up and his hand had gone to his inside breast pocket for money, but with his hand there he had changed his mind and felt in the back pocket of his trousers for his own money carried in a shabby morocco billfold... He was asleep while he still considered it.

When he awoke, his head had a muzziness which a plunge into a basin of cold water failed to remove. His mouth and tongue dragged against each other like damp chamois leather.

At the station he had twenty minutes before the train went. In the railway hall he stopped at a kiosk to buy himself a magazine and some cigarettes. As he turned away he found himself facing Gufo. He wore a light Italian raincoat drawn over his shoulders cape-fashion. The large face was freshly shaven and powdered, the small eyes blinked good-humouredly behind his glasses. Seeing his bland, beaming face

Mercer found it hard to imagine that this man was a murderer.

'*Sono venuto a dirvi addio, signore,*' he said pleasantly, walking with Mercer towards the barrier.

'To say good-bye – and to make sure I go?'

Gufo shrugged his shoulders. 'Signore – I'm here because I like you. Also – these days one has to think of such things – to let you know that if you ever want anyone to help you, you can always call on me. You never know when you may need a companion, or where. I speak French and German, and I have nothing to keep me in Venice.'

'So you're feeling the pinch too, eh?'

'Men like us can't advertise or go to an employment exchange, signore. When the time comes you will remember me?' They were at the barrier now. Mercer said nothing as he felt for his ticket. Gufo went on: 'You can always get me with a letter through Gostini. *Addio, signore, e buon' viaggio...*' He made a movement to hold out his hand, but Mercer ignored it and walked through the gate into the station. On the other side of the barrier he turned, looked at Gufo for a moment, and then raised his hand in a short salute and swung away to find his train. Something in the man's last words had roused in him a feeling of nausea.

In this carriage there were two other

people, a young English couple, not long married, he guessed; both of them spoke with loud, unself-conscious voices. At home, he thought, they would have kept their voices low, but out here – and probably thinking him Italian and unable to understand them – they proceeded to make the carriage their own.

'If only they allowed one to bring more money. The things, darling! I could have spent our whole allowance in that little leather shop near the Luna. Don't you think we were a bit mean about the gloves for Martha?'

'Nonsense, angel. She'll like the scarf just as much and it saved us at least a thousand. Damn it … we've barely enough left for our food on the train as it is. Relations can't expect you to starve just to bring them the presents they want. She's lucky to get the scarf. I'm sure there was something wrong with the hotel bill. Five hundred more than I'd worked out…'

He leaned back in his corner, shut his eyes and tried not to listen to them. But their voices ran on, high-pitched, irritating. His head was still aching from his heavy sleep. Against their open voices, he heard others, echoing inside his mind; Adriana saying coldly: *'I understand. But you're wasting your time!'* Gufo's voice, saying: '…*Men like us can't advertise… Men like us… You and I*

*understand each other, signore... You and I...'*
He stirred suddenly, wanting to escape, and the movement made the notes inside his pocket crinkle, brittle dry noises that seemed to explode frighteningly in the echoing carriage.

He stood up suddenly and went into the corridor. Why didn't the damned train start? He wanted to get away from this place. He'd done very well here, hadn't he? Now he wanted to get away. And Gufo's voice seemed to echo his thought. *'I couldn't have done better myself.'*

And that, of course, was the real trouble. Not only Gufo, but other people, Adriana and the Count, saw him for what he was, a shabby adventurer without scruple or conscience, a man whose mouth could be shut with a bribe. People had tried to buy him off before and he had always refused. Always before he'd been loyal, even to people like Gevlin Frères. It was a quality one had to preserve because in the long run it was good business and because, more important, without it one became entirely lost, over the crumbling edge and thrust down into a crowd of Gufos and Morettos... But what the hell did that matter? He had to join them sometime if he wanted to go on eating. He had joined them. He couldn't even claim now a professional loyalty or pride. He was for sale to the highest bidder; marked unreliable, cheap... In front of him a shabby, blowsy future, and one day he'd end up with a knife in his back, or wandering around Les Halles picking half-rotten vegetables from the market gutters to make himself an old man's soup... Even giving the money back wouldn't... Damn, that was ridiculous and he was letting his fancy take him too far. He had the money now, he could make a clean start. If he went back he mightn't get an inch nearer Uccello, he wouldn't do Gevlin Frères' client any good, and almost certainly he would be beaten up... Maybe it wouldn't stop at that. No, one thing was more than certain. He wasn't going back.

He went into the carriage and sat down, shutting his eyes and leaning against the cushions. The English girl's voice fluted over him, bird-sharp and excited: '...If only they'd let us bring more money abroad. I still think it would have been quite safe to let that man cash a cheque for you. He said it would be all right.'

'Don't be an ass, darling. He was the kind who'd say anything. It just isn't worth it, old dear. It just isn't worth it...'

The engine whistled far down the platform, and the carriage gave a sudden jerk. Mercer stood up swiftly and reached for his battered suitcase. He swung it down and slipped into the corridor, but at the door he turned and looked back at them and then, smiling suddenly, he said: 'You're right. It just isn't worth it...' He ran down the corridor and swung off the train as it began to pull out.

From the station waiting hall he rang up his hotel and got his room back. Then he gave his suitcase to a porter, paid him and told him to take it to the hotel. He was in no hurry to go back there himself. He wanted time to think. There was no sign of Gufo.

Outside the station he swung away to the left down the Lista di Spagna, following the great curve of the Grand Canal, intent on working his way back to the Piazza San Marco. Now and again he lost his way, but an enquiry put him right.

If he'd had any sense, he thought, he would have gone to ground somewhere in the great warren of Venice, not be going calmly back to his hotel. But the matter now was less one of sense than pride and the arid distaste of making any compromise. This had nothing to do with Adriana. She was dead to him. He had a right to be in Venice and a straightforward purpose here ... not that that would worry Gufo and Moretto and the people behind them. Anyway, whatever he did or wherever he went to ground they would soon know about it. There was little point in putting a difficulty in their way which they would soon overcome... There might be some point, however, in going to Spadoni and presenting all his facts to him. But would Spadoni believe him? No, he wouldn't. What had he got to offer him? A tale of overheard conversation, the fact that Grandini was Boldesca – which he had already withheld. All of it too vague. Even if Spadoni questioned the Count, the authority of the man's denials and evasions would weigh more than his, Mercer's, word. Spadoni had no love for him. He would look for the double game which he would imagine was being played, doubt him. That was the trouble with himself and the police, they worked under and over truth too much to recognise the line of frankness when it came to them.

Spadoni occupied him the whole length of the Via 28 Aprile and at its end he threw him away, knowing, as he had known when he left his carriage, that for better or for worse he was on his own. But, at least, he wasn't without weapons, and not without a certain cold relish at the prospect of fighting. Loyalty, to his work – unsavoury as it was – and to himself – unsatisfactory as he might consider himself – remained. And loyalty to any cause was some virtue. Perhaps the only one he could claim, claim fiercely now since he had come so near to losing it.

It was one of those evenings when the

brilliance of the sky, a great fold of blue silk, displayed in the window of the heavens, is suddenly withdrawn as though by the hand of an impatient shopkeeper. One could almost hear the rustle of its long folds as it was pulled aside. A warm little wind blew up the curving gulf of the Grand Canal. Idle puffs and currents loitered through the narrow streets and channels on either side of it. And smelling the wind and the evening, all Venice came into the streets. The movement of air and humanity stirred up the odours lurking in torrid suspension all day, just as the sudden churn of steamboats as they drew away from a landing stage spewed up the dark canal waters and released the aged smell of the black mud. Oil and vinegar, and the sandal-wood sappiness of cabinet-makers' dens, the friendly gusto of soap and shampoo from hairdressers' salons, the sudden assault of frying pimento, the sweet child's-breath of bread, the vulgar veils of cheap scent, the clean, aseptic statements of eau-de-Cologne, the plebeian flavours of *pasta*, stuffed veal and red mullet, and the coarse spread of cigarette smoke ... the moving air drew them forth and the moving crowd mingled them, and in the movement and the richness was a happy, brawling strength and fertility which crowded and jostled for elbow room in the evening spaces of the grey and gold and ochre framed city...

In the Campo San Angelo Mercer met Signore Orlino – Adriana's brother-in-law. His wheeled chair was drawn up facing the wall of a building next to a café, and he was starting at a poster on the wall. Mercer stood for a moment at his side before he was recognised. He saw that the poster was the same kind as the one he had watched a man paste up on the quay that morning, the same as many others which he realised now he had seen displayed about the city. It announced the visit to Venice on the following Sunday of the poet, Madeo Nervi – Rosa had mentioned him – who was to have a civic reception, followed by a ceremonial gondola procession down the Grand Canal to the Piazza San Marco where he was to open an Exhibition of Proletarian Art of the 19th and 20th Century, and during the following two days was to give public readings of his own and other poems.

Orlino, seeing Mercer, swung his chair away and said with a good-humoured bitterness:

'Just my luck, signore! All my life I've wanted to see him in the flesh and now, when he comes to Venice, I have to go away.'

'Where are you going?'

'Turin. On Saturday. The doctors think there is a hope they can do something for these.' He smacked his blanket-covered legs as he drew his chair into the side of one of the café tables. 'That's what they think. But I know that whatever form of intelligence controls this stupid little world has long decided I shall never use my legs again. Doctors are an arrogant lot. In all their talk they haven't once asked me if I want to walk again.'

'Don't you?'

'Maybe not. I never did myself much good with them. Without them, I can live the life of an idle man – isn't that what we all want? – and tyrannise my family and friends by demanding a sympathy for myself which, frankly, signore, I find very flattering. Let me buy you a drink and over it you can explain why you've never come to see me. You see I'm beginning to bully you like all the rest.' He smacked his hand noisily on the table-top for the waiter.

'Why are you so disappointed at having to miss Nervi?' Mercer asked when the drinks had been brought.

'Because, signore, he is a man. Italy could do with more like him.'

'Do you say that because of his poetry or his politics?'

'He is beyond politics – he is a force. To the peasants and the working men of this country he means more than any party. He's a man with greatness born in him. His head's up in the stars but his feet are on the good earth. He was born a peasant, educated himself, suffered under Mussolini, fought as a partisan, and when he opens his mouth every man with a load of trouble, every woman with a burden of making two hundred lire stretch to do the work of five hundred, hears the voice inside their own heart speak. Stand up in this café now, signore, and say a word against Nervi and you'd start a riot, not only Liberals like myself but Communists, Christian Democrats, would be after your blood. Even those who hate his politics love the man.'

'If he's so good, why isn't he the leader of a party?'

'Because he knows he can do more good outside all parties. When Togliatti was nearly assassinated, it was Nervi – not Minister Scelba with his police – who kept civil war from this country. He spoke then, pointing his finger at the disaster we invited on ourselves, and his word held us. But if it had been he and not Togliatti who had been shot – then a red flame would have swept this country. You can smile, signore. Go and listen to Nervi – if I were here I would take you – and then perhaps you will understand and see why I, who doubt most men, have no doubts about him. You don't understand Italy, signore. It's a powder magazine and any day the match may be dropped. The peasants are hungry for land ... the workers in the towns are hungry for decent homes and a fair share of their labour. We're tired of the people who have ruled us and fed us with promises.'

Mercer listened to him, to the rich, sincere voice. The man believed all he said, spoke from some controlled, almost sad passion, as though the future he saw, the moment of change, was to be regretted since it need never have birth if only men and women would bring to the problem of living as a community some of the courage and self-lessness they could find to preserve them as families.

For himself, he had no politics. He had walked too long in the shadowed ante-chambers where deputies and officials whispered and schemed to have any faith. But he made up his mind to go and hear Nervi if he had the opportunity. He would like to see the man who drew such admiration and loyalty from so many conflicting parties.

He walked alongside Orlino as the man wheeled himself slowly back to his house near the Fenice Theatre, and pushed him up the little wooden ramp which had been laid over the house-steps. He stood with him for a while in the darkened hallway, refusing to go in for a drink, but promising, if he could, to come and see him before he went to Turin.

Orlino looked up at him in the half-light

and a tight smile twisted his large, expressive mouth. 'You promise, signore, like a man whose mind is on something else. What are you thinking about? I make no apology for my curiosity?'

'If I knew I might tell you.'

'Perhaps I can tell you, signore. I have lost my legs but not my eyes. Maria Pia told me this afternoon that she heard you were to leave Venice on the six o'clock train. But you are still here.'

'That's true. I changed my mind.'

Orlino nodded his head gravely. 'You are wasting your time. You know that yourself – otherwise you would come in for a drink. Adriana will be here very soon with some books for me.'

'You've got me wrong. I'm not interested in Adriana.' He spoke curtly.

Orlino laughed gently and, raising a hand rubbed the stubble of his chin, and for a moment the garlic-flavoured breath struck Mercer. 'Even if you were, signore, you would be wasting your time. But I allow myself the privilege of not believing you, and the liberty of advising you to change your mind again. If it is for Adriana you've returned ... there's still a train that leaves at ten tonight for Milan. You can make a Paris connection there. She's not for you, signore...' He wheeled himself away and the tone of his last phrase hung strangely in

Mercer's hearing. There was a bitterness in the words and a suggestion of warning.

He walked slowly down the hallway to the street, lost in his thoughts. A woman came up the shallow flight of steps to the door and, abstracted still, he stood aside for her to pass.

Adriana's voice said evenly: 'Good evening. I was told by Minelli that you were leaving on the six o'clock train.'

He looked up sharply at the sound of her voice. In the soft evening light her hair was ebony and the long oval of her face was warm ivory. She held three books under her arm and the coldness in him gave him a perception he had never had before. Her right fore-finger picked at the frayed binding of a book. There was a spray of blossom pinned to the loose collar of her open coat, the leaves pearled with a drop of water. He could see her picking them from a jar before she left work and pinning them to her. The scent she used, a tiny scar of dirt across the toe of one of her shoes, the slight rise and fall of a thin gold chain about her neck... Small, intimate things, each with a heritage of habit, movement and life behind them which only in imagination he could share, a life closed to him irrevocably.

He looked at his watch.

'It went nearly two hours ago. I'm still here.'

206

'You're not going tonight?'

'Or tomorrow.' His voice was quiet, unhurried, but only he knew the coldness it came from, a coldness more painful than any open anger.

'I don't understand...'

His hand went into his breast pocket. 'It seems to be taking us a long time to understand each other. But whatever your feeling about me is, I should have thought you would have understood that I'm not the kind who can be bought off.'

'I don't know what you're talking about.'

'You don't have to act with me.' He held out the neat wad of thousand-lire notes and snapped the rubber band around them with his finger. It was a vicious, brittle noise in the fading light between them. He handed them to her. 'You'd better take them back to whoever they came from, and tell them I'm still poking ... in the darkest and dirtiest corners I can find.'

He walked past her and went down the cobbled street.

She heard the great clock in the Piazza San Marco strike one and then, with a kind of hurried apology, the other clocks over the town followed it. She lay in her bed in the dark room and she knew that the anger which had been with her all evening had settled to a firm conviction which was not to be shaken. She had been angry with Gian before, but never like this. Before it had been his stupidity, his impatient carelessness which had disturbed her. Now, her anger was compounded of love and anxiety for him, and sharpened by the arrogance with which he had acted.

She heard the bedroom door click open. In the quiet room his breathing was like the sound of some distant engine.

'Awake?'

'Yes.'

'I couldn't get here before. It's not always easy.' She heard him cross the room and then the sound of the water carafe being lifted and the liquid stir of a glass as it was filled. His silhouette wavered for a moment against the brighter darkness of the window and then was fuzed into the room's gloom as he sat down. She heard his shoes drop one by one to the floor. Before he could move she said:

'Stay where you are for a while.'

'Why?' Surprise echoed gently in the dark room.

'It's easier to say what I want to say if you're not touching me.'

He laughed quietly, confident in himself and with the knowledge that her anger would be as short-lived as he cared to make it. But he stayed at the window. 'What have I done, *cara*? Finish the scolding quickly.'

'Where did you get a hundred thousand lire?'

'What do you know about that?'

'The Englishman's given it back to me.'

'To you?'

'Yes. Where did you get it?'

'I borrowed it from Boria. Mercer was making me nervous. With the end so near I wanted to be rid of him, to make sure he went!'

'He's still here.'

'I know.'

'What are you going to do about him now?'

'I shall have to see Boria first. There must be no more mistakes.'

She sat up in bed, laying her arms on the cool stretch of silk cover. 'The mistakes you make ... all of them could have been avoided if you had stopped to think. All the other men in the world are not like you, Gian.'

'You are very angry with me?'

'Yes. If you had asked me I could have told you that this man was not to be bought.'

'A hundred thousand lire ... all new notes? He must be a saint. *San Eduardo dalle Centomila Lire.*' He chuckled, hoping to soften her, but her voice went on with a stiffness which he knew was also in her body and would stay there until he put his arms about her. He imagined the warmth that would come to him through her thin nightdress and he stirred uneasily on the chair.

'He's no saint. But he has one thing you will never have. He has a pride in himself, and it is the stronger because he hates what he does. With you it is the opposite. You have a pride only in your work.'

'And which is the more admirable, *colombella mia*?'

She hesitated for a moment. Then she said slowly: 'It is harder to be as he is.'

He stood up impatiently and when he spoke the jealousy was quick and harsh in his voice. 'You think too much about him.'

'I think too much about you. All your life you have been unfortunate, but I have loved you. It is enough for a woman to say that. But now, when it is so near – your freedom and mine – it is not the moment to make mistakes. Did the Count ask you why you wanted the money?'

He stood at the side of the bed and she lay back, drawing her arms from the cover, wanting, for some reason which she could put no name, to remain untouched until he answered.

'But, of course. It was his idea.'

'He suggested this man could be bought off?' There was surprise in her voice.

'Yes. Since he broke into the palace, and after his visit to you, talking all that nonsense about Boldesca, and showing he suspected I was alive ... we had to do something.'

'I should have been told. It wasn't the way to handle him.'

'Boria thought it was. You can't argue with him.'

'A hundred thousand lire ... it's a lot of money.'

'I've told Boria that I will regard it as payment for the tapestry, and the other designs I shall send him.'

She was silent. Somewhere in all this was a confusion which raised doubt in her.

From her silence he knew that she was not satisfied. He said gently:

'What are you worrying about, *cara*?'

'I don't know... Sometimes I feel that I don't understand you or the Count, that there is something between you which is hidden from me.'

'He is helping me to leave the country. What else?'

She would have answered him, but his hands fell on her bare shoulders and his mouth was against hers, then slipping across her cheek and teasing at her ear as he whispered to her. She felt the anger and anxiety in her pass away, and the only word her lips held was his name.

# Chapter 11

Tio, the barman, deputising for a waiter who was ill, brought him his breakfast tray. Mercer sat up in bed and reached for his cigarettes. The man went to the windows and drew the curtains. The morning sunlight made the room shabby.

'Hell,' said Tio, turning round and smiling, 'no matter what the priests say, is any number of things.'

'Such as?' Mercer poured his coffee and passed his lips cautiously over the thick edge of the bowl.

'A cork that breaks in a bottle, a woman who says "Don't – you'll crush my dress", a *padrone's* wife who visits the agony of her Stromboli belly on her staff, a cat that litters in the darkest corner of the bar cupboard... So many things, signore. A tablecloth after a family *anniversario* party, a waiter who falls sick to spend an extra hour in bed with his wife...' He caught the cigarette Mercer tossed at him.

'And Heaven?'

'Heaven, signore, is time to waste, and the felicity of small things. A dress that slips easily from the shoulder, a cigarette and a

212

newspaper while someone rattles on the privy door, a row of bottles with coloured labels like the banners of the Pope ... or a girl's face coming into the staleness of a hotel hall, a face as fresh as one of Lippo Lippi's angels. Heaven, maybe, is a small blue envelope with a woman's handwriting ... or maybe it's Hell.' He tossed an envelope on the bed. 'It was left for you half an hour ago. From her sister, she said.' He went out whistling softly.

It was a letter from Adriana, and as he read it he surprised in himself a sudden lift of hope. He suspected his feeling, knowing that the strength of his disappointment in her kept him covertly searching for some justification of her behaviour. He couldn't help that. No matter how irrational, even infantile, his love for her had seemed, it was still there, avid for reconstitution. 'I must see you again, to tell you how mistaken you are about me and my understanding of you. I also need your help. Please don't let your anger with me keep you from coming.' She wanted him to meet her at two o'clock that afternoon on the Fondamente Nuove where the Rio dei Mendicanti ran into the lagoon.

The Fondamente Nuove, he knew, was the long quay which formed the northern side of Venice, facing across the wide stretches of the Laguna Morta towards the great raft of the Public Cemetery and the distant islands

213

of Murano, Burano and Torcello. It was a side of Venice generally left alone by tourists. They usually went as far as the Campo San Zanipolo to see the equestrian statue to Bartolomeo Colleoni and then turned back. It was a distant part of the city for her to have chosen as a meeting place. He knew he wanted to go, but he treated his desire cautiously. What could she say which would change anything between them?

He went down to see Rosa Melitus that morning. There was something he wanted to ask … a phrase overheard in the palace, possibly the last lead open to him.

Rosa showed no surprise at his return. She was sitting at a table under the window doing her accounts, a coffee tray by her side. She poured him a cup and laced it with a little cognac.

'Just before you came in,' she said, holding her hand to her large breast as she belched gently against the heat of the coffee, 'I was thinking of Patrick Smith. There must be something about indigestion, dear boy, which sharpens the memory. Do you remember Patrick? He went to Spain with me in thirty-six.'

'He owes me a thousand francs still and I'm sure his real name was never Smith.'

'You'll never get your money. He's dead. Though for sentimental reasons, I'd be glad to pay his debt to you.'

214

'No thanks. I'm throwing money away at the moment.'

'The trouble with Patrick was that you never knew when he was going to change his mind. In the end the strain became too much for someone. He was picked out of the Ebro at a little place called Pina. There was a hole in his head as if someone had been burrowing to see what kind of mind it was that changed itself so often.'

He said suddenly: 'Someone paid me a hundred thousand lire to leave this town and forget a certain Gian Uccello. I don't defend my insanity, but I gave the money back and here I am.'

Rosa sighed and drew her wrapper which had slipped back across her unstockinged legs. 'Unless you're playing for a bigger bonus, and made it clear, I think you were temperamental.'

'No.'

'Then you should carry some insurance.' She pulled open the drawer of the table. 'It has no pedigree, unregistered, a mongrel – but its bite is keen. Take it, dear boy.' A small automatic pistol lay in her hand.

He shook his head. 'I never use them. You know that.'

She sighed again, slipping the revolver back into the drawer.

'Survival is so often a simple matter of being able to change one's habits at the right moment.'

'I prefer to stay in my groove.' He drained his coffee and lit a cigarette. It was the thirteenth he had smoked that morning and he tugged at it as though anxious to be soon past the ill-omened number. 'If someone said they'd meet you at Orfeo's at six – where would you go?'

Rosa was silent for a while. She was thinking about him with far more concern than he would ever know. He wasn't going to get anywhere. Not because she knew anything about it, but because she knew a lot about him. With an effort he could be cruel but not ruthless. The strain of doing that left him without other resources. Before and during the war he'd got jobs because there were more jobs than men. He spoke five languages and was intelligent, but beyond that he had nothing except half-formed virtues and uneasy faults. All of them disadvantages. He was pathetic … that's why she loved him like a mother… Life should have been sensible and insisted on his being a corn-chandler. One day they'd pick him out of some offal-scummed canal and lay him like a net of cabbages on the dusty quaystones. And she'd cry her heart out for a day and be drunk for three with Bernardo.

'No one ever asked me to meet them, but if they did and they said Orfeo's they'd have to qualify it. There's a cake-shop of that name close to the Rialto bridge, a brothel with the same name over in the Dorsoduro district, and a glass works somewhere on Murano.'

'Orpheus gets about a bit.'

'Take my advice and ask for your money back, dear boy.'

She was sitting in the stern of one of the shallow little skiffs which the fishermen used for rowing or poling about the wide stretches of lagoon. He saw her as he came down the steps of the bridge which crossed the Rio dei Medicanti. She gave him no greeting, but said to the small boy who was holding the boat into the steps: *'Bene, Carlo. Al ritorno lasceremo qui la barca.'*

The boy held the boat as Mercer got in.

'You row, or shall I?' she asked.

'I need exercise.' He pushed the boat off and the small boy watched them go out into the wide spaces of the lagoon.

He rowed, watching her, and neither of them spoke. She kept her eyes from him, looking at the grey and green veined whorls of water that spun away from the bow of the boat. He saw the firm, splendid body, the set of the still head, the curve of her chin, and all the promise of love and warmth that lay in the half-parted lips. It was no good, he thought, he still wanted her, searched

217

himself for excuses for her, and waited absurdly – but with all the fervent hope of his deep, forlorn longing – for her to reach out and restore what she had taken from him. The thought made him pull angrily on the oars. She turned her face, and he saw the glimmer through the lace border of her blouse of the gold crucifix she wore about her neck. Then, as though she had trapped some vibration of his thoughts and had need to defend herself, she began to speak.

'In the past I have lied to you.'

'Obviously.' Openly, at least, he could make no capitulation.

'Whether you believed me or not, I do not propose to lie to you any more.'

'But you are going to make a proposition?'

'No. I wish you to know the truth.'

'I may take advantage of it.'

She was silent for a moment, and he had the impression that it was a point she had considered, seeing in it danger.

'I have thought about that, but I do not think you will take advantage of it. If I thought you would I should not be here. When you gave his money back, I learnt a lot about you.'

'I came as near as damn-it to keeping it.'

'I don't think so.'

It was stupid how the few words warmed him, brought him closer to her; but in speech he tried to keep away.

'Perhaps it wasn't enough … you can't know.'

'I do know.' She was emphatic, almost cross with him for talking about himself like that, sensing the bitterness in him. Her concern touched him so that he avoided her face, looking down at the movement of his hands on the oars. She went on: 'I never knew it had been given to you. It was done without consulting me… I am sorry it happened.'

'Why do you say "his money"?'

'Gian Uccello's.'

He rested on his oars for a while and watched the thin green sea grass floating by. A seabird, seated on one of the tripod channel marks, rose and screamed away from them.

'He is alive, of course?'

'Yes.' He saw her lips tighten after the word was gone as though the effort of saying it persisted still. He tried her further.

'Tell me his real name.'

'Lucio Gianbaptista Martellore.'

The relief in him raised his hopes. There was truth between them now. If there might never be love, there was at least a mutual respect, and as long as that existed he knew it was useless to curb his hopes.

He paddled on gently, watching the channel marks streaming in a curved perspective back towards the low, heat-smudged huddle of Venice.

'For a hero, he's a hard man to reward. That's all I wanted to do. Put him touch with his benefactor-to-be. I don't turn people over to the police.'

She nodded and said quietly: 'That is why I am talking to you now. Gian Uccello has a police record. Long ago, in self-defence, he killed a man. After that he was desperate and did foolish things. He was young and impatient. During the war he was a partisan and when he saw the chance to bury Gian Uccello for good, he did so. He did no harm to the unknown man who bore his papers... I do not know how much of this you know, but I am telling you the truth. Under the name of Cerva he was taken away by the Germans... You now what that meant? Six months ago he came back to Venice and asked my help to get him out of the country, to South America where he could make a fresh start. He is a man with more than talent ... one must forgive men like that. In a few days he will be leaving. Count Boria, who has known him since he was a boy, understands his character and his possibilities, is helping. Without him ... I could have done nothing. It has taken a long time to arrange.' There was a weariness in her last words that escaped almost without her knowledge and he had an indication of the strain which had been with her these months and stayed with her still, drove her to talk to him now. 'If you had found him there would have been publicity ... the police would have known and their memories are long. He thought he could bribe you to leave Venice and forget him. He borrowed the money to do so. Now, I am not bribing you ... I have nothing to offer. I am asking you ... please ... please go away from Venice and forget him. He did a good service once for the man you represent. Let his reward be that you tell that man he is buried at Mirave.'

He made no answer at once. A feeling of cleanliness and pride had grown in him. She had thrown herself on to his hands, relied on his decency, and had judged him the kind of man who would not take advantage of her desperation. He could forgive her everything for that. He couldn't even be cautious about the restoration of his pride. To doubt her was to doubt himself. What she had said about Uccello, too, was the truth. He found himself suddenly less concerned with truth than with curiosity about the man himself. He had been in the shadows so long, he now wanted to give form to the hazy figure.

'Does he know you have come to see me?'

'No. He would have stopped me.'

'Where is he in Venice now, and what does he call himself?'

'I have promised you the truth... I can't tell you that. One can risk so much for another, but that... I cannot tell you without his permission.'

And he knew that there was nothing to be gained by pressing the point. She would know exactly how much she could risk for Gian Uccello without his knowledge. She would know exactly... Because... And now there was left to him only the question which had risen while she talked. And since it was all that remained to him he found it hard to put. He turned away from her, looking at the whirling pock-marks left by his oars, seeing the slow, caressing swell of the shallow waters as though underneath some great animal breathed gently. They were abreast of one of the tiny islets that studded the lagoon, a deserted military look-out, a few low trees and a ragged cross-hatching of broken walls marking its surface. In the distance the tall tower of Burano leaned over its reflection and the westering sun caught the cypresses on the far island of San Francesco del Deserto so that they were like raised short swords, their edges sharp with light and the body of the blades dark and corrugated with shadows. There were a few other boats widely spaced on the lagoon, but these points of life made their own isolation more complete. They sat a few feet apart and from them stretched the distances of water and sky, a wide bowl with Venice itself no more than a coloured daub of paints smearing the far rim.

'Tell me,' he said, watching the dip and rise of his oars carefully as though some importance in the neatness of his stroke carried significance for him at this moment, 'what is this man to you? What claim has he?'

She said slowly. 'I am his wife. I was married when I was seventeen. No matter what he has done out of his wildness, I know the good in him, and I love him. If this were not true I should not be here.'

Each word rang in his mind with a slow, lingering shock. He felt his heart beat labouringly within him, a deep echo of sound in his ears as though it pounded against the shell of a dry, time-hollowed tree. He knew then what it was in her which made him want her, not just the warmth and the flesh of her, but the force which was herself. Until now he had only recognised it as an undefined quality that drew him blindly towards her, a weakness and loneliness in him responding instinctively to the strength and comfort in her. To love she added, as so few other women ever did, the rare quality of loyalty. Some women loved like that, making their loyalty the first article of faith... It was this which all his life he had looked for in a woman, and now here it was

… but not for him. And recognising it, accepting his own bitterness of loss, he knew he could do nothing against her… He heard her voice, strained and strange with emotional fatigue: 'For years before the war he was out of my life… Sometimes I used to wish he would never come back. But when he did I was glad. There's something in the heart which can't be put out. I don't care what he's done … we're man and wife. I live and work now for the day when our love can come out into the open, the day when he will no longer have to visit me secretly, the day when we shall be able to go into the streets together in another country without fear that someone seeing us together may recognise us…'

He pulled the boat round gently and swung it towards the little island. The bows of the skiff grated on the mud and stones of the beach. He drew the oars inboard and as the clatter died away into the wide spread of lagoon and sky, a few sounds struggled for a moment against the absoluteness of silence; a train whistled on the unseen causeway running to the mainland, an outboard motor somewhere beyond the island puttered gently to itself and then died in a faint, surprised cough, and a low flying seabird went by, its small head swinging gently, its wings breathing through the calm air.

He lit a cigarette and leaned forward on

his knees.

'If Gian Uccello is what you say, a man of genius who now wishes his past to be dead so that he can start to live again in another country, then I am not interested in exposing him to the police.'

'That is all there is.'

'I don't doubt that you believe it.'

'What else could there be?'

'I don't know. But there are certain things that make me wonder. Would Uccello have killed Boldesca because the man had learnt his secret?'

He saw the colour flare into her face and she answered him quickly.

'Boldesca is alive. I have told you that. I have seen the letter from Milan written by him. Gian killed once. The police may call it murder, maybe it was, but it was also self-defence. He was young and he was wild and he was afraid... But now. No! No!'

'All right. I'm only trying to get things clear for your sake as much as mine. The Count might have forged the letter from Boldesca.'

She laughed at that. 'You do not know the Count. He would have no part in anything like that. He is the only other person in Venice who knows about Gian.'

'Boldesca knew about him. He was going to tell me.'

'He could have told you only what I have

225

told you. The Count sent him away because of that.'

'The Count ... what is his interest in all this?'

'He is helping us because he has known us since we were children, and because he recognises Gian's genius. For the Count that excuses so much... You must believe me.'

'You are going away with ... your husband?'

'I shall join him later.'

He threw his cigarette away. What she said, he wanted to be true, but he could not rid himself of the uneasy feeling that there was more between Uccello and Count Boria than even she knew and, feeling that, he also recognised how difficult it was to make her even suspect this. She loved the man too much to be able to step outside herself and consider him dispassionately. Women like her, he thought, had watched their lovers sentenced to death for murder and had cherished a belief in their innocence for the rest of their lives. You could do nothing against it.

'What will you do?' Her voice was tired, unemphatic.

'I have already told you. It is none of my business to tidy up the police records ... if that's all there is to it.'

As he finished speaking there was the

sound of stones falling on the island behind him. He looked round. Gufo had just climbed one of the low walls and was coming slowly down to the beach. Behind him walked Moretto. They came down, across the thick turf and the pads of sea-thrift, silhouetted against the far pearl wash of the sky with a blackness that seemed to increase their stature, drawing them up until they were gigantic and grotesque against the light. Mercer had a feeling, flashing sharp and fearfully through him, that he had lived this moment before, seen the two men come down across the mud and stones, heard the watery slime suck at their heels, watched the short curve of Gufo's cigarette as he tossed it away to hiss for a second like a snake on the wet stones, and seen the brown, stupid face of Moretto twisted in an ugly grimace like some animal mask.

He jumped out of the boat, the water coming up around his ankles, cold and matching the coldness in him. He bent to push the boat off and saw Adriana's face, white and amazed, but meaning nothing to him, a woman's face stupid with its surprise, a something as irrelevant now as the jagged crest of distant Venice. A hand fell on his shoulder and drew him back with a slow force which was so sure that it seemed almost gentle and vanquished resistance in him.

'There's no hurry, signore. We want to talk to you.' Gufo held him and his face beamed gently, but it was a face without eyes for the sun took the ovals of his glasses and gilded them and his mouth was drawn tight like a firmly healed scar. Moretto raised his foot to the bow of the skiff and pushed it off. It slid out and rocked with a series of idle, lapping explosions. Moretto called to Adriana:

'You can come back when we've finished, signorina.'

Gufo dropped his hand from Mercer and he nodded along the beach towards a ruined block house which had once served some military purpose.

'We will go there, signore.'

'What you want to say ... or do, can be done here.'

Gufo shrugged his shoulders and without looking at Moretto said:

'All right, Moretto.'

Moretto leaned forward and hit Mercer above the right eye, a short, angry stab that sent him backwards on the mud and stones. As he lay there with his eyes closed against the shock, he heard Gufo say viciously:

'Not the face, you ape!'

Then, as he raised himself, Gufo went on: 'Let's go along the beach to the building signore.'

Mercer turned and walked along the

228

beach. Gufo and Moretto followed him, so close that he could hear their breathing, and the beach, under the pressure of their weight, sang with gurgling water noises, small laughing voices that rose up in tiny gaiety from the hidden holes and pockets of mud and stones.

Gufo, behind him, began to speak: 'You must understand, signore, that with us this is business. Since money means nothing to you, we have been asked to persuade you in our way. What did you hope to gain by coming back?' There was a note of quite genuine solicitousness in the last phrase, a kindly professional enquiry.

'You wouldn't understand, Gufo. I find it hard to explain to myself.'

He went up to a small path and through the ruined framework of a door. The roof had gone from the place, weeds grew in the cracked cement floor and the dark corners were littered with filthy paper and dried excrement. On the wall before him was scrawled in red paint – *Cristo fu il primo Comunista. Perchè i preti hanno sempre difeso i maestri?* Christ was the first Communist. Why have the priests always defended the masters? And underneath was a great sickle and hammer and the slogan *Viva Togliatta.* The wall to the right was broken away and he saw the smooth grey back of the lagoon drawn in a faint curve across the horizon with the tiny islet of San Francesco del Deserto borne on it, immaculate, formal, like a palanquin on the back of an elephant. And he was cold, cold in the body and the mind, concerned only with an icy ferocity which, rising from some primitive conjunction of time and place and blood, withdrew him from intelligence and left him a simple animal, cornered, but unable to accept the neat design of the trap in which it stood.

He turned round swiftly. The two men were close to him. His fist crashed into Moretto's face and he was surprised to find its apparent hardness a pad which seemed to absorb his strength. The man went down, grunting with sudden anger and pain. He leapt for him, but Gufo, with the deliberation of a spectator suddenly deciding to take sides, raised his foot and kicked Mercer in the groin. The pain was like a fine, frayed flame of fire running up into his stomach. He doubled over to quench it and Moretto, panting with little animal coughs of delight, swung up towards him from the floor and hit him below the heart as he straightened to meet him. His head went back as he fell and he felt the loose wall plaster collapse behind him. His hands, spread to give him purchase for rising, crushed the soft shards that had fallen. He came forward swiftly and swung at the brown, grimacing face, hitting and careless of himself.

Moretto took his blows with an indifference which widened his own viciousness into despair. He felt the shock on his body of Moretto's fists, and their power drove him backwards, threw him from wall to wall and beat from him an agony of breath and sudden, unwilling cries. Pain spread in him like a sickening intoxication which must go on and on until it spent itself, and while it lasted there was an intense clarity of perception which forced him to identify himself minutely with each second of torture. When he staggered backwards and Gufo, laughing, kicked his feet from under him, the pain against his ankle was distinct, enduring, refusing to merge into the general body of anguish. The feet that drove into his side as he lay sprawled on the ground added another spasm of torment to the convulsive catalogue. He fought back, but never knew at what point pride and instinct abandoned him and he became abject flesh and his senses a burning humiliation. He lay on the floor and they kicked him, their feet hard and vicious against his body. Moretto picked him up, holding him by the breast of his jacket, and he heard Gufo say: 'Remember, not his face,' and then a fist drove into his heart, boring through him. He went backwards, heavy with relaxed muscles and the ground joined forces with them and struck him. The same power that kept his mind alive to each agonized moment, forced him also to keep his eyes open so that he saw, not only the cruel stance of a body leaning to kick and strike, but the minutiae which embellished each piercing moment ... the slight gleam of saliva which marked the corner of Moretto's mouth, the gay angle of Gufo's bow-tie, the outthrust yellow tongues of a pad of purple toadflax which sprouted from a crack in the ruined walls, the word *Cristo* and the tears of red paint which had run from its rough letters... Then, this clarity of sight and sensation seemed to detach itself from him and rise in a soaring curve, a noiseless crescendo of drawn nerves, and going from him gradually allowed him to subside into a vacuum of stupidity which was a sudden peace without oblivion.

He heard Gufo say: 'That's enough.' He saw the large, bland face bend down to him. But he closed his eyes against it, and found a dull pleasure in the power which had come back to him and, like a child practising a newly acquired trick, he opened and then shut them once more to confirm his power. The world left him.

'He's out,' said Gufo.

He turned and went out of the place and Moretto followed him, sucking at the knuckles of a raw fist.

She had filled the baling tin from the boat and was sponging his face with water. He could feel her fingers on the back of his neck and smell the perfume from her wet hand-kerchief. When he sat up she said nothing. He leaned back against the wall, breathing hard, dazed. When he moved, and habit forced him to begin to brush from his clothes the dust and plaster, he put out his hand to stop her from helping him. But when they went down to the boat his stupor made him unaware of her hand which held his elbow, helped him and now and then took his weight as he swayed unsteadily.

As she rowed back to the city, he shut his eyes against the waves of giddiness that swept through his head. All he wanted to do was to lie there, uncaring, heedless of where he went, and what was done for him. He heard her speak, felt her help him from the boat. He seemed to be passing through a slow nightmare, impatience growing for the waking moment which would comfort him with reality.

Then, as his brain cleared, he found he was lying on the divan in her flat, his jacket off, and a glass of brandy in his hand. Adriana was leaning over him, fixing a strip of plaster to the cut above his eye. She stepped back and picked up his jacket to brush it.

He said suddenly: 'You knew this was

going to happen?'

She stopped brushing the coat and came over to sit at the foot of the divan.

'No! I swear to you. Gian is a frightened man. He did not know I was going to speak to you. Fear makes us stupid and he must have felt that what money could not do force might.'

'I don't believe you.'

'But you must believe me—'

'For God's sake! What do you think I am?' He was confused, bitter, angry – and more than all these, humiliated. He went to the french window. He wanted air. He couldn't even begin to think straight. He walked across the loggia and leaned over the wrought-iron rail.

Adriana followed him. She was helpless and although words were useless she had to try. 'You must believe me. You mustn't hate me—'

'Leave me alone.'

She was standing beside him, but he kept his eyes from her, leaning forward over the rail. His body ached and he could feel his bruises stiffening, and the brandy on his weakness was exaggerating everything he saw and heard into an almost unbearable clarity. The roof stretched gently away beneath him and then rose again to a sharp pent which ran out on to the flat leads of the buildings around the Piazza San Marco.

Under the dying sun he could see the yellow moss patches on the mellow tiles, a tiny forest of tipped hairs rising from each pad. Dead plumbago and mimosa blossoms from the creeper over the loggia choked the gutter below the iron railing, and the slight breeze that stirred them seemed to set up a tumultuous sound. The surface of the balcony handrail in the angle where he stood was lined with silver streaks scored against the blue paint. He stood up, feeling a little giddy. She saw the movement and understood it.

'You need rest ... and perhaps a doctor.'

As she spoke he had to hold the rail to fight back giddiness. The long perspective of little gables that sprang from the roof running away to his right suddenly began to buckle and curve, and a sequence of broken tiles below the rail began to shift in a fantastic pattern, kaleidoscopic and confusing. He stood there, shutting his eyes against the vertigo and heard her voice come to him after a while.

'Drink this.' A cold glass and colder water touched his lips and he drank greedily.

He went slowly back to the room and put on his jacket. At the door he paused. She was standing in the middle of the room watching him and the folds of her lace blouse free of her body had a pale, silver luminosity against the window, but neither

her body nor the anxiety in her face touched him now. He went out.

That night Adriana was awake until four, waiting for Uccello to come. There were times when he did not see her for days. As it became clear to her that he would not be coming, she was almost glad. For the first time in her life she was waiting for him, unsure of her attitude. And the uncertainty, she was well aware, came from the strength of her feeling for Mercer. She was thinking of him far more than of Gian. He had been hurt and humiliated, and some part of both she shared with him. All her compassion had been roused, but the exercise of it had been denied by the bitterness in him against her. Now, she found him driving Gian from her thoughts ... found herself searching for some way to show him that she had contributed nothing to the brutality he had suffered... It was a new experience to wait for Gian and not to know how she would feel or what she would say when he came. And for a while, towards the end of her vigil, before sleep took her, she even found herself trying to explain the uncertainty of her own feelings by examining the possibility which Mercer had raised that there was more to be known than had been revealed to her. But it was a postulate which even in the confusion of night thoughts she could not hold for long.

At twelve o'clock the next day, which was a Friday, she telephoned the Albergo Adriatico to enquire about Mercer. The answer the desk-clerk gave her left her poised between relief and an odd sense of disappointment. Signore Mercer had paid up his bill and had left to catch the mid-morning train to Milan.

## Chapter 12

Mercer had left on the mid-morning train. He had taken the water-bus up to the station and had not been surprised to notice that Gufo and Moretto had followed him, but they kept well clear. He was a little more surprised to notice on the boat the street photographer Cassana and he wondered if Spadoni had got wind of his beating up and was watching him and Gufo and Moretto.

At Mestre, the first stop after Venice, he got out of the train. In the town he caught a bus back to the Piazzale Roma, the road terminus in Venice. From here he hired a private motor launch and, seated well back in the cabin, went to Rosa's house, stepping out on to the small quay a few yards from her house. She was in the hall when he entered.

237

'I want a room where no one will bother me. A bed and food when I call for it. I've left Venice. Milan train this morning.'

'Certainly, dear boy.' She turned and began to lead the way upstairs. There was no need for explanations between them.

'How long will you want the room?'

'I've an appointment at six o'clock tomorrow evening. After that I'll let you know.'

She opened the door of a small attic at the top of the house.

'Not even Bernardo?' she enquired, wheezing heavily from her climb.

'No. Not even Bernardo is to know.'

'Very well, dear boy. The sheets are clean, but you'll find it a bit noisy perhaps. My girls are a jolly crowd.'

She pulled the key from the outside of the door and handed it to him.

'The bell works whenever you want me.'

'Thanks Rosa.'

When she was gone, he locked the door and threw himself down on the bed. Within ten minutes he was asleep, not only because he was tired, but also because he wanted to be free of thought and he had long ago acquired the habit of this escape.

It was eight o'clock in the evening when he woke.

He rang for Rosa and was not surprised when she appeared with a tray. There was cold tongue, a salad, two bottles of iced beer, and a pack of Guibek cigarettes.

'What would I do without you?' he smiled.

For the moment she was without humour.

'Exactly what you'll do with me. End up on a mortuary slab. I don't want to know what it's all about, but I know you and I know this town. Why don't you leave Italy?'

'Because I've got an itch to know something. Because I'm going to make myself bloody awkward.'

'I see you've been walking into another wall.'

'Yes. How did you know it would be beer I wanted?' He began to fill his glass.

'Because the corn-chandler half is on top, that stubborn and rather stupid side of you. When you come to your senses, I'll present you with a bottle of Veuve Cliquot to drink on the train.'

She was quite right, of course, he thought. It was the stubborn and stupid side of him. But there was nothing he could do about that now. He turned it over in his mind, after she had left him. Adriana had ceased to exist for him. The days of that blind foolishness had gone. His presence had worried the Count and Uccello and they had thought themselves judge enough of his character to know how to rid themselves of him. Pay him off and if that fails, beat him off, and if that fails... And they had been so near right about him that their acumen had had the effect of opening his eyes to himself. A man will find ready ways of avoiding the truth about himself. But when someone else speaks it, he must either accept it, or prove it wrong by acting a falsehood. That's what he was doing. He *was* the kind of man who could be bought off or beaten off, but he was unable from some residue of pride and damped-down virtue to acknowledge it. He was staying; but even so, he had not lapsed into a stubborn and stupid arrogance that set no limit to his staying. To keep his actions clear and his position sound, he had decided that he would take the risk of one more probe. An enquiry, through Tio, at the hotel that morning before he left had brought him the information that the Orfeo Glass works were owned by Count Boria. He was going to be at Orfeo's at six tomorrow evening to see what he could learn about the Count and the affair which was so deep that it had involved Boldesca's death and their attentions to himself. He felt vicious in a cold, hard settlement of feeling. Vicious, and cautious – for he had no wish to end up in a canal.

He lay back on the bed and smoked. The room was small and shabby, and he felt comfortably at home. On the floor below a gramophone was playing, and now and again he would hear a girl laugh, the low note of a man's voice and once the rapid beat of feet along the landing outside his room. There was no silence in the house, it seethed with noises, warm, busy, human sounds. As he flicked his cigarette over the ashtray by his bed he noticed that the little china dish was marked with a saying – *'Uomo ammogliato uccello in gabbia'* – 'A married man is a bird in a cage.' It was a good motto for this house. But all escape was only from one cage to another. Uccello, the bird he was most interested in, had his cage. He could hate the man, but even that was not sufficient to force him to deny any good to him. No matter what evil he held, there was the other side of him ... the hero who had risked his own safety to help another man, the artist whose hand freed an imagination and power which was locked in most men, the lover with a magic which could charm Adriana to the point of blindness...

At five o'clock the next evening he was on his way to Murano. Rosa had arranged for a gondola to pick him up on the canal edge a few yards from the house. She had provided also a felt hat which he wore pulled well down and a light, Italian type raincoat. She had offered, also, the revolver but he had refused it again.

They swung through the maze of canals

beyond the house and were soon out on the lagoon north of the city. It had been a dull day, and the evening was moving in with occasional warm squalls of rain which swept across the grey waters in sudden, dark stipplings. Mercer sat huddled up in his coat, smoking, and watching the geometric island of the Public Cemetery move slowly abreast of them. Once a black canopied funeral gondola came rocking by them, oared by two rowers, a disturbing sight in his present mood of depression. He touched wood, smiling at himself.

After a while they turned out of the lagoon into the main canal of Murano. The place was unimpressive; quiet grey houses and buildings with a narrow strip of cobbled walk along the canal, and an air of gentle decrepitude. He paid off the gondola at the steamboat stage and went ashore. He walked up the narrow cobble strip, passing a café, a cabinet-maker's shop, the dark alley entrances to two glass factories and then almost at the bridge which spanned the canal, another alleyway with a white and black notice board plugged to the wall. It read – *Vetreria Orfeo*. A few steps beyond was another café. He went in and sat close to the door where he could watch the alley mouth.

He had the place to himself, except for a slatternly looking girl who brought him a bottle of beer. She turned up the radio

242

behind the bar counter and then disappeared into the back of the place. One or two barges filled with crates moved up the canal, then a motor launch, and for a time three children in a punt, paddling with lengths of wood, played about close to the opposite bank. The outlook reminded him of some of the sluggish canals which run through little towns in the North of France. There was a drab somnolence over the scene which gave an aggressiveness to the ugliness. A scud of rain drew erratic runnels on the dirty window and the bar cat, its ears scabbed from fights, came and rubbed itself against his foot.

When Mercer had stepped into the gondola at the canal edge by Rosa's house, Cassana had watched him from the shelter of a lean-to against the wall of the furniture factory on the opposite bank. He had recognised him at once, recognition made easy because he had known that Mercer had returned to Venice and had gone to Rosa's house.

He smiled as the gondola drew away. He gave it five minutes start and then went down to the water and got into a skiff moored at the canal side. He rowed slowly after the gondola, pulling his raincoat collar up against the sudden rain-squalls. Mercer, he was thinking, was a most interesting character. Interesting because it was still far from certain what he was after. And stupid, too. A man who had left Venice once and come back might do the same thing again. He had taken a chance on that, knowing how easy it would be for a man to get off the train at Mestre and catch a bus back. Four boring hours at the bus-station had brought their reward.

He whistled as he rowed, and looking back at the broken line of Venice against the darkling sky, he found himself pleased with the picture. It was unusual, a grey, rather sinister city now, no brightness, no heat, no longer a gilded mirage … just a dark raft afloat on the steely waters.

He idled at the Murano canal mouth until he saw Mercer make his way into the café. He tied up his own skiff well below the steamer stage and went ashore. He walked slowly up the strip of cobbles and stopped at the open door of a cobbler's shop.

An old man was sitting on a stool cutting lengths of blue felt to make slippers. The thin blade of his worn knife slipped like a silver fish through the blue material. Cassana watched him in silence for a while, leaning in the doorway out of the occasional licks of rain.

'Waiting for the steamer?' The old man raised his head.

Cassana nodded. 'How's trade?'

The old man's face came up to him again,

his tongue pushed against the side of his grizzled cheek, and he shrugged his shoulders. Quite close a steamer's whistle blew and there was the sudden sound of water churning under screws. Cassana turned and watched the white bulk of the boat crab noisily towards the landing stage.

Mercer heard the steamer come in and then after a little while the sound of voices. He went to the door. A party of French sight-seers with a guide was coming along the walk. The guide kept a little ahead of them, like a chief with his tribe behind him. They turned into the alley leading to the entrance of the Orfeo Works. Mercer followed them, moving unobtrusively into the tail of the party. They went down the alleyway picking their way carefully around the puddles.

At the end of the alley was an arched doorway that led into a small courtyard littered with cases, piles of ash and rusty heaps of iron. The far wall held a row of dirty windows, guarded with wire mesh, through which came a warm glow of furnaces.

The guide led them through a small door into a long showroom, its walls lined with wooden shelves on which the products of the factory were displayed. Down its length long tables were set out with glass-ware. The crowd broke up and wandered around the room. Mercer stood undecided, listening to their cries of delight. A factory salesman, who had been talking to the guide, broke away and moved amongst the crowd, explaining that everything was for sale and when they had seen the foundry they were welcome to come back and buy, but for the moment would they please not touch anything. This last injunction was ignored with typical French good humour. Mercer pretended to be admiring a great glass dolphin on whose back a nymph rode. In the corner of the room, he noticed, was a half-open door revealing a flight of stairs.

The guide, rejoined now by the factory official, let his party debauch their first enthusiasm over the glass display, and then clapped his hands importantly.

*'Messieurs! Dames! Suivez-moi, s'il vous plait...* You can return here later. We are now going into the foundry where all these lovely things are made. I should explain something of the glass-making history of Venice... This is not a factory in the sense you may perhaps understand that word. Here work only five or six men ... their art has come down to them, a family treasure, through the ages...' Mercer listened to him as he went rapidly over the history of glass-making. The Count was to be here at six for an important meeting. As he owned the place the meeting would probably take

246

place in his own office or room, and that was most likely to be somewhere above the ground floor. Somehow he had to shake off this party and go up the stairs. 'Come then ... and the ladies will be pleased to mind their dresses since the foundry is not a clean place.'

He was taken forward with them. The foundry was long and dark-shadowed like some cave, the floor was loose with ashes and there was an acrid tang in the air. They grouped themselves about the open mouth of a low furnace from which the glow of molten glass struck sharply at the eyes. A troglodyte in a leather apron, a face that was dirty with smuts and two days' growth of stubble, plunged his blow-tube into the glass and drew out a great golden bubble. Then lifting the tube to his lips, he stood before them like an ancient priest and demonstrated his mystery. The long tube supported on one knee, rolled in his hands. His cheeks tight with air, his free hand drawing out the glass with his clippers, he worked from the great bubble a slow miracle. A vase with simple grace of a Greek amphora, a bird, wings high poised as it alighted, a drinking goblet and a family of small animals ... all these in turn rose skilfully, inevitably from the end of the rolling tube, from the quick, deft movement of tongs, and then were tossed back into the melted glass. He did it all with a stolid grace and complete indifference to the circling party, and when it was done he turned his back on them and ignored the lire notes they dropped into a bowl set on a box near him.

The party was led down the foundry and shown the various processes in the making of glass, but some of them grew disinterested in this and drifted back to the showroom. Mercer went with them. He waited until the salesman's attention was taken by a couple who were debating a choice of coloured glass figures and slipped through the half-open door. He went quietly up the stairs and found himself in a long, well-lit room whose large windows looked out towards the lagoon and the straggle of buildings on the marshy edge of the island. Here, too, there were shelves and tables of glass ware, but the floor was crowded with packing cases, some of them already nailed down, others in process of being packed. Straw, paper and strips of wood littered the floor. At the far end of the room one of the corners had been cubicled off by a half-glass, half-wood partition to form a small office. The long panes of glass, rising from about breast height, had been given a light wash of white paint to ensure privacy for whoever worked within the room. A small door set in the side facing Mercer was marked in black lettering – *Direttore*.

Keeping close to the windows he moved down the room until he was at the partition. Edging round a pile of crates so that he was screened by them and confined in the narrow angle between the outer wall of the room and the partition, he listened. There was no sound from within the office. Examining the pane of glass before him he saw that in one of its lower corners the paint had begun to peel away. He picked delicately with his fingers at a loose curl and exposed a ragged segment of plain glass the size of this thumbnail. He half-crouched, and looked through.

Inside the office were two men. Count Boria and the naval officer, Longo, wearing civilian clothes. The Count was seated at a table going through a business file. He was completely absorbed, leaning forward as he read and tapping his teeth with the end of a silver pencil. Longo was seated behind him near the one window which served the office. His chair was tilted and, although Mercer could hear no sound, his lips were half-pursed as though he were whistling gently to himself. Across his knees was a rifle which he was cleaning and oiling. After a moment he dropped his chair square to its legs and said something to the Count who nodded. To Mercer there came only a low murmur of sound, indistinguishable as words.

Mercer watched them for a while. Then he straightened up to ease his cramped legs. The sound of footsteps from the stairway at the far end of the room made him drop quickly into hiding behind the piled cases. Through the overflow of straw and paper-filling from the crate against which he huddled, he could watch part of the room. He saw the salesman come through the door, sling an order book on to a rough desk by one of the tables and then cross to a small cupboard against the far wall. He took out a hat and a raincoat, humming gently to himself. Then he came down to the office door. He gave a brief knock and opened it.

'The place is empty now, signore. Do you wish me to wait still?'

Mercer heard the Count reply: 'Yes, you must wait. He cannot be long now.' His voice was testy, impatient.

'Very good, signore.' The salesman closed the door and came back through the room. He stopped at his desk and made a brief gesture of disgust. He stood there for a moment, undecided, before lighting a cigarette and going away to the stairs. He disappeared with a noisy clatter of feet.

Mercer made himself comfortable behind his crates and decided that he must wait, too. Somebody was coming to see the Count. He wanted to know who it was. He might not be able to hear what the stranger would say but at least he would see him. He waited patiently. From where he sat he could twist his head and see dark rain clouds massing above the lagoon. A trail of creeper on the front of the building began to tap imperiously against the window in the freshening wind. He remembered a remark one of the Frenchwomen had made in the foundry as she had watched the old man. *'Faire comme ça, il faut avoir un peu de Dieu dedans...'* And it was true, to create the miracles in glass the old man must have a little piece of God within him. How he envied the man his skill and craft. A job you could be proud of ... that was worth having. It was a virtue in itself. And Uccello, for all that he hated him and for all his evil, had something of that... But what had he got? A large slice of the Devil in him, he supposed, to do his job. Here he was again, more animal than man, prowling, watching ... and all for what? Exactly nothing in terms of the currency with which the old glass-blower was rewarded.

Footsteps sounded on the far stairs and the salesman came into the packing-room again. With him was a short, dapper-looking man with a thin moustache. Mercer had never seen him before. He wore a loose coat over a navy blue suit and carried a brief-case under his arm. They crossed the room and Mercer heard the office door open and the scuffle of feet and chairs as the two men within rose. There was a confusion of voices in greeting for a moment and then the Count's voice came clearly: 'There's no need for you to stay now.'

He heard the salesman give them good night, the click of the closing door and then the man came hurriedly back across the room. He paused to switch off the lights and then his feet hammered on the wooden stairs. A few seconds later Mercer caught the distant slam of a door.

He crouched there in the darkened room and from behind the partition came a low, unintelligible murmur of voices. The pale radiance filtering through the glass panels filled the packing room with long shadows. He raised himself and looked through his spy-hole.

Longo was standing by the window. The Count was leaning back in his chair, a small frown on his forehead, and Mercer had the impression that the man was impatient. The stranger was standing by the table, opening his brief-case and talking. Now and again the Count nodded.

It was a dumb show which told Mercer nothing. From his brief-case the stranger took a sheaf of papers, referring to them as he talked, and once he spread out what looked like a map and indicated something on it. Longo came and examined it, but the

Count nodded his old head and stared straight before him. Then the man's eyes half-closed and he began to speak, emphasising his points by touching the palm of one hand with his finger...

Mercer watched it all and slowly he felt an intense irritation rising in him.

From some distant church he heard the chimes of a clock strike seven. He stood there with his eye to the glass. For all he knew the dapper little man might be a Milan buyer who was discussing a contract. Then Longo suddenly picked up the rifle from the table, balanced it in his hand and said something which made the little man smile and brought a brief gesture of annoyance from the Count. The stranger began to shuffle his papers back into the brief-case. The Count rose and moved towards the door. They were coming out.

Mercer dropped down behind the crates. He heard the door open. The voices of the men came clearly to him.

'...if you weren't pressed for time, Colonel, you could stop and see Uccello for yourself.' It was the Count and he spoke with a faint touch of asperity. 'He's coming out here this evening to pick up the rifle.'

'Yes, yes. I wish I could – but I must get that train. As long as you've got everything arranged for him...'

'Everything. Today, so far as the people he

works for in Venice are concerned, he's going off to Turin, visiting a sick mother, and he won't be back for two weeks. Tomorrow he'll do his work here for us and then remain in hiding for two days until he leaves the country. It's a precaution we felt necessary … this town will be overrun with police reinforcements in the next few days.'

'Yes, yes, that's a good idea. Keep him out of the way.' Mercer could hear the half-impatient, half-nervous note in the colonel's voice. A worried man, he thought, involved in an affair which was too big for him to accept comfortably. 'Well, I must get off to my train.'

'You'll be in good time,' said the Count as they moved out into the room. 'In fact, you need never have come. Everything is in perfect order. The Navy haven't worried me half as much as you Army people.' You could hear it, Mercer thought; that touch of intolerance and authority, an old man who didn't like to have his arrangements questioned.

'Their responsibility is not quite the same. However, I agree that my visit may have been unnecessary. But I was in no position to tell my superiors that. They take the real risk, you know.'

'There is only one real risk, and by this time tomorrow it will be over. After that everything is in the hands of our friends in

Rome. If they need reassurance send them to Machiavelli and remind them that prayer by itself is nothing. The armed prophet always conquers.'

As he finished speaking the telephone in the office began to ring.

'See who it is, Longo.' The Count came into Mercer's view as he spoke, a tall, stiffly held figure. He picked up one of the glass ornaments from a table and turned it over in his hand. Mercer heard Longo go back into the office. There was the occasional murmur of his voice and then he came out. He stood by the Count and Mercer saw the long, tight-lipped face taut with emotion. He said very clearly, anger sustaining his voice: 'The Englishman Mercer has not left Venice. From what I've just been told it's likely that he's in this building now.'

It was some moments before the Count said anything. Then he quietly put down the glass ornament and turned to the colonel.

'The man who was making enquiries about Uccello. I thought he'd left. He seems to be an extremely stubborn person.' He nodded towards the end of the room. 'Put the light on, Longo. We'll start with this room and go through the factory.'

Longo began to walk down the room, threading his way past crates and tables. To Mercer it seemed as though he moved with an agonized deliberation, like a man pushing his way through a tall tangle of weeds. He watched him as though he were hypnotised, his mind numbed so that time dragged itself out, a dream-like infinity of suspense in which it was easy to believe that Longo would never reach the switch, that the light would never blaze over the white scars of loose packing-cases, that the three men would never turn and search and find him...

Longo switched on the light.

The sudden brilliance was a physical shock which brought Mercer to his feet. In that moment, standing upright, his body leaning to motion, the whole room was printed on his mind as though by the vicious precision of lightning searing across darkness. He saw the prism-blurred edge of a chandelier on one of the tables, the words *New York* stencilled on a loose case cover, the milky intaglio of monograms cut into the sleek cheeks of a set of drinking glasses, and the three men ... the Count's face with a surprised, uncontrolled vacuousness, the Colonel with a hand to the top button of his overcoat, one knee raised to save the briefcase under his arm from slipping lower, and Longo, his back to him, a hand still at the switch, the rubbed material of his jacket momentarily colourless from a high sheen across the shoulders. Then, Mercer was moving.

He swung round a crate and raced down the side of the room.

'Longo!' The Count shouted a warning and Longo turned. Mercer had outflanked the other two and Longo alone stood between him and the door.

Mercer saw the lean, angry face, the outstretched arms, and he drove his right fist forward as they came together. It took Longo on the side of the face and sent him backwards, lurching with widespread arms, fighting for a balance. He stumbled sideways and hit against the glass-packed shelves on the wall. There was the crash of glass as Longo's flaying arms swept ornaments to the ground. Mercer swung through the door and raced down the stairs. At the foot of the steep flight he could see the light-framed door of the showroom. He went down three stairs at a time. As he reached the bottom he heard the sound of feet thundering behind him.

In the showroom he ran around the long display table and made for the door which led out to the courtyard. He threw himself against it, twisting at the handle desperately. It was locked from the inside and his fingers sought wildly for the catch, clumsy and stupid in his haste. He heard a shout from the stairway opening. He turned to see Longo move into the room. The man swept up a great glass bowl from the table and hurled it. Mercer half-dropped, drawing his head down and throwing up a hand before his eyes. The bowl crashed against the door and splintered into a thousand pieces. On the backs of his hands Mercer felt the sudden bite of a spray of vicious glass. Then Longo was upon him.

For the next few seconds they were creatures of wild desperation. Longo hit him as he twisted away and he went back, thudding against the display table, and there sang in his ears the musical ring of vases, bowls and glasses as they swayed and rolled. A pair of hands clamped about his throat and the long body of the naval officer was flung upon him, forcing him down to the table. Mercer drove upwards with his knee, felt the whistle of the other's pained breath on his face, and then rolled. They crashed across the table in a pandemonium of glass and flaying arms and legs and the table lurched and swayed drunkenly on its trestles. They hit the ground and broke apart and, as Longo leapt up, Mercer kicked at his legs and sent him tottering backwards to come to rest against the wall shelves.

He drew himself up to one knee, panting. He saw the Count and the colonel come to the open stair door and the movement of the Count's hand as it went slowly upwards, holding a revolver. When he could shoot without danger to the others he would.

Mercer swayed to his feet. Longo came at him, and raised in his hands was a great confection of coloured glass shaped to the form of a massive cornucopia. The bare bold light of the great bulb hanging from the ceiling lavished the multi-curved purple of grapes with high lights, drew a fire from the rose and jade of apples and spilled a moving sheen over the blunt ridges of bananas. The coloured mass hung poised for a moment and then smashed down at Mercer. As it came, he threw himself forwards and sideways. The cornucopia shattered on the ground at his side, a vicious explosion that sent sharp fragments scudding into the air whining like angry bees. He hit Longo below the chin, feeling his fist drive indecently against the warm neck and the man went down.

'Stand away, Colonel!' The cry was petulant, almost childish, and Mercer, swinging round the table, saw the Colonel who was coming for him with a length of wood stop. The revolver in the Count's hand rose. As it came up covering him, Mercer grabbed a paperweight from the table and hurled it at the ceiling light, letting the movement of his arm take his body forward, heading for the door which led into the foundry. The light bulb broke with a low, almost human sound, a dry *pop* like a man eructating unexpectedly. A flicker of flame drove through the darkness, the room echoing to the sound of the shot, and Mercer heard the sullen plug of the bullet boring into the plaster of the wall. He found his hands on the foundry door and plunged through into the cavernous darkness, hitting himself against the obstacled gloom.

Half-way down the foundry the low light from a single furnace threw a soft glow against the shadows. He ran towards it, stumbling and falling, his hands driving deep in the loose ash of the floor. He heard the men shout behind him and the Count, angry, imperious, calling: 'The switch, Longo. Where's the switch?'

He picked himself up and raced past the furnace and in its gentle gleam saw a low door in the far wall. He wrenched at it and as he closed it behind him the lights came on. He swung the door shut and, in the darkness as he leaned against it, his fingers found a bolt. He threw it across and moved a step into the room. A few feet from him was a wall with a small window. Through its dirty panes came a feeble light from some lamp in the courtyard.

Someone threw himself against the door behind Mercer, but for the moment the bolt held. He went to the window and tried it. It was fastened permanently in its frame. He picked up a chair and raised it towards the four-small panes that made up the window.

As he did so, heard the Count call to Longo–

'Get round into the yard. The window's the only way for him.'

He smashed the chair into the window, jabbing and thrusting at the rotten sash. He heard the glass strike musically on the stones outside and a gust of cool air flushed into the room.

He straddled over the frame, working quickly and precisely now, holding himself clear of the jagged margin of broken glass, and then dropped to the cobbles. A veil of heavy rain swept into his face as he began to run across the yard towards the alley. Once out of the alley there were people, lights, security…

Cassana was standing in the shadows at the alley mouth when he heard the revolver shot. It was faint but, to him, unmistakable. Instinctively his hand dropped into his coat pocket, fingering his own revolver. For a moment he stood there, biting gently at his under lip, a frown creasing his brow.

He turned and keeping to the side of the wall, moved without hurry towards the arched entrance. The last party had long left the works and he knew that Mercer had not come out with it.

As he reached the archway, he heard the smash of broken glass. He drew back swiftly into the shadows. He saw a man drop from the window and begin to run across the yard. It was Mercer.

Cassana watched him race towards the archway, saw the white circle of a face caught for a moment in the pale gleam from the meagre light which hung over the entrance. Then away to the right the showroom door opened and a hard block of fierce yellow light wedged into the darkness and was shot with black streaks of rain. A man's figure was silhouetted in the door and he heard a shout.

Mercer came swinging through the arch. Cassana heard the swift, angry breathing, saw the loose edge of a collar lift like a broken wing under the neck and, as Mercer passed, he put out his foot and tripped him.

Mercer went down with a sprawling, heavy abandon, his body striking against the wet cobbles with a savageness that drove all breath from him. He lay there, sick and shaken, not knowing what had happened. He had to get up, to go on, and the desire was an agony of grief in him. He pushed with his hands against the wet stones.

Cassana stepped forward and hit him on the back of his head with his revolver butt. Mercer's body relaxed and his face flopped sideways, mud-stained, dewed by the falling rain, the eyes closed.

Longo came running up to them.

'*Dio mio!*' Framing his relief, the words echoed harshly against the arch of the gateway. 'Thank God you were there, Uccello!'

Cassana laughed and bent down to the body. 'After I telephoned you I thought it might be wise to wait outside. Most rats come out the way they go in. Give me a hand with him.' He put an arm under Mercer's shoulders to lift him.


# Chapter 13

Spadoni was worried. He stood at the window of his office and watched the wet gleams of light on the Rio dei Greci. One hand rubbed at his cheek and his great body rocked gently on his thin, ludicrous legs.

Luigi, his assistant, sat on the edge of the desk whistling gently against the thin edge of a sheet of paper held against his mouth. It was a teleprint – decoded now – which they had received an hour before.

'If there's any truth in this,' said Luigi softly, 'there's going to be all hell and high water.'

Spadoni swung round slowly and for a moment his mouth pursed in an ugly grin.

'Hell – the army, and high water – the navy?'

'If it's true.'

Spadoni took the sheet of paper from him and read it again. Then he dropped it on the desk with an impatient gesture and snapped: "'Reliable indications not susceptible to proof, but bearing a circumstantial authenticity which cannot be ignored." There's a phrase for you! I can see the first-grade secretary who composed it, smacking his lips over the words and then going off for the day feeling he's earned his money. And what does it mean? That there's a whisper, a rumour, a few words spilled out by a stool-pigeon or a frightened servant who knows very little but infers much more. In a thing like this you expect leakages. The bigger the plot the more holes to be plugged. But the more rumours and half-baked information you get the more helpless you are. They sent me up here on a chance. Now they expect results without giving me any facts. Just a theory. A popular figure is going to be assassinated. That'll touch off fireworks which will put this country in a blaze, and then after a few days the interested parties in the army and navy will step in and take control. You know what that means – just a blood-bath. And when it's over the army and navy chiefs concerned will be in power and we shall have them running the country. We shall have Fascism again.'

'If they fail?'

'They won't fail. Every party will claim him as a martyr. They'll let the Communists, the Democrats, the whole angry bunch, light the fire and set the pot boiling for a few days, and then they'll step in and kick the fire and pot to hell. If it happens our only hope is to make every political faction see they're being used and have them keep quiet. You know how difficult that will be if a man like the poet Nervi is killed.'

He went back to the window and stood there rubbing his hands through his hair. 'A police escort, all the precautions in the world can't help if they're really after him. If we could lock him away in a room... But you know what he's like, and, anyway, he and his people would just think it was a Government trick to stop him appearing in Venice. No, the only thing that would help is to get our hands on the assassin now. Easy, isn't it?'

'We could take into custody every likely man in this city within a couple of hours.'

'That's what we're going to do. But it still doesn't close the net. The man who's going to do it may be unknown to us, or may already be safely tucked away somewhere...' He turned and came back, standing close to Luigi, frowning and biting at his thumbnail. Then he dropped his hand to his pocket and pulled out a photograph and handed it to Luigi. 'I haven't shown you this before. At the back of my mind I thought it was a false line. Now I'm not so sure.'

Luigi looked at the photograph. It had been taken by Cassana and showed Mercer, Gufo and Moretto sitting at a café table, drinking together.

Luigi grinned. 'He must have needed company badly. I can pick up Gufo and Moretto in ten minutes, but not him. He's out of the country by now.'

Spadoni took the photograph back. 'He left on a train for Milan, that's all. He's been mixed up in this kind of thing before. He needs money. He could have come back. If he has he won't show his face until the last moment. But you and I and a few men are going down to his friend Rosa's house now, and you'd better see to it that every likely man is pulled in – including those two, Gufo and Moretto.' He sat down at his desk and pulled out his fountain-pen.

'I'll need an hour for this,' Luigi said, rising.

'That's all right. If he's there he won't move. I've a dispatch for Rome to do anyway.' He sighed as he pulled a sheet of paper towards him.

From a console table at the far end of the room a Louis XVI clock in marble and ormolu struck the hours of ten in bright, silvery notes that vibrated sweetly in the long reaches of the great room.

'What is it that worries you?' The Count rose from the desk and walked slowly to the wide fireplace. With his toe he pressed the electric fire switch. It was getting cold in the room. A twisting sequence of artificial flames turned slowly, pink and green ... crude, ugly colours compared with the burning cadmium filaments as they glowed into a fine intensity.

'I'm a naval man,' said Longo suddenly. 'When a plan is laid down I like to stand by it. There are other ways of dealing with this man.'

'But none so effective and certain as this. A plan at the best is only a rough sketch for the final thing. If you compare Raphael's sketches for a cartoon with the finished work you will see that all plans are only guides and must be re-shaped as one proceeds.' The man, he knew, had already agreed in principle. It was just another example of a stupid, tiring tendency one found so often in his kind. They judged the virtue of an expediency not on its intrinsic logic but on the effectiveness of its advocate in persuading them to forget their own prejudices against change. Not that he would hesitate to give the direct order to Longo if necessary. He had authority for that. But it amused him to handle Longo in his own way. The man was a savage, of course, the son of some peasant who had done well and with money had covered his tracks and got his son into the navy ... but he was a reliable worker and cunning enough to see the advantages which would become his when all this was over.

'Our people in Rome – what do you think their attitude would be if they could be consulted?'

'We haven't time to consult or convince them. But if we had they would agree with me. My dear Longo' – the voice became paternal, invoking a deliberate intimacy and confidence as he meant it to, knowing how it would inflate the feeling of importance in the man – '...think of the obvious advantages. In the old plan Uccello would fire the shot and disappear. We should have an assassination and an assassin still alive ... a mystery which would tease people's minds and keep them restless, no matter how secure we should eventually become. We can rely on Uccello and he will soon be thousands of miles away, but the mystery would remain and mystery carries odium for those closest to it. Already I've accepted that unpleasantness. Remember, it is from this room that the shot will be fired. But the other way–'

'Uccello will still be the assassin.' Longo stood up and came over to the fireplace.

'Of course. But you become a hero and there is no odium attached to me. And over there by the window will be the body of the assassin, Mercer, whom you will have caught in the act and will have shot when he attacked you. A body, lieutenant, without the power of speech, a mercenary Englishman with the blood money tucked into his wallet, and a man, so far as I am concerned, who has already broken into this place and has now used it for his own purposes. A man who can have no possible connection with me. From the point of view of convenience, too, it saves us having to kill him some other way and dispose of his body. There's a neatness about it which delights me. Don't tell me that you have objections about playing the rôle of hero?'

Longo laughed. 'If I had you'd find an argument to overcome them.'

'Or that you have any personal feelings about Mercer?'

'No. Shooting him will be easy.'

'And when this country is in the hands of a strong government, when we have rid ourselves of milk-and-water democracy and the threat of a proletarian paradise, you will not be forgotten.' He watched Longo as he spoke. The man was hard, ambitious with a kind of animal vigour and instinct reminiscent of many of the peasants on his Lucania estates.

'We've got to do something with him. I think what you say is the right way.' Longo pulled out his cigarettes and lit one.

'Then we'd better get the details right.' The Count moved back to his desk. He sat down and smiled at Longo, but there was no humour in the smile.

Adriana leaned on the loggia rail, her face cupped in her hands, staring at the moon-struck shapes of the housetops. It was a cold, hard world of geometrical planes, a dead stone-coloured world slashed with variegated shadows. Uccello walked slowly up and down in the shadow of the over-hanging creepers behind her. Now and again, when he drew strongly at his cigar-ette, the glow flushed across the leaves of the trailers which curled down the iron support at her side and the tiny leaf veining stood out in a warm pattern of filaments.

'You say I was wrong. Stupid and head-strong ... how many times have you accused me of that? But this time I did the right thing.' His voice was pleasant but she knew that behind it was the same unreasonable anger which lingered in her. 'He's left Venice – that's what I wanted and that's what's happened.' The lie was unimportant. Mercer would trouble him no more. 'How could I have done the wrong thing?'

'There was no need for violence. I could

have got him to go without that.' The memory of Mercer lying on the dusty floor of the blockhouse was painful.

'Maybe, but you didn't tell me what you were going to do.'

'You would never have agreed.'

'No. I've asked you to do a great deal ... but not that. You don't have to go down on your hands and knees and plead to any man for me. You never got to that, did you?' He asked the question sharply.

'No.' She said it calmly.

He came up behind her and touched her on the shoulder.

*'Cara* – if you had said "Yes" it would have made no difference. We don't have to hide anything...'

'I didn't tell him anything.' She lied, knowing that for all he said the truth would have roused him.

He laughed quietly, satisfied. Then, one hand playing with the loose tendrils of hair over her neck, he went on: 'I didn't like having to arrange it. In a way, I quite like him. Sometimes I wonder if he was as stupid as he seemed.'

'Stupid?' The question rose almost to the point of defence, and hearing herself speak she wondered why she should want to defend Mercer.

'Throwing away a hundred thousand lire–'

'All men can't be bought.'

271

'He could have kept the money and saved himself a beating – if he'd been wise.'

'Sometimes we do things we can't explain to ourselves even.'

'Like coming back for a beating you know you can't take? Nonsense.'

'That doesn't seem strange to me. The body is a weakness which betrays the strongest mind...' And feeling his hands touching the warmth of her neck, knowing that even as she spoke she had turned her head to bring her chin close down against the palm of his caressing hand, she wondered whether she had spoken for Mercer or herself. Gian's hands on her now were smoothing the anger from her.

She went on: 'There was a time when I wondered if he had some other purpose here. All that about Boldesca...'

He was silent for a moment, wondering how far he dared go. He had lied to her in the past because he knew that even with her there was a limit to loyalty and love and their love was too precious for him to risk. She was never to know the price which Boria had demanded of him for providing him with a new identity, hiding him in the heart of the enemy's camp – it was lucky that no photograph of him existed in the police files – and finally helping him to a new life in another country.

'Spadoni had been unhappy about him

272

ever since he came. He thought he was after something else… I've never mentioned it before, but he has bad record here. Years ago he was mixed up in an assassination in Rome–'

'I can't believe it!'

'It's in the records… He's a strange man. I think our way of handling him was best.' He paused, his fingers playing with the chain about her neck. 'He's gone, anyway. Let's forget him.' His arms went round her slowly, cupping her breasts, and his face slid against hers, and his voice soft and with a quiet richness of feeling went on. *Cara mia* … only a few more days. Things have been hard for you… But in a little while you will come to me and we shall be free… We shall walk together in a land without evil for us… Free to sit in the sun together… No darkness around us so that sometimes we come close to losing each other in it.' His hands brought her round, holding her gently against him, and the tenderness in him seemed to take from her all anxiety and strain. She felt his lips touching her ear and the languor of relaxation in her body stirred, wakening expectation as he began to whisper small absurd words of love.

They stood there as the clocks began to strike midnight, held together by the low, measured strokes in a dark enchantment.

# Chapter 14

Let into the ceiling there was a small light, protected by a thin wire grille. The grille reminded him of ones he had seen over flower-pots on graves. Damp, grey autumn days and the steady seep of rain on the deliquescing heads of tawny chrysanthemums... That was Père Lachaise and his mother's grave. He had been cold and tired and lost that day... Perhaps ever since. Moisture seeped and thin water noises overlay one another in a fretful series of complaints.

Turning on his side, his brain still hazed with sleep and unconsciousness, he saw that a runnel flowed across the floor in a wide gutter, pouring blackly out of a hole in the base of one wall and disappearing beneath the opposite wall. Under the pale lemon light the flagstones of the room seemed varnished, damp and sticky. He dropped back on the raised stone dais that ran the length of the wall and heard the straw creak in the bolster under his head. He struggled to keep his eyes open fighting off sleep. Above his head, springing hideously from the stone joints were one or two fungi, pale, flat, bloodless tongues, their under-surfaces marbled with grey veins... There had been one holiday with his mother when he was a boy, coming to her from England, when she had laughed at him for his belief that only mushrooms were edible. In the woods around the villa where they stayed she had picked little pink and grey fungi she called *prunelli*, and they had tasted like oysters... His eyes closed against his will and he drifted into sleep.

It might have been five minutes or five hours later when he awoke. There was nothing in the room to help him mark time, and his hands were tied behind him, denying him a sight of his watch. He rolled over on the dais and sat up, muscling his shoulders awkwardly to ease the stiffness from them. A sharp, putrid smell came up from the gutterway.

He stood up and walked carefully round the room, working the stiffness from his body. His head was throbbing. He would have given a great deal to have his hands free to rub his eyes which were sore with sleep grains. There were no windows to the room and from the dampness he guessed that it was below water level. There was one door, a heavy, iron-ribbed structure with a great lock and no handle. He tried it with his shoulder but he might have been butting against the wall itself.

He went and sat down on the dais, noticing for the first time the grey army blanket which had been under him. The blanket, the bolster, the cords about his wrists behind him... He began to remember now. His race across the courtyard at the glass-factory. He'd tripped and as he lay there someone had hit him. And now this place. But between the two although there was a gulf of time which he could not assess, there were dark, dreamlike impressions. Voices hovering over him. Hands on him, and then the purr of a motor and the slap-slap of water and opening his eyes, coming up momentarily like a man under an anaesthetic, to see the floodlit façade of the Salute stand out in swimming greys against a moon-pale sky before he dropped back into a troubled limbo of dream.

'I'm in a bloody hole, and I asked for it.' He said it aloud, suddenly. A score of echoes repeated it for him around the room.

Anything could happen now. He was stowed away in this cellar while they decided what to do with him. He knew too much now to have any hope that they would decide to deal less than ruthlessly with him. He had to go. For them it was simply a problem in disposal... For him there was no problem at all. He could only wait with no advantage except the doubtful one of knowing that all the anxiety he had about his future was now resolved for it had been reduced to the dimensions of the present ... these four walls.

A key grated in the great lock and Longo, in naval uniform, entered. Behind him a steep flight of stone steps ran upwards and a sharp bar of sunlight lay rigidly across wall and stairs. Mercer stood up, and as he did so Longo came across to him. The lean, bitter face had a hard, humourless smile.

'If you'd been going to stay with us longer, signore, we should have made you more comfortable.'

'Whom do I thank for the blanket and pillow? Not you?'

'No. Count Boria provided those. Perhaps he wanted your last impression of him to be a kindly one.' The tight lips were sucked back taut as he finished speaking and the cold, dark eyes never wavered from Mercer's face.

'I'd like to see him.' He knew what that was, the desperate hope of being able to make some compromise with the Count, a feeling prompted by the menace which filled the man before him.

'You're not going to see anyone.'

As he finished speaking Longo jerked his right arm forward with a sudden, savage grunt. His fist took Mercer on the jaw and his head, snapping back, tightened up the throat muscles so that a quick, animal gargle of sound was forced from him. Mercer

277

dropped to the dais heavily and lay still.

Longo rubbed his knuckles reflectively for a moment. Then he rolled Mercer over and untied the cords around his wrists. From his pocket he took a pair of thin wash-leather gloves and a long envelope. A little awkwardly he pulled the gloves on Mercer's hands and then slipped the envelope into the inside pocket of the tweed jacket.

This done, he pulled Mercer's body up to a sitting position and, holding him with one hand, crouched at the side of the dais and drew him across his shoulders. He rose, unsteady for a while under the weight, and moved across the room to the stairs.

The sunlight was thick, yellow butter across the worn pillars of the little vestibule at the stairhead. As he crossed it a warm bumble of voices from beyond the wall poured over him. He put his shoulder against a low door and went up steep, worn stairs, twisting, grunting under the weight and hearing the scrape of Mercer's boots against the wall as he took the narrow turnings. At the head of the stairs he freed a hand and slid back the bolt on the Count's secret door.

He went in, the door swinging gently to a close behind him. He slid the body to the ground at the foot of an armchair near the window, where it lay like a collapsed puppet.

At the window the long, half-drawn curtains ballooned in the warm afternoon air which came through the open lattices. A voice from behind them said with a faint stir of laughter in it:

'How long's he good for?' Uccello's head peered round the curtain.

'Long enough.'

'Ten minutes should do it now. Cigarette?'

'You can smoke when you get out of this room. Not before!' Longo went to the window.

'An order?' There was laughter under the questioning tones.

'Yes – and keep that damn thing down until you have to use it!'

'Nervous?'

Longo sucked his teeth irritably, watching a gloved finger rubbing the long blue rifle barrel. He made no answer. He looked down at the packed waters of the canal. A thick drift of gondolas and launches nosed gently upstream and the rough freeway between them was like a brown run across a bright cloth where a thread has been pulled.

Uccello went on:

'Never killed a man before? That's your trouble. I don't blame you. It's not a nice thing to do – the first time. It's better when you're angry or frightened, or even drunk. Better still if he's coming for you. That gives you an out with the priest – if you worry about that kind of thing… But when he's just lying there like a bag of clover–'

'Shut up!' Longo turned back, looking at Mercer, and standing there his hand went down to his pocket, feeling the hard lines of the revolver... Inside himself he heard someone praying, a voice that repeated with an angry monotony, *Sante Madre*... With his foot he hooked Mercer's legs straight.

Longo went over and tried the door-handle of the room. It was locked now, but before he shot Mercer he would have to unlock it, give the impression when they all streamed up that he had just rushed in. His was a dirtier job than Uccello's. They would have to make that up to him...

Uccello, reflective, went on: 'Fifty yards. Above La Spezia we used to pick off the *tedeschi* dispatch-riders at eighty in the dark... Sometimes the machines used to go on without them. That was war and the peasants fought it. They're always fighting – for the right to eat black bread. What did the Navy ever do, except sail out to hand over to the English? *Mare nostrum!*'

'You're talking too much.' Longo dropped into a chair. He was all right now.

'Yes. I'm talking ... that's to keep my hands steady. Strictly professional, *amico mio*. I was born a peasant, but I always knew it was a mistake. I want cake, not black bread. A man has one life. He can live it for himself or for other people.'

Count Boria had heard every word the two women were saying. When they paused he answered them with easy, fluent words that slipped into the cracks of conversation with a felicity that came from years of habit. What would they say or do, he thought, if they could know that they were addressing only the shell of a man. He wasn't with them. He was up there in his room, awareness spreading from him, reaching up the canal across the tightly-packed boats … extending himself towards the coming moment of death. It was a brutal moment he would hate, yet one which he would do nothing to prevent. It had to be … the only way from a dilemma which had slowly gathered around him and his kind. No subtlety, no argument, no nicely graded compromise could keep for them the things which gave their life meaning. They were fighting for survival … and if he had a suspicion that the fight would be useless, he still had to fight. It was the contradiction between his sense of historical inevitability and his inborn loyalties which exhausted him so, made him aware of his years – a great longing to be left alone in peace… But he had to struggle on, hiding himself from his friends, pouring out for them now the facile words which told them that this was the man they knew, civilised, affable, and kindly…

He said: 'It's not age, my dear Lea, which

kills institutions, but economics.' She smiled at him, one of his oldest friends. Minelli came towards them through the crowd on the palace front, holding a silver tray with drinks. 'In fifty years there won't be a gondola left. The motor ferryboats and the launches are killing them.'

He took a glass and handed it to her. 'Three hundred lire from here to the station on the ferryboat, a thousand if you take a gondola. People count their lire these days... Even in the season, a gondolier is happy if he makes six thousand a day. It's not enough for survival. Unless the Municipality subsidises them they will go, and then the workshops over on the Giudecca will be still... And the wash from the launches will slowly shake our palaces down...' He laughed gently, raising his glass.

'The Count is always pessimistic about the future,' a man said, leaning back against the grey balustrade.

'*Au contraire*,' he smiled. He moved over to the great run of steps that led down to the water, watching the gondolas packed around the tall mooring-posts which bore his colours and arms. Some of the faces in the floating crowd turned curiously towards the terrace, watching the movement of well-dressed women and men, the gleam of glasses and silver where Minelli moved. A gondolier in a blue and white shirt called with happy malice:

'When Adam delved and Eve span, who was then the gentleman? *Viva Nervi!*'

The Count laughed with them. Then his eyes looked beyond them, up the far reach of the canal. Very soon now Nervi would be coming, sitting with the city officials about him in the State gondola. The brightly dressed rowers, the ribbons from their wide straw hats streaming in the breeze, would bend to their strokes, the voice of the crowd would rise ... pageantry and homage, and then into it all would come the master of the final ceremony, heralded by one echoing rifle shot...

Minelli came by him and he put his empty glass on the tray.

'Signorina Medova is not here?'

'No, signore.'

'Or Tenente Longo?'

'A little while ago he was here, signore.'

'Maybe he has gone up to the next floor. One would see better from the windows there. Bring some more glasses, Minelli.'

Minelli moved away to the doors of the palace, sidling through the guests. At the door, standing on a raised plinth, one arm about a pillar, was Ninetta. Her other arm clasped the puppy to her. He stopped for a moment, easing the heavy tray against his chest.

'You should see well from there, *piccina*.'

She shook her head. 'Do-do can't see.' She

283

lowered her chin to the puppy's head and rubbed it affectionately. 'Can't I go to the edge of the terrace?'

He shook his head. 'The Count would not like it. When the boats come you must hold Do-do up. He will see fine then.'

'But there are so many people in front.'

He smiled at her. 'I will come and lift you both. Stay there and be a good girl.'

He went into the palace with his tray.

From beyond the curve of the canal a slow swell of sound rose in the hot afternoon air, rippling over the heads of the crowd in a strengthening murmur.

'He's coming...'

He is coming, thought the Count ... towards the moment which holds everything and nothing for him. Without personal malice, without pity he could wait the moment. And knowing what was to be taken from Nervi, he could hold in his mind with a curious prescience the whole of the man's life; see the boy going barefooted under the grey olives, scaring the birds from the thin green lines of young maize pricking the sullen clay of the south, the boy who watched the black-draped women file up the hillside when early morning was a purple and pink wash in the waking sky; see the young man over his papers in the dark, goat- and hen-fetid squalor of the living-room, the brown, work-seared face above the knotted table boards which shone dully with wine and oil and years of fret from the thin elbows and hard hands ... the poet, the humanist, the unconscious force which, destroyed, would loose other forces. And thinking about him, Boria had neither sympathy, nor anger; no emotion except the high, dead level of his own purpose. His eyes went up to the open window in the face of the palace and then to the overhanging slope of the great stone shield, held firm in the knotted hands of bearded tritons, which leaned ponderously above the great door-way on to the canal front. The weathered stone was cut deep with the device of his own family... There was no escape, he thought, no escape from oneself.

Uccello said: 'They're coming now.'

Longo stepped over Mercer and stood a few paces from the window. The gondolas and small craft were drawn tightly together. Below him a yeast of heads and arms moved with an aimless fertility. He was quite calm now, the moment racing on him seeming to push a deadening lull before it.

'When you've done, drop the rifle by him and get out.'

'Don't worry. I'm not staying to be congratulated.'

Longo saw the barrel lift in a small arc and settle on the wooden window-frame and he heard the creak of flesh and muscle as Uccello steadied himself on one knee. Two gondolas, high-pooped, ceremonial, four-rowers apiece, each man dressed in gold and maroon velvet, swung by under striped oars and then with a boiling of dirty water spun about and lay drifting, facing upstream. A husky breath of applause steamed up from the crowd.

'*Bello*... I should have a pencil not a gun,' he heard Uccello say softly.

Longo shifted his weight from one leg to the other. Time seemed to be sucked out of the room leaving it cold and small and barren. The prow of a barge nicked the edge of the silk curtain and with the caution of a sluggardly monster the boat edged into view, riding flat-chested on the dark waters. He saw the rowers ease their oars, the sheen of sunlight on the silk of their knee-breeches, and the three men in the stern: two sitting, blunt, truncated figures, their heads moving in ritual bobs and the other, standing alone, tall, an arm spread to the sky, the leonine head and hair like worn marble against the black hulls of the far gondolas. The hungry voices of men and women, rough with emotion, chanted raggedly: 'Nervi! Nervi! *Viva Nervi! Viva*...!' Then like a long thirsty sigh, sucked voraciously into the black heart of the crowded boats, '*Vivaaaaaa*...!' Let Nervi

286

die, he called silently and shut his eyes against the brightness. Let him die. Let the braid be on his own arm and the hunger of ambition inside him be stilled.

Uccello fired. The tall figure in the gondola spun round suddenly as though somewhere in the crowd a familiar voice had called unexpectedly. A hand was raised to his breast. The echoes of the shot bickered angrily over the canal. Nervi fell, and a great sigh tore itself painfully from the packed boats. The noise died, and it seemed that all the silence in the world was slowly gathering out there on the waters.

Longo turned, jumped across Mercer's body, and went to the door, his hand going down to the key. Behind him he heard the movement of Uccello, and then the thump of a rifle being tossed to the ground.

'*Addio...*' The whisper floated across the room and he answered it with a lift of his hand, his head drawn back now to the window where a fury of noise had risen. He turned the key.

The rifle lay on the carpet by Mercer. One hand was thrown out as though he reached for it and the other sprawled away towards the armchair. Longo put his hand in his pocket for his revolver. As he did so he kicked one of the arms away from the rifle, destroying the cruciform sprawl of the body. He brought the revolver up in his right hand, steadying it towards the still head, and with his left hand he made the sign of the cross against his own body and conscience, knowing that in three seconds the dull face would be a stupid splash of brain and shattered flesh, and as his left hand dropped to his side and the shouts of the crowd massed savagely between the tall walls of the canal outside he stepped closer to the body.

'Signore?'

A child's voice called to him gently. Longo swung round. Ninetta had opened the door and was standing, watching him. Her right hand clasped the wriggling puppy to her breast.

'Ninetta – get out of here!' His voice was harsh, edged with panic, and he made a movement towards her.

'But I want a better view, signore. Down there...' She came forward, smiling at him.

Longo moved forward swiftly between her and Mercer and put a hand on her shoulder.

'You must go, Ninetta.'

The urgency in him was desperate, but with an effort he kept his voice soft, his gentleness masking the savageness he felt. So long as she was in the room he could do nothing. Even now it was bad enough. He would have to say that Mercer had recovered when the girl had gone, and had attacked him again, and he had been forced to shoot.

'But I want to see the–' Ninetta half-twisted from him, her voice breaking off as she saw Mercer lying on the floor. She turned and looked up at Longo, her eyes solemn. 'It's Signore Mercer. Is he hurt?'

Panic had begun to take Longo like a fever and he fought to keep control of himself.

'Yes... Yes, it's Signore Mercer. But he will be all right. Now go.' He held her arm, pushing her roughly towards the door. Every second counted. Five minutes' grace was all Boria had allowed for him.

'But why–?'

'Go!'

He pushed her forward through the door. He could have struck her, strangled her, feeling the tension of his nerves and muscles strung to breaking point, his mind aflame with an impatience which fought off crowding disaster.

'Did he faint?' Her voice trembled with an innocent concern for Mercer.

'Yes.' Longo's hand forced her through the door and he reached to shut it.

'What's going on, signore?'

Minelli was facing him, breathing heavily from the stairs.

'I was looking for her when I heard a shot...' His words trailed off as he saw the revolver in Longo's hand. Then, with an alacrity which surprised Longo, he pushed the girl behind him and reached out for the gun.

It was out of his hand. Everything was out of his hands. 'Don't be a fool, Minelli,' he said wearily. 'It's the Englishman. I heard the shot, too. He's there.'

Minelli rushed past him and looked across at Mercer.

'He did it?'

'He was just making off when I arrived. I had to hit him before he could use his gun...'

'*Dio mio!*' He looked from Mercer towards the window and shook his head. 'If that crowd ever get their hands on him they'll tear him apart.'

Voices and footsteps sounded on the stairs and Ninetta drew back from the door as the Count appeared with some of his guests behind him. He stood there for a moment taking in the scene and Longo watched his face anxiously. Then he turned to Longo, holding out one arm to keep the people behind him from entering. 'Is he dead?'

'No. I knocked him out as he was trying to escape.'

The muscles of the old face tightened gently.

'Who is it?'

'Signore Mercer, the Englishman...'

The Count made a gesture to Minelli. 'Take everyone downstairs and keep them there until the police come. You stay here, Longo.' He turned as Minelli crossed the room and raised his hands to the people outside. 'Please … it will help if you do as I say. Minelli will make you comfortable…'

When they were all gone, he went over to Mercer who was beginning to stir. He stood above him, observing him.

'Close the window.'

Longo moved over to the window and shut it.

'Why didn't you shoot him?'

'That damned child! I couldn't risk being caught in a locked room with him.'

'It was a risk you should have taken.' For a moment he would have said more. Then the futility of protest stilled him. The past was a dead weight they carried into the present … nothing was simple, isolated, the sword which should have cut the Gordian knot had slipped. They had the frayed, unravelled mess before them now, a challenge which dispersed his fatigue.

'We could do it now.' Longo nodded at the revolver which the Count had taken from Minelli and which he still held.

The Count shrugged his shoulders and moved towards the desk.

'After all those people have seen him lying here helpless? When there are two of us, one armed and the other able to take his rifle? No, Longo – the police must do what you bungled. They will take longer, there will be a trial but the final result will be the same.

He has been caught red-handed. Anything he says about us we can deny. The police will take our word before his...' He picked up the receiver and asked for a number then, covering the mouthpiece, he said gently: 'We shall have a little time before they come. I want you to listen carefully...'

Longo nodded, dropping into a chair and lighting a cigarette. The Count was showing no anger, but he knew it was there; knew, too, that the blunder would be held against him for a long while. Yet there was a curious lightness in him as he looked across at the uneasily stirring figure of Mercer. The police were welcome to take him over... Standing stubbornly behind lies was no hardship to him compared with the other thing which he had so nearly wrought. The thought struck him that if he had not paused to make the sign of the cross before shooting then Mercer would now be dead...

## Chapter 15

He had asked for a drink and someone, Minelli he thought, had brought him brandy mixed with water. Lying back, his eyes shut, his head cushioned against the padded back of the armchair, he could hear their movements in the room, feel the tremble of his hand holding the glass along the chair-arm. He took another drink and then slowly opened his eyes.

The room came into sharp focus. The telephone on the desk began to ring and he saw Spadoni pick it up. Spadoni looked smart, Mercer thought. He wore a clean white suit and against his shirt the tie was a broad blue tongue. He saw that the man's hair was sleek with pomade. As he spoke Spadoni ran his hand gently over his hair, touching it like a woman, knowing that soon it would lose its glossiness and order.

Mercer turned his head stiffly. Count Boria was standing by the fire place, rubbing the facet of a signet ring on his hand, his long body relaxed in a watchful abstraction. Beyond him, half-seated, half-standing against a gilt and painted *cassone* was Longo, one leg swinging slowly, tapping the side of the chest which gave out a hollow note. Mercer saw the Count turn and make a gesture with his hand and the tapping ceased.

He raised the glass again and finished the drink, feeling the warmth and strength of the brandy expand within him as though it had touched some desiccated core of energy which now flowered miraculously. Minelli came from the window and took his glass. He put it on the desk and then stood by the door where another man sat.

Spadoni put the receiver down and leaned back in his chair, his fingers spread on the edge of the desk as though it were a keyboard and he about to play. Then he stood up suddenly, and came round the desk. Mercer saw the movement of heads following him.

'Through both lungs. They think it's only a matter of hours.' Spadoni spoke quietly but the bitterness in his voice trembled across the room like the note of a wasp in a still attic. He went to the window and looked out at the great spawn of boats which spread across the canal from the palace. There was no open anger now, no shouting, only a quiet murmur and a disturbing stillness of bodies. They were waiting. 'When he dies the lid of the pot will go flying.'

'When who dies?' Mercer heard his own voice, thick and uncertain.

Spadoni looked at him, but said nothing. Disgust and contempt marked the large loose face. He went back to the desk and sat down.

The Count said suddenly: 'This man ought to be taken away now. There's a crowd in the *campo*. They might break in here.'

Spadoni shook his head.

'If I tried to take him out now they'd tear

him apart. I've sent for more men. When our launches have cleared the canal we'll take him.'

Mercer stood up and he could see how the movement alerted them, brought out the quiescent hatred in them.

'If you're talking about me, I'd like to know what I'm supposed to have done?'

'Sit down!'

But Mercer ignored Spadoni, shaken by a spasm of anger. 'But I want to know. Who's dead?'

Longo came forward a step. 'As though you didn't who's dead. You dirty swine–'

'Longo!' The Count put out a hand to him and the man dropped back. Then he looked across at Mercer.

'You may have no feelings about Nervi's death. Please spare us by discontinuing the pretended ignorance.'

'Nervi–' So that was it. He looked around at them. They watched him as though he were a dangerous beast, and he was filled with a sickening sense of being trapped and bereft of right that made him drop back into the chair and, relapsing there, feel with a slow spread of understanding that he stood at the centre of evil.

Spadoni began to speak, his voice formal now, driving out all emotion:

'While we're waiting, I want to get things straight. Luigi?'

Luigi by the door nodded, sucked the end of his pencil and settled his notebook on his knee.

'Signore Longo – you were first here?' Spadoni glanced across at the man who rose.

'Yes.'

'Full name?'

'Marcello Longo. *Tenente di vascello*, corvette *Medea*.'

'She's tied up at the Dogana. How did you come to be in the palace?'

'When we're in Venice I rent a room in the basement from Minelli. Most of the officers rent rooms for leave, it's…'

'All right. What happened?'

'Count Boria invited me to watch the procession from the palace front. I didn't know any of the other guests and felt a bit uncomfortable there. Also I thought I could get a better view from the first floor, so I came up here. I was sitting at one of the windows on the stairhead watching the procession. When Nervi's barge was opposite the palace I heard a shot and saw him go down. The shot came from this room and I ran in. This man' – he nodded towards Mercer – 'was coming away from the window with a rifle in his hands. He saw me and raised the rifle. I hadn't time to get my own revolver. I hit him and he went down. I think his head must have struck the chair. Anyway, he was out, but I drew my revolver just in case.'

Mercer listened to him and each word dropped into him like an ice-cold stone. His mind was clear now and he was aware of the tangle of deceit into which he had been drawn. This was how they were going to get rid of him. Anger rose from his desperation.

'The man's a liar!'

Spadoni grunted, ran his fingers through his hair and turned his pouch-weighted eyes on Mercer.

'Your turn will come. Until then be silent!' Contempt fined the words and Mercer knew that there was no help for him in this room except from himself.

'As I stood over him,' Longo went on, 'the girl Ninetta came into the room with her dog. I pushed her towards the door and as I reached it Minelli came in. He took the revolver from me. A few seconds later Count Boria arrived with some guests. The Count got rid of them and Minelli, and then telephoned the police.'

'Thank you.' Spadoni rolled the end of his tie between his fingers and bent his shoulders forward over the desk. 'Minelli.'

Minelli braced himself, staring at the far wall to avoid the confusion of other faces, his decency troubled, his embarrassment honest.

'Pietro Minelli. I'm caretaker and attendant here. My apartments are in the base-ment. Everything he says is true.'

'Tell it your way and begin at the begin-ning,' said Spadoni softly.

'I've been here twelve years. Ninetta's my niece. She's a good child but fanciful. Count Boria doesn't like her to come above the ground floor and I have trouble sometimes … I was serving drinks to the guests and then I missed Ninetta. She couldn't see very well from the place where I put her in the doorway. I was coming up the main stairway when I heard the shot. I ran up here and found her standing in the doorway with *Tenente* Longo. He had a revolver and for a moment – please forgive me, *tenente* – I thought he meant her some harm. Then he brought me in here and Signore Mercer was lying on the floor by the chair. It was very hard for me to believe … but it is the truth.'

Mercer listened to them. He didn't doubt Minelli. He knew he must have been lying there on the floor. He didn't doubt the Count who now took his turn and said that he had heard the shot overhead and then had come up with some of his guests to investigate. But he was sure that the Count knew what to expect when he arrived, and he, himself, knew that whoever had fired the shot was now safely away. And the man who had fired the shot, he was pretty certain, was Uccello.

Whatever happened he must keep his head. It was no good storming against them, losing his temper. So far as Spadoni was concerned he knew that the old rancour between his kind and their kind had come up strongly, and having been caught red-handed he could expect no sympathy for any protest of innocence. Fact only would touch Spadoni, and any fact which would show his innocence would have to stand without a shred of dubiety about it... Such a fact must exist because he was innocent, but he would have to search for it.

'Have any of you ever seen this man before?' Spadoni looked around at them and Mercer saw them move their heads affirmatively. He was 'this man', set apart from them, stripped of personality and being, a 'this' which sat there between them.

The Count said: 'He's visited the Gallery once or twice, just as other people do, and a little while back Longo, Minelli and I found him here late at night in very suspicious circumstances. At the time I accepted his story that he had fallen asleep here. Now...'

'That's very interesting.' Spadoni reached into his pocket and pulled out a packet of cigarettes. Then very deliberately he flipped a cigarette across to him. 'Now you can talk.'

The cigarette fell at Mercer's feet and for a moment he wanted to let it lie there. The movement of the large hand had been an insult, the gesture according him no humanity. But desire for a smoke was too great. He picked it up and lit it.

'I didn't shoot Nervi. Why should I? He was only a name to me.'

Spadoni shrugged his shoulders and lifted an envelope from the desk. 'You must do better than that.' He tipped the envelope and clean thousand-lire notes slid from it. 'One hundred thousand, signore. And perhaps more waiting for you. I myself took the envelope out of your pocket. I think that answers "Why should I?" Your price has probably gone down since nineteen thirty-eight.'

Mercer stood up angrily and he saw the movement of the men in the room, the half-step, the sudden turn of a shoulder, the jerk of muscles being tensed, but Spadoni shook his head at them. 'Let him move about if he wants to. I don't think Signore Mercer's going to be foolish.' His broad hand patted Longo's revolver which lay on the desk. 'Let's have you story, signore. Begin where you like but don't be surprised if I interrupt you now and again.'

Mercer sat on the arm of the chair, forcing anger from him. He wouldn't do himself any good by going off the deep-end. He had to talk convincingly.

'Nervi was shot either by Longo or a man

called Gian Uccello. I can't tell you which because while it was all going on I was lying unconscious on the floor here.'

Longo laughed dryly. 'The musketry records of my training establishment would prove that I couldn't hit a motor-launch at that distance, let alone a man on it. I have a defective vision of the right eye... In fact, it was only through a great deal of influence that I was passed for a commission.'

Spadoni nodded. 'I don't think there's any need to go further into that.' He turned to Mercer. 'Now, about Uccello. I shall be interested to hear how a man who – on your own evidence – is buried at Mirave came to be in this room today?'

'He's not dead. That's the whole truth. I came to Venice looking for Uccello. A man who worked in this place offered to give me some information, but he was murdered before he could talk.'

'You're talking about Grandini?'

'His real name was Boldesca. He was a porter here.'

'You told me another name, and nothing about him working here?' Spadoni frowned.

'At the time I wasn't in the mood to help you, any more than you're in the mood to help me now.'

The Count stirred by the fireplace. 'It might help this confusion of names if I said that I received a letter from Milan two days ago from Boldesca.'

Spadoni nodded. 'Go on, Signore Mercer. You came to find Gian Uccello and you finally found him, buried at Mirave.'

'I got that from his wife – Signorina Medova who works in this place. That's what I was to believe, that he was buried at Mirave. But he is alive still. He was a stone-mason's assistant at Mirave and worked off his papers on an unknown body after an air raid. Paolo Cerva he called himself, and the Germans took him off when they retreated from Mirave and he was never seen again. But on the night I was found in this place I heard him talking in this room. I was here to take another look at a tapestry design being made here – the design is the same as the one done by Uccello. I got more and more interested in Uccello and began to poke my nose into things and then someone – Count Boria – began to be worried by my insistence...' He was talking quickly now, as though in speed there was some potency which would carry Spadoni with him... 'First they tried to buy me off, and then they tried to beat me off, and finally when I got too close they worked this on me. Out at the Orfeo glassworks I overheard the Count and Longo and an army colonel discussing the details of Nervi's assassination. They want to stir up trouble in Italy so that the army and navy hotheads can walk in and take the country over. I tried to get away but I was knocked out and kept somewhere in this palace until today. An hour ago Longo came to me and knocked me out again. When I came to, all of you were in the room looking at me as though I were something that smelled too high!' He sat back, breathing heavily, and for a moment there was silence in the room.

Spadoni sat very still, his eyes on the loose lire notes.

'You're suggesting, signore, that Count Boria and others were to use Uccello for this assassination and, when your strictly professional interest in him became too close, they framed you for a crime which, in fact, he did?'

'Yes, it's obvious.'

Spadoni rose. 'I don't know that it's obvious, but it's certainly ingenious. I must congratulate you on being a quick thinker.'

'Damn you, I'm not lying!' He was on his feet, anger springing from the hopelessness which struck him in Spadoni's words.

'Sit down, Signore Mercer, and be calm. I assure you it will impress me more.' Spadoni went to the window and looked out. The crimson coloured police launches were nosing slowly through the mass of gondolas, forcing them away, working at a widening semi-circle of water along the palace front. It wasn't, he thought, a question of this man's guilt or not. The real trouble lay out there, the trouble would spread unless something were done, the right thing, the restrained action and common-sense which it was so hard to induce into passionate men and women...

'Count Boria, I think one or two points have been raised which you might like to comment on?' Spadoni turned to him.

'Thank you. Perhaps I may speak for other people as well as myself?' His voice was assured, the tiredness long lost now to the necessity of meeting a threat. Not that Mercer worried him. The threat lay in the future, a looseness of speech, a wrong phrase which might be uttered, but against which he was preparing himself. Mercer, himself, had disappointed him. The man was almost pathetic, making a bad case for himself. In a similar position, he felt, he could have done so much better. 'Gian Uccello,' he said, 'is a name well known to me. He was born on my estate near Potenza. When she was very young, he married Signorina Medova, a woman for whose talents I have the highest respect. After he took up a life of crime she had no more to do with him. I brought her to Venice just before the war, to work here, and she assumed her present name. She learned of Uccello's death at Mirave through a stonemason's assistant there. I forget his name, but no doubt it was Paolo Cerva. He came to see her once and because he knew she worked for me he brought with him some designs he had done. I purchased one. Incidentally, it's a very fine design and had he not been taken off by the Germans I might eventually have employed him... The rest of his story is nonsense. I have neither tried to buy nor beat him off. The Orfeo glassworks belongs to me but I have not been there for two weeks. You are welcome to question my employees. Longo I know simply as a lodger of Minelli's with whom I pass a word occasionally. And quite frankly, though I respect Nervi more highly as a poet than a politician, I should be an extremely stupid man – if I wished to assassinate him – to arrange for it to be done from my own palace.'

Mercer was on his feet. 'You know that shooting Nervi from this place doesn't affect you a damn! It's practically a public building. Anyone could get in here to do it!'

'That's obvious. You got in here.'

Mercer turned angrily to Spadoni. 'Can't you see the truth that's right under your nose? They're framing me. Uccello shot Nervi.'

Spadoni ran his fingers through his hair. 'Uccello's dead, signore.'

'No he's not. Get hold of Signorina Medova and ask her. She admitted to me

305

herself that he was alive and in Venice and that Count Boria was going to help him leave the country.'

Spadoni was silent for a moment, his eyes on Mercer. Then he jerked his head towards the Count.

Count Boria raised his hands in a weary gesture of hopelessness.

'The man has the most fantastic imagination. It's not true, of course. But I suggest that you send for Signorina Medova and ask her.'

Spadoni grunted. 'I'm not sending for anyone at the moment.'

Mercer stood there with hopelessness growing in him. If they had sent for Adriana or if Spadoni questioned her later he knew that she would not help him. Whether she knew the full truth or not, Uccello and the Count would make sure of her. She loved Uccello. She would say what he wanted her to say. There wasn't a hope for him. He could argue and protest, but for everything he said they would have an answer. If it came to a trial the proceedings would be dragged out and, with the Count backed by his own people in power, there would be no help for him. Witnesses could be suborned, could be spirited away, lies with a fine legal backing would meet his blunt, unsupported statements and, if truth showed any signs of breaking through then he, himself, could be attacked. Men died in prison, men committed suicide conveniently... He caught sight of the Count's face, old, the thin lips touched with the twist of an inner smile, and he knew the man was unworried. They had him.

Spadoni came back from the window and stood by the desk. 'All right. I'd like to talk to Signore Mercer alone. Luigi, you stay.'

He went to the door and held it open. As he did so and as the other men went out of the room Mercer had a glimpse of two armed carabinieri standing outside. Spadoni closed the door and came back. He picked up the revolver from the desk and dropped it into his pocket, keeping his hand on it. For a while he walked slowly the length of the carpet before the fireplace, lost in thought, biting gently at the thumbnail of his left hand. Then as he moved, without looking at Mercer, keeping his eyes on the design of the carpet he began to talk...

'It's ingenious, but it won't hold water. When it came to a trial it would all be knocked from under you.'

'You don't believe me?'

For the first time a touch of anger showed in Spadoni.

'For God's sake stop being stupid, man! In front of the others you had to put up a show. But not with me. Of course, I don't believe you. I'm not even thinking about you. That's what's worrying me – that, out there!' He shook a hand vigorously towards the window. 'All hell's going to break loose unless something's done quickly. And you know it.'

'Of course I know it – but I'm not responsible for it.'

Spadoni flopped down into the desk chair and gave Luigi a despairing look.

'Signore Mercer – I'm not a child who believes in fairy stories. You're caught here in this room, wearing gloves and with a hot rifle. You're a professional agent. You've been mixed up in an assassination in this country before. All your life you've made a living on the dark side of the fence. You're hard up. Times are bad. You come to Venice on what I'll grant may have been a legitimate job. You run into the end of it and your expense account goes bang and you've only a few lire between you and the next job. Why didn't you go back to Paris? Because you found another job here. You've been keeping company with men like Gufo and Moretto. Two days ago you leave Venice openly. Today you're back – but in between you were hiding somewhere. *Corpo di Bacco* – what do you take me for?'

'I know it looks like hell. But I didn't do it. It was Uccello. He's alive I tell you.'

Spadoni shook his head. 'I don't care whether he's alive or dead. I don't care whether you live or die. That's all I care about' – his fingers stabbed viciously towards the window. Then his hand dropped with a bang to the desk and in a changed voice, calm, unctuous, he went on: 'But you care whether you live or die – and a life sentence on one of our islands is death. Now listen, you tell me the truth, give me a lead to the people behind this, the men who want that trouble to boil up out there... Give me anything so that I can tell our people where to watch, where to keep a tight or loose hand, and I'll do a deal with you. When Nervi dies the Government will have about two days to act and they can only pull it off if they know exactly where the danger is. You can tell us that, or help us to it, and I'll see that you don't lose by it.'

Mercer stood up and came over to him. 'I've told you. Count Boria and Longo know all about it. I know nothing. Uccello's the man you want.'

'I see,' Spadoni leaned back. 'You don't mind sticking it out. The trouble will come, and your friends will be on top and then everything will be fixed and you'll go off with another fat roll to add to this one. But you won't, you know. No matter what happens the people out there will shout for your blood and your friends with the thousand-lire notes will push you over to them – a nicely wrapped corpse just to stop

309

you from speaking. You stupid animal, whatever happens you lose!'

Mercer turned his back on them, walking slowly across the room, and they watched him, Spadoni for a time taking hope in his silence.

Without turning, his eyes on the chamfered panelling of the wall, he said quietly, 'I've helped you already. I've told you – Count Boria knows what it's all about. Make him talk, or get hold of Uccello–'

'Uccello!' Spadoni gave a gusty sigh of exasperation. 'The man's dead and you know it. Listen, Mercer, I'm offering you a chance. Give me the truth and I'll do all I can for you. In this room we can be frank. There's no question of loyalty or good faith between you and whoever you worked for. Cash and your personal safety – that's all you need to think about. Be sensible and make the best of a bad job...'

In the silence as Spadoni waited for him, he felt the anguish of rising fear. He was alone, as he had always been alone, and there was only his own cunning between him and the menace ahead. He turned and leaned against the wall panelling, his hands behind him moving slowly over the wooden rosettes.

'You're right about me, Spadoni,' he said evenly, but his body was stirring now to the rising beat of blood and the hammering of his nerves. 'Cash and my own personal safety mean everything to me. If I could do a deal with you I would. Doesn't that prove I'm telling the truth?'

'No.' Spadoni stood up and took the revolver into his hands, his eyes on it as he weighed it gently. 'It means the deal you've done with the others is a better one. I'm not wasting any more time. By midnight I'll have you talking – out of a nightmare which won't let up until you've said everything.'

Mercer felt the wooden rosette give under his fingers and, his back against the panelled secret door, held the weight of wood from moving inwards.

'The man who needs that treatment is Uccello.'

'He's dead!'

'But if he were alive?'

'Then I might believe your story. In fact, I'd take a chance on it. I'd make Boria talk. The whole country would know the truth and there wouldn't be a chance of success for whoever's behind all this.' Spadoni stepped forward angrily. 'Give me names, man. Names of the people in Rome to jump on – anything, and I'll make it worth your while!'

'Only Boria or, maybe, Uccello, can do that.'

'Uccello!' Spadoni spat the word from him, and then spun round. 'Luigi – call the men in. We're wasting time with this assassin–'

As he spoke Mercer slid aside and the door opened. He twisted through it and pulled it after him, his hands reaching for the bolt. He heard Spadoni shout. The bolt went over with a dry, screeching sound and he flung himself aside. The wooden panelling splintered as three revolver shots tore through it, and then he was racing down the narrow, twisting stairs. He went down the steps three at a time, his arms widespread, his hands dragging and fending him off from the walls. At the last turn, twelve steps below him, he saw a carabiniere framed in a great plaque of sunlight from the pillared vestibule. The man looked up at him, his face relaxed with surprise, and then his hand dropped for the revolver holster at his hip.

Mercer jumped the last six steps, saw the sallow face, the drab olive mass of body, and the tugging hand at the holster race up to him. His feet struck the man on the chest and they went down in a heap, the full weight of Mercer's body crashing on to him. The man's head smacked against the paved floor and as Mercer rose he lay still.

He raced across the vestibule and out into the narrow walled garden. His appearance sent up a handful of pigeons perched on top of the wall. A small doorway in the wall, he knew, led out on the quayside. He brushed himself with his hands and tidied his clothes.

Listening for the first sounds from the stairway, he walked to the door and slipped quietly through. On the quayside was a thin sprinkling of people, watching the palace with a quiet, sullen concentration. Mercer felt their eyes on him. A man reached out for his arm, holding him for a moment. It was a carabiniere stationed at the door to keep the crowd out.

'What's happening in there, signore?'

Mercer smiled, shaking his head. 'Don't ask me. I'm a journalist, they won't tell me anything.'

A woman in the crowd shouted: 'Why don't they bring the swine out!' The crowd stirred, a corporate movement of animosity.

He pushed through them and they let him go, their eyes turning back to the palace. He went up the quayside, keeping his pace deliberate, waiting each moment for the hue and cry to break out behind him. Walking without haste, a control which tortured every step with the mad impulse to run, he turned off the quayside up a side street. He swung away through an under passage and in a few moments was lost amongst the Sunday evening crowd which moved restlessly towards the palace. No one knew him, no one had any interest in him. In an hour things would be different. In an hour he knew that he would not be able to go five yards in daylight without being picked up. He worked away right-handed behind the Piazza San Marco heading for the only refuge he knew.

## Chapter 16

He turned off the Via Garibaldi. Half-way between him and Rosa's house a bunch of children were playing, dancing round in a ring and singing: *'Gira, gira, tonde, il pane sotto il forno...'*

It was still light, but in the alleyway there was a lingering gloom, a sadness of shadow which clung nostalgically to all these unsavoury passageways where the crowding tenements offered always some angled barrier to the sun. As he passed the children something of the urgency and desperation in him lifted a little. So long now had he schooled himself to walk without hurry that the last half-hour had become a dream-like sequence in which, lifting his face to the crowds, he had dared them to see in him a man burdened with any weight of fear. Walking through the streets had been a child's game with carefully observed rules.

Once inside Rosa's, the fantasy would be dispelled.

The children's voices followed him as he turned into the house. Then, the closing of the door cut them off and he was conscious of the great brooding weight of the house, its ancient smells and the slatternly comfort of the dark stairs and disordered bedrooms.

The sitting-room was empty. He went up to Rosa's bedroom and pushed the door open. She was leaning over a wall basin washing her hair. The top of her slip had dropped to her waist and the spread of her great shoulders was splotched with crisp soap froth. She turned, peering at him through a wet trellis of hair, and the water ran from her breasts in hasty globules like rain from the backs of storm-passive sows.

'Most people knock, dear boy.' She raised her head, flicking the hair back in a noisy whip that drew a fan of dark water marks across the wall.

'Most people have time to knock.'

She picked up a towel, wiped herself, then twisted it round her head in a turban. Drawing up her slip she pointed to the bed. He brought her a yellow, peacock-spread *peignoir*.

'In five minutes the police will be here, asking if you've seen me.'

'They've a habit of repeating themselves. They were here asking the same thing last night. Anyway...' She paused. 'Bernardo 'phoned a little while back. He thought you might come here. He keeps his ear to the ground pretty well.'

'Well?' He thought she was going to fail him. She was biting her lip and the fat, puffed face suddenly had a stern, accusing expression which increased his sense of isolation.

'I liked Nervi's poetry and his politics. If you shot him, I'll give you five minutes grace before I 'phone for Spadoni.'

'For God's sake Rosa – don't you start believing that.'

'I'm not starting to believe anything. I'm asking a question. Yes or No?'

'No. I didn't shoot him. I was framed. But, anyway, I can make it on my own.' He turned towards the door. He thought – self-pity standing out like a rock from the sea of anger and apprehension which swept him along – even she is ready to believe it. The shock was like that of a child who runs to a mother for help and is met by a buffet.

He had his hand on the door when she spoke.

'All right, dear boy – there's no need for heroics.'

She came over, and it was Rosa now, the old Rosa, smiling, comfortable and assured. She put up a hand that was hung with heavy trails of soapy perfume and patted his face.

316

'You didn't shoot him, but you've dug yourself a hole as deep as any man ever did. Come on.'

She opened the door and he followed her.

They went up the stairs to the room where he had sheltered before. She locked the door behind her and then crossed to the clothes cupboard against the far wall. She opened the door and drew the clothes back from the centre rod and then reached up and twisted one of the hooks fastened to the rear panelling. The back of the cupboard slid away. Seeing his eyes on her she laughed quietly.

'During the war quite a percentage of the population in Venice lived on the roof-tops. It was a habit that used to annoy the Germans.'

He climbed through and then reached back to help her. They were directly under the roof, a jagged stippling of light seeping in between the old tiles. He went forward, bowing his head, feeling the crunch of loose plaster under his feet. After a few yards the roof space broadened into an angled recess made by the upthrust of a chimney stack. Against the stack was a mattress.

'This will have to do until we make other arrangements. Don't smoke, and don't move about more than you have to. Have you a watch?'

'Yes.'

'If you hear anyone coming up here before midnight, go out of the skylight. What you do then depends on the time you have.' She put her hand on a sloping wooden skylight in the roof. 'You can jump for the canal. That's a hundred-foot drop, or you can go along the roof to the next skylight and down. It's a carpenter's and undertaker's place. There won't be anyone there until tomorrow morning.'

He held her arm for a moment. 'I should have taken your advice long ago – and cleared out.'

'You don't have to make any pretty speeches, dear boy.' She put her hand on his shoulder and pushed him towards the mattress. 'I'll do what I can for you. I'll be up here at midnight with some food and a bottle of wine.'

'Thank you, Rosa.'

She turned away from him.

Back in her room, she let the soapy water out of the basin. She was setting her hair when she heard them coming up the stairs. There was a knock and Spadoni came in alone, leaving the door open. Three carabinieri stood outside. She smiled at him, her mouth full of hairpins.

'Professional or private visit?'

'Your little boy's been playing with fire-arms, Rosa. I'm in no mood to be fooled.' He turned to the men. 'All right – go

318

through the place. I'll see to this room.'

'Don't you think you ought to go with them? Some of the girls are sleeping. It might make your men forget their proper business.'

Spadoni closed the door and came further into the room. He looked under the bed and in the wardrobe, the only hiding places.

'Whatever he's done – he wouldn't be likely to come back here.'

Spadoni sat on the edge of the bed.

'He's shot Nervi.'

He waited, watching her, knowing that even if there was surprise in her she would not show it.

'You know what that means?'

She nodded.

'Certainly, but I don't think he did. He isn't that kind.'

'You can tell, eh?'

'Why not. Psychology comes easy to me. Freud and I are in the same business – the relief of inhibitions.'

'You won't be in business for the next few days. I'm going to have a man sitting in your hallway just in case he comes back.'

'Pick one that can play patience.'

Spadoni was silent for a moment, watching her as she went on dressing her hair. He tried not to think of her as he remembered her back in 1938. He got up and went across to her, standing behind her and watching her face in the mirror.

'Wherever he is, you probably know it. He may be wounded. I shot at him.'

'A man can run a long way with a bullet in him.'

'Put your finger on him for us and I'll see you get the money he was carrying. A hundred thousand lire.'

Rosa smiled at him in the glass and slowly withdrew the last hairpin from between the red rolls of her fleshy mouth.

'I wish I could earn that money.'

Somewhere in the roof there was a hole or missing tile. He lay on the mattress and felt the funnelled draught sweep over him. Occasionally he heard the flicker of a bat's wing as the animal came swooping in from the night. He lay there smelling the faint smoky odour that seeped through the chimney stack and listened to the distant sounds of the city. He was thinking of Rosa's face, ugly and strange, in the moment when she had asked him if he had shot Nervi. There was never any full understanding of other people, never a complete faith. As well as she had known him, there had been a moment in which she had conceived him capable of an act which he knew he could never do. There was the core of true human loneliness. There was no person in the world who could share the inner truth of oneself.

And thinking that, some other part of his mind held parallel course and considered Adriana. In the press and passage of his danger, he had had little time to give her. Bitterness was now unimportant. He could think of her without emotion. Either she knew the whole design, or only part of it. She might know that Uccello had been the assassin... He had no way of telling. The whole business – Boldesca, the buying-off, the beating up – had been worked out to keep him, not from proving that Uccello was alive, but from interfering in a rôle which Uccello had accepted. Did she know that? Did she guess that he was innocent? Even Rosa, who knew him so well, had doubted for a moment. What would this girl, who knew him so much less, who had already betrayed him, yet for whom he felt so strongly, what would she believe? If she had never been party to the full plot, then already Uccello and, maybe, the Count would have worked on her, maligning him, building against him...

He lay there in the darkness, hearing the clocks labour through the hours to midnight, thinking about her, sorting out the disorder of his mind, keeping apprehension held down, and wondering what he should do.

It was just after one when Rosa came. He heard the door swing at the end of the roof and then the soft stir of her breath as she came through the darkness towards him. A bottle of wine was pushed against his hands as he sat up and there was the gentle clink of a plate on the floor.

'Eat and drink while I talk.' He heard her settle at the end of the mattress and the creak of her large body, the smell of her in the gloom was a comforting presence. He drank and lowering the bottle said:

'*Lacrima Christi.* Reminds me of Rome – nineteen thirty-eight.'

'There's cold ham and tomatoes. Ideal food for garret picnics. I had to smuggle them up in my blouse so don't complain if the tomatoes are a little warm. There's a carabiniere in the hallway killing time and my week-end business.'

'What's happened outside?'

'Nothing much yet. A radio announcement of the shooting and a description of you, and a demonstration in the Piazza San Marco because the police let you get away. Someone threw a brick through the window of the Spanish consulate. They thought it was the British. The balloon will go up when he dies.'

'He's still alive?'

'Yes. They're giving him blood transfusions. You can tell from the bulletins on the radio what they're expecting. You're in a mess, dear boy.'

'I've got to get my hands on Uccello. He did it.'

'You've got to get out of this country and go to earth for a few years. You know that.'

'Maybe.'

'No maybe about it. Forget Uccello. Just write *finito* under the name Mercer, and hope that we can work something for you. I've spoken to Bernardo – got him down here as my lawyer to protest about the gorilla in the hallway. It's strained him a lot but he's going to help. Tomorrow morning you move out of here on an underground ticket.'

'It's a bright future, isn't it? Where do I finish up – growing raisins in South Africa?'

'There's nothing wrong with raisins. They're in short supply everywhere. You do as you're told and do it fast – and forget Uccello and any other bee you may have in your bonnet. Now eat and drink up. I've got to get back in case our friend takes it into his mind to have a stroll round the bedrooms.'

When he had finished she handed him a packet of cigarettes and matches. 'Be careful with them.'

In the darkness she pulled at one of his ears affectionately.

'I was offered a hundred thousand lire for you tonight, dear boy.'

'You should have taken it. In the open

market I'd be lucky to get ten.' He stood up and put his arm around her.

She gave a contented little grunt. 'You're one of the stupid ones who should have stayed at home.'

'I'm not complaining, and I won't ever forget you.'

'Gratitude is about all I ever get from my men. Send me a packet of raisins when you get to the end of the line.' He felt her hand against his pocket, and then she moved away from him and indicated the boarded skylight. 'If you hear someone tap on that three times, don't be alarmed. It'll be the undertaker.'

'For me?'

'Yes. Open up for him and do as he says. Don't argue. His name's Tallius and he deals in contraband as well as corpses. Good-bye, dear boy, and don't forget the raisins.' Her hand reached out to his cheek, touching him softly and then she was gone.

He put his hand into his pocket and pulled out the revolver she had left there. It was heavy and cold against his palm.

The clocks had just struck five when the taps came on the skylight. Mercer pushed it open and saw a man's face framed in the pale, grey square of early morning. It was a lean, tight-skinned face, the thin lips pursed as though on the point of whistling. Iron-grey hair was cropped closely over the broad head. The man made a motion with his hand and Mercer climbed out.

Far out over the lagoon, beyond the Lido, the sea was turning to a pearl blush as the sun rose. Islands and houses were black silhouettes against the growing light, and a thin wind trembled across the roofs spreading out ochre veils of chimney smoke.

Tallius touched his arm and moved forward over the flat roof. He stopped at a little pent and pushed the door open with his foot.

They went down a series of dark, narrow stairs, the sweet smell of planed wood rising stronger to them as they descended, and finally stood in a long workshop on the ground floor. The windows were filthy with dust and the double doors to the yard and canal side were bolted. Down one side of the room was a row of carpenters' benches and on trestles in the middle of the shop stood three newly-made, unvarnished, unadorned coffins. Against the far wall a cardboard plaque displayed a selection of tarnished brass and chromium handles and hinges. A cat was curled up in the shavings under one of the coffins and by the door was a tall, chipped marble angel from whose outstretched right hand hung a card with the words – No Smoking.

Tallius stopped by the coffins, turned and

eyed Mercer up and down, and for the first time spoke.

'Five feet ten-and-a-half, and about a hundred and forty pounds?'

Mercer smiled. 'Five ten and about a hundred and forty-five.'

Tallius nodded and slid the top from the centre coffin. He stood back and motioned to Mercer.

He came up and put his hand on the smooth run of the side. The coffin had a fresh, wood smell, sweet and clean.

'Do I make the journey all the way in this?'

Tallius shrugged his shoulders and tapped the side of the coffin. Mercer climbed in and lay down. Tallius folded up a sack and put it under his head and then lifted the lid and slid it part way over the coffin. He disappeared for a moment and then came back with a screwdriver and screws.

'There'll only be a couple of screws, top and bottom. You'll get enough air.'

The coffin top slid over him and he was in darkness.

Tallius screwed home the lid and then went across and opened the double doors. The yard, stacked with piles of wood, sloped gently away to the canal. He sat down on the plinth of the marble angel and lit a cigarette. He sat there stroking his chin and watching the grey waters slowly take a rippled gilt as the sun rose. The cat came and rubbed against his legs and he scratched its ears.

Half an hour later a gondola came up the canal and drew into the side of the yard. It was a long, black, funeral gondola, rowed by two men. Its centre was taken up entirely by a palanquin of black velvet curtains hung with black tassels, its four supports crested with stiff sprays of black plumes.

The two men came across and Tallius rose to meet them.

''*Giorno, padrone.*'

''*Giorno.*'

He went with them into the workshop and under his directions they lifted the centre coffin and carried it down to the gondola. Straining under its weight they placed it on the dais of the palanquin and one of them drew the black curtains.

They stood for a moment on the yardside facing him and their faces had a dull curiosity. One of them asked:

'*Cosa c'è dentro, padrone?*'

'Inside?' Tallius looked at them solemnly for a moment, then the top of his tongue curled gently over his upper lip. 'Salami.' He smiled, nodded to them and walked away.

A few moments later they were rowing down the canal, the black curtains shaking a little in the morning breeze.

They came out of the mouth of the Rio della Tana under the bridge by the Veneta

Marina steamboat station and swung right up the great lagoon towards the Grand Canal. The sun was up now and the quaysides and town were stirring. The water-front was busy with people hurrying to their work, water-buses and steam-ferries chugging in from the Lido, and in mid-stream opposite the Danielli hotel the great white liner still lay at her moorings, little sighs of vapour curling from her stacks and a black mass of lighters crowded about her stern. When they were abreast of the Punta della Salute at the mouth of the Grand Canal, a crimson-painted police launch drew up from behind them and throttled down. For a while the two boats travelled abreast, a foot of water between them. A police captain leaned over the side.

The gondolier in the stern smiled at him. *"Giorno, capitano."*

The captain nodded, and said: 'Who is it?'

'It's empty, Captain. Tomorrow it'll be full. Aberto Amati – the post-card seller from San Marco. He died yesterday. Too bad, just as the tourist season was getting going.' The gondolier raised a hand and crossed himself.

Inside the coffin thin voices came distantly to Mercer. He lay there, his body stiffened against the effort to ward off the claustro-phobia which had crept over him. There were times when the crowding walls of an

328

hotel room could give him a choking, breathless sensation, as though he were trapped in damp, clogging layers of wool. Here it was a hundred times worse. He had to shut his eyes, brace his body against the irrational fear, and the strain made him sweat so that he could feel the cold runnels break across his face and neck. He pressed his elbows outwards against the hard walls of the coffin, obsessed with the idea that if he relaxed they would close in on him crushing him. The sound of his breathing he felt must be heard, the long, angry draw of lungs sucking for air in the close, hot darkness.

The captain pulled the curtains aside. He eyed the coffin for a moment and then let the curtain drop. He raised his hand to his cap in a perfunctory salute and then waved them on as the launch circled away.

The gondola swung across stream and turned into the Rio di San Moise. For a while they worked between the narrow houses, moving right-handed in a ragged circle that brought them eventually to the head of the Bacino Orsento, a dark back-water, hemmed in between hotels and workshops. They drew in against a narrow strip of a quay footing the back of a tall building which bore a sign across its middle floor – *Casa Tallius. Pompe Funebri.*

The coffin was carried into the building

and laid on trestles in a small workshop lit by unshaded electric light bulbs that dangled from the ceiling. An old man in a green apron was screwing a plate to the lid of one of the four other coffins in the shop, and in a far corner a youth was varnishing another coffin. The old man nodded to the two gondoliers as they settled the coffin, and then ignored them as he went on with his work. When the two had gone he turned to the youth and said:

'Tell the signore outside to come in, and then you'd better get down to the post with those letters the *padrone* left.'

The youth went out through a door at the end of the workshop that led into a small display room which faced the street. Avvocato Bernardo was sitting on a chair reading a newspaper. The youth picked up a pile of letters from a small counter.

'You can go in now, signore.'

He held the door for the lawyer. Then he put the letters into his pocket and went out into the street.

The old man was unscrewing the lid of the coffin as Bernardo went across to him. He took the screws out, dropping them in the pocket of his apron and then lifted off the lid.

Mercer sat up, blinking his eyes against the dim light.

Bernardo smiled.

'With a little imagination you can get some idea of what the real thing will be like.' Mercer got out and brushed himself down. He felt limp, exhausted. He said nothing, not trusting words. A glance at Bernardo's face, the smile gone now, showed him that the man understood. The advocate said:

'During the war, we had some who just wouldn't do it. Not only Italians.'

'Hurry, signore. The boy will soon be back.' The old man lifted the lid and began to screw it in place.

Bernardo went across the workshop and out to the shop. Behind the counter was a small door. Mercer followed him. They went up the stairs to the top floor and turned into a room whose windows were open on to a narrow balcony. On the balcony Bernardo paused, his hands on the iron balustrade. He turned to Mercer:

'You're not the first Englishman who's used this route ... I've seen a general scramble along there like a roof cat.'

They were facing a little triangle of roofs, a sharp valley, blocked at one end by the blank upsweep of a wall. On the far slope of tiles was a small gable. Standing there Mercer was reminded of the view from Adriana's flat... The same kind of balcony, the same steep roof scarps and the same scaly pattern of weathered, moss-marked tiles.

During the trip in the gondola he had been as near pure fear as he had ever come. Bernardo could never know the joy he had felt when the lid had slid back to show his wine-soaked, wrinkled plum of a face. Up here now, he felt free and removed once more from the apprehensions which had been with him ever since he had entered Rosa's house. Now he was moving along a route which others before him had used... How many British and American soldiers and hunted Italian civilians had come this way? How many times, he wondered, had men stood as he now stood with their hands on the iron rail, waiting to make the first step towards freedom?

Bernardo raised a foot and began to clamber over the rail. Mercer, preparing to follow him, lifted his hands and smiled to himself at the tell-tale scratches on the top of the rail. They were old now, but he would leave his own marks, bright scars against the dead green paint... He followed Bernardo down the slope of the roof. There were no windows over-looking this little valley, except the one they had left and the gable to which they worked their way. Bernardo slipped slightly on the tiles and Mercer saw that a great many of them were broken and cracked.

In a few seconds they were through the gable window and standing in a narrow room which held a truckle bed, a small bookcase, a table, and a sink with a glass-fronted tin cabinet over it.

Bernardo closed the window carefully, and said:

'You can wash and shave. Everything you want is in the cabinet. Smoke if you like but don't move about too much. There are families on the lower floors. Lock the door after me when I go and don't open it again unless it's knocked like this.' He tapped the table in a three-one knock.

'Right. How long do I stay here?' Mercer lit a cigarette and moved to the window, looking back across the roof trail.

'That depends on other people. Maybe until tonight, or tomorrow night. I'll see you get food.'

Mercer turned back to him.

'What did the morning bulletin say ... about him, I mean?'

'He can't be expected to last. His priest is with him.'

'I didn't do it, you know.'

'Stay in this room. An angry crowd won't stop to argue with you.'

'I could give myself up and stand trial. Damn it, I'm innocent!'

Bernardo came across to him and took a light from his cigarette.

'What has innocence or guilt got to do with politics? You might just as well go back to the workshop and let us screw you down for good.'

Mercer turned away. The window drew him again. He stood there, watching the warm sun drawing thin-lipped shadows under the edges of the tiles.

Bernardo began to move towards the door. 'Lock it after me. There's wine behind the bookcase. I'll be back in an hour with some food.'

When he was gone Mercer went to the sink and washed and shaved himself. Afterwards, going to the bookcase for a bottle of wine, he found the wall to one side of it marked with old inscriptions. *Good old Walham Green, E.C.H. June, 43. You can bribe everyone except the bed-bugs. Paul Klein, p.f.c. To Scragger, if he comes this way – see you in the Chandos Arms, a year from now, if it's still standing. Tim.*

He sat by the window in a warm angle of sunlight. The quiet triangle of roofs was as still and remote as an upland mountain valley. Now and again a few pigeons flew over, drawing swift, dark shadows across the sun-bathed tiles. Across the way he could see the loggia railing over which he had come with Bernardo and below it, trailing up to the window where he sat, a broken line of tiles marking a route used by so many before him. Where would the trail end, he wondered?

He felt he knew exactly what would happen. Rosa and Bernardo's influence would take him so far. With luck he would reach the end of the line, and then he would be dropped, a man without a true name ... a curious nonentity with a whole past history to be forged and memorised, and a future to be lived under the shadow of a threat which would never diminish. Rosa had said write *finito* under the name of Mercer. That left him nothing. Before this he had faced a future which had little recommendation except the continuance of his own identity. He might have starved, been miserable, raised enough for an occasional drunk, opened himself to a passing elation, even have found someone who would have given him a little of what he had hoped for from Adriana... All this without fear of his own tongue or features betraying him. Men had long memories, and memory backed by rancour lasted longest. There would be photographs of him plastered over Italy. Any man or woman who had loved Nervi, respected the politician or praised the poet, would hold the assassin's face in memory easily. Even when they thought it forgotten if they glimpsed it in some African bungalow or Syrian bazaar, memory would flash back, sharp, detailed and endowed with the passions that lived at this moment out there in the sunlit squares and the crowded streets. What defence had he got against all that? Only truth, the truth in him which Spadoni would not accept. The truth which only he could establish by producing Uccello. Produce him and Spadoni would make him talk.

A pigeon swooped down into the roof valley and paraded with aldermanic pomposity across the tiles, pecking now and again at the loose mortar. He watched it, his mind tired and confused... Then, suddenly, the thought and memory bringing a wild exhilaration to him, he remembered how he had stood on Adriana's loggia, looking out at the roof. He remembered the bright scores on the railing beneath his hands, the broken line of tiles and the tiny tufts of green and yellow moss and fifteen yards from the loggia rail the pent of a small gable... Someone had passed across that roof to her loggia often enough to leave a trail. He remembered Adriana telling him how she and Uccello met secretly, remembered the Count saying that after Uccello's work was done he would hide up for a few days before he left the country. Uccello would be going off soon by himself. It was natural that he would hide near Adriana, spend all the time he could with her before they were separated... If only he could get his hands on the man, prove to Spadoni that there was a living Uccello...

Bernardo knocked on the door. Mercer crossed and let him in, hardly conscious of him. Bernardo dropped a parcel of food on the table.

'I'll be back this evening with some clothes for you. Things are bad...'

Mercer saw his face then, became aware of him and knew that the man was frightened. He said slowly: 'It's happened?'

Bernardo nodded. 'He's dead. Two hours ago. The place is swarming with police. There's been a free fight in the Chamber of Deputies – every party claims the other had a hand in it for dirty reasons, to stir up trouble and take power. If the government lasts a week it'll be a miracle. By tomorrow there'll be riots and strikes... *Povera Italia.*'

'And after that?'

'Then the people who started all this – your friend Boria – will walk in with the interested sections of the army and navy, and we shall have Fascism again – only it'll have a different name.'

Mercer moved impatiently. 'Why the devil didn't Spadoni take a chance on my story and get to work on Boria!'

'Because he's a policeman, because your story didn't even begin to sound true. Boria's too influential a man for the police to tamper with unless they have some clear evidence–'

'If they had Uccello – knew there was such a man living – then they'd have something and there'd be a chance to stop the trouble.'

'Yes. Give them a reason to jump on Boria and they'd make him talk. They'd pull everything into the open ... the various political parties would see the design behind this affair, and the Government would clamp down on the army and navy people who want this trouble before it comes to a head. But time is running out–'

'If only I could get my hands on Uccello–'

'You look after yourself. There's nothing you can do.' Bernardo helped himself to a glass of wine and drank it nervously. Mercer realised that without Rosa's influence Bernardo would never have helped him.

He said quietly: 'If anything goes wrong and I'm caught you don't have to worry about all this. I won't talk.'

Bernardo smiled humorously, the old, veined face pursed: 'Even if you did we're covered. It's a precaution one takes – not against treachery, but against weakness. Men talk even when they don't want to.' He began to move to the door. 'I'll be back as soon as I can with the clothes.'

Mercer nodded and turned towards the window, watching the sun on the roof. 'You know where Signorina Adriana Medova lives?'

'Yes. Why?' He could hear the slight

surprise in the man's voice.

'I want to know who owns, rents or lives in the house on the right of her block.'

'Why?'

'I'd like to know.' Mercer turned and faced him. For a moment he thought Bernardo was going to argue, but the man slowly shrugged his shoulders and went out.

It was just growing dark when Bernardo returned again. Opening a parcel he had brought with him, he tossed across the bed a shabby blue suit, a light raincoat and a wide-brimmed Italian felt hat.

'Change into these. There's money in the suit pocket. You'll be moving out first thing tomorrow morning. You know where the steamer pier is for Chioggia?'

'Yes. Just beyond the Danielli.'

'That's it.'

'How far is that from here?'

'This house backs on the Bacino Orsento, not a long way from San Marco. But don't you worry how you'll get there. I'll tell you everything in the morning. If you make this stage the rest should be easy.'

'If–'

'There are very few things a man can guarantee.' Bernardo moved towards the door. Mercer went over with him and reached for the handle.

'Did you find out what I asked you?'

'Yes. The house next to hers is a furniture

depository owned by Boria. Take my advice and forget whatever you're thinking about...'

But lying on the bed after Bernardo had gone, he went on thinking about it. If he did get his hands on Uccello... It meant going out into the streets on a long chance, walking and waiting for the shout, for the moment of panic. If he were recognised the crowd would take him and, instead of a future of quiet misery, he would have the sharp agony of a vivid few minutes during which hate would use his body. The thought of the crowd obsessed him. They'd tear his guts out and kick him to a bleeding pulp in the gutter before any carabiniere could save him. He'd seen an angry crowd in this country before ... the women were the worst. It would be madness to take the risk... It was safer to follow Bernardo in the morning and make what he could of the future.

## Chapter 17

A moon had rolled up ponderously above the ragged line of roofs, a hazy plaque of white metal. He stood at the window, listening to the clocks striking nine. He was

340

dressed in the blue suit and in the shadowed room behind him the raincoat and hat lay on the table.

He was saying to himself: 'You don't want to go, but you're going. You're scared stiff of going out, but you know what'll happen if you don't. Every time in the future when you feel desperate, you'll think back to this moment and wish you'd done it. It's your one chance. Hours of thinking about it... Now you've got to do something, make the choice.'

He went over to the table and poured the last of the wine. He drank it slowly. It had no taste, no meaning. Nothing had any meaning except the fear of not knowing ... the fear which would last the rest of his life if he stayed in this room tonight.

He picked up the coat and slipped it on. Hat in his hand he went to the door and felt for the key. Then with an urgent clumsiness, he opened the door and was outside, cramming the hat over his forehead.

He went down the stairs. In a corner of the first landing a man and a woman were huddled against the wall. The girl's arms were about the man's neck as he kissed her. Raising his head Mercer saw the string bag she carried in her hand roll gently across the man's back. It was full of vegetables. On the next landing two boys were wrestling in a curious, silent ecstasy. They swung against

Mercer as he passed and for a moment his hand touched the thin, hot neck of one of them. In the hallway a door opened as he crossed. A voice bellowed angrily and a young man came out and slammed the door behind him. He pushed past Mercer and went into the street.

Mercer stood on the doorstep. Opposite him was a stone balustrade along the edge of a canal. People passed before him and he heard their voices and the sound of their steps as though it were from a great distance. He put his hands in his pockets and left the doorway.

Before he had gone ten yards he was aware of the change in this city. The streets were full, the lights from shops, cafés and restaurants drove back the evening darkness, leaving here and there obstinate wedges of shadow and gloom. This should be night-time Venice – careless, gay, expanding after the day's work and fret. But it was that no longer. In his heightened imagination sound and movement acquired a new significance, distorting the strangeness and preoccupations of the crowd. The passing figures seemed more than human, moving slowly not from leisure, but as though their laborious saunter was imposed upon them by some unseen weight. Their voices came to him, not now gay and brittle, but taut and sullen. When someone laughed it had a hard, lingering trace of shrillness that seemed near hysteria, and he had the impression that the whole town was abroad, restless, prowling through the dark labyrinth of alleys and passages as though an agonising hunger kept them going. The noise and movement of them were a menace. A woman turned suddenly ahead of him and he saw the wild flare of her silk skirt and a sudden flash of blood-red nails as she reached for her companion's arm. He felt in imagination that same lean hand grasping at him, the long frenzied pull of nails scoring into his flesh and he could not prevent himself from gripping the butt of the revolver in his pocket fiercely. He went down the street, his legs stiff and awkward as he fought to stroll as they did, and he kept his head lowered, watching their legs under the brim of his hat. The darkness of an archway closed over him and he paused, raising his head like a man who surfaces from a long dive and swallows at the air.

Beyond the archway and in the light he looked quickly up at the name of the street to get his bearings. As his head came down a face smiled at him from the wall beside a shop window. He stood there, stupid. It was his own face. Above it in thick black letters were the words – AVETE VISTO QUESTO UOMO? HAVE YOU SEEN THIS MAN? There it was, his own face, smiling, puffed-up and coarse from enlargement and he knew when it had been taken, the morning he had sat drinking with Gufo and Moretto.

A man and a woman pushed at him from behind and he heard the woman's voice, fat and angry and hoarse with the accent of slums: 'I'd do a better job on him than the police will. I'd pull him to pieces and miss nothing.' She stepped forward and spat at the poster and he saw her, a troglodyte in a worn, black dress, her breasts and belly straining at the shiny cloth, her face red and pocked with moles about her lower lip which carried a dark line of hair. He moved away quickly, threading his way through the people who moved along the narrow channel of the street. He felt his heart pounding, his fingers crushing against the diamond-scored pattern on the wood of his revolver butt, and he was fighting down the impulse to turn and go swiftly to the safety of his room. But he went on.

At the end of the street a flight of steps rose to a small bridge over a canal. He went up them and at the top a hand touched his arm. He spun round, vicious, startled and found himself, as the crowd brushed his back passing over the bridge, staring into the still, impersonal eyes of a tall nun. A crucifix swung gently across the flat board of her bosom and she held out her hand, intoning a mumble for alms. The relief in him was so great that he smiled and fumbled in his pocket for a note. He gave her something and she bowed her head, the movement of her headdress stirring a truant fragrance of incense about him.

He dropped down the other side of the bridge and began to cross a small square. It was darker here and there were fewer people about. A few stalls in the centre of the square, lit by naphtha flares, had collected a small crowd of people and he could hear the loud voice of a hawker, rasping and husky. He walked a little quicker now. He had taken his bearings and knew the way he must go.

He turned the corner of the square. Standing against the wall five yards ahead of him was a carabiniere. He stood there with his thumbs tucked into his belt, his carbine slung over his shoulder, watching the thin trickle of passers. Mercer hesitated. To turn back abruptly might attract the man's attention. He forced himself to go on, drawing out his steps with a casual movement which was all agony. He held his head down and, as he neared the man, raised a hand and stroked his chin as though, walking, he pondered some thought, his hand masking the lower part of his face. He saw the drab uniform, a bilious green in the street lights, and the worn leather belt. Then he was by.

Ten yards beyond him, he had the feeling

that the carabiniere must be following him. He wanted to know, but dared not risk the danger of turning to see. A flood of light from the end of the street beckoned him and he fought with his desire as he moved towards it. The light came from behind a great wooden trellis of arches thrown across an empty space between the houses. Through the trellis, twined with artificial creepers and starred with great coloured paper-flowers and painted electric light bulbs, he saw the movement of waiters and an idle drift of dancers tracing a slow pattern in the space between the tables. He halted and looked up at the notice over the main arch – *Pista da Ballo*. With a slight turn of his head he glanced back along the street. The carabiniere was coming towards him with slow, ponderous steps, his face as round and bland as a moon-struck yokel.

Mercer went into the garden and sat down at a table which gave him a view of the entrance, a table drawn back in the shadow of a streamer-hung alcove. A spotlight with revolving discs threw a kaleidoscope of colour over the dancers. A waiter paddled up to him and with a gentle 'Signore?' hung suspended almost at the limit of his attention.

'Cognac,' he said and the sound of his own voice suddenly seemed unnecessarily loud and strange. Two young girls who had been

346

dancing together came to the table and settled opposite him, reaching out for their glasses which he had not noticed. They gave him a quick look and then ignored him, whispering to one another in a long, excited *frou-frou* of sound, giggling and turning to the dance floor, animated by some interest which centred out there among the dancers. Over their heads he saw the carabiniere standing at the arched entrance. The man's eyes went round the place, on his face a placid smile, paternal, approving, no trace of regret in it for this pleasure which belonged to others while he worked. One of the girls gave a high laugh and, momentarily, the carabiniere's attention was held by them. Mercer dropped his eyes to the table, holding his knees under cover of the cloth to give firmness to his shaking hands.

The waiter's shadow darkened the table and a glass was put before him. He drew out a note for the man and waved away the change. He drank slowly, the liquid an anonymous presence in his throat. When he looked again the carabiniere was gone. At once a tremendous impatience took him to be out of the place. Every moment he was on the streets increased his danger and built up in him a rising head of strain. It needed only a shout, a second glance from one of the two girls before him and this garden of dancing would become a garden of

347

violence, a jungle in which he would be trapped, crowded upon by angry, lust-stirred people. His skin crawled with the suggestion of his fancy. He got up and went to the entrance, skirting the floor, his head down watching the changing mosaic of colour on the concrete.

There was no sign of the carabiniere in the street. Half-way down it the shrill ringing of a bell made him look up. He was bathed for a while in a warm pulse of air, thick with tobacco smoke and murmurous with distant voices. A knot of people broke past him and went up the broad steps of a cinema portico. A poster held his attention for a moment showing a tall, desperate-eyed man, one hand holding that of a ragged boy, and then, to one side of it, a police bill with his own face. He hurried on, losing the sound of the programme bell.

As he did so, a young man in a raincoat who had been examining the framed photographs in the lobby of the cinema turned sharply, threw away his cigarette and moved up the street after him.

In a little while Mercer was passing the crowded front of the Post Office behind the Piazza San Marco. He turned a corner and the doorway of Adriana's apartment house was twelve yards from him. He moved along the wall, loafing. The doorway before hers was a tall, double-leaved affair with a small inset door. He leaned against it, his hands behind him trying the handle. It was locked. He stood there, undecided. The evening crowd drifted by him.

He tried the lock again. The rattle of the door drew the attention of a man passing, and Mercer moved away. The only windows were high up and barred. Something like panic began to grow in him. He should have thought of this. He had risked the danger of the streets, all his mind concentrated on that, only to find he was unable to get into the depository.

He found himself outside the entrance to Adriana's apartment house. By going up to her flat, he thought suddenly, he could reach the depository. But what about her? Once she saw him she would ring for the police... He would have to deal with her, use force... It had to be done. He was desperate. He stood there undecided. Across the way gondolas were moored under the wall of an albergo, black, silurian shapes in the night shadows, men loafed against the canal balustrade and the wooden soles of women's shoes clattered by him. A blue neon sign for beer flickered from the window of a restaurant, and round the open door of a radio shop a knot of people listened to a bulletin. It blared at him, seeming to reach out over their heads in some inanimate spleen: *'A statement from the*

*Ministry of the Interior this evening indicates that the assassin, Eduardo Mercer, is still in Venice. Within the next twenty-four hours the police are confident that he will be found. The Prime Minister has issued the following appeal for calmness on the part of all sections of the public...'*

He escaped from it through the doorway of the apartment house. There was only one way left for him to reach Uccello – through her flat. He went up the stairs, remembering the first time he had climbed them, not so many days before, but now it seemed a whole age away, so that the man then and the man now were different creatures. With each step he took he heard the thudding of his heart, felt the itch of sweat between his neck and collar and a cold sensation of apprehension turn in his stomach.

He went up, smelling the same damp smells, picking out for a moment the wall scribbles under the dim landing lights, and finally he stood before her door, reading her name typed on the little card. He stood there for a while letting his breath even down and very deliberately he wiped his hands free of sweat against his coat. He pressed his thumb against the bell-push.

He heard it ring within the flat and his hand dropped loosely to his side. He was conscious of an unexpected relief which relaxed his body and mind. The horror of the streets was behind him. With relief came a partial confidence, a freshening surge of spirit that lifted him up.

The door opened and he saw her against the light. The silk of her black skirt swung gently in the door draught and across her dark hair ran a smooth palm of reflected light. He took off his hat and saw surprise sweep across the long, oval face, saw the warm lips half-parted to speak, but before she could say anything he had stepped by her and shut the door.

She moved backwards into the room.

'You...' Her voice was a whisper, low and accusing. He was a ghost who had walked into the room, the visible memory of a man who, having excited liking, pity and guilt in her, had gone, destroying all feeling except loathing for his last monstrous act.

'Yes, me.'

She held herself taut against the distress which fear imposed upon her, and tried to drive from her mind the echoing word, 'assassin.'

'What are you doing here? What do you want?'

She tried to keep her voice firm but in it there were the hurried tones of alarm.

'I want nothing from you.'

She went to the mantelshelf watching him over her shoulder and the movement of her body raised a pang in him. Many times, in the privacy of thought, he had imagined himself coming here, moving into this room to find the privilege of affection. Each time he came, each time he saw her he felt that there was something here for him, and always it escaped him. He had found here suspicion and humiliation ... never the thing he wanted, never the right to drop into a chair and have her come to him intimately with a drink and cigarette, to stand or sit by him while he talked and to accept the tender licence of his hands or kisses. All that was a dream compounded from his own lone-liness...

Absently she picked a cigarette from a box and lit it. He saw that the few seconds away from him had brought back courage.

'Uccello shot Nervi. He's the one who's going to help me.'

She made no answer, standing there, watching him, her body drawn up into the guarded tenseness of an animal which feels its safety threatened.

He saw her look towards the telephone that stood on a small table near the door. Crossing to it he jerked the flex free of the wall attachment.

'You must know I wouldn't be here unless I were desperate. If you try to give any warning I shall know what to do.'

In turn he went to the doors of the other rooms and looked in. There was no one else in the flat. Now he was here, and they were alone, his urgency died, leaving a curiosity about her still and a faint reluctance to move on yet across the roofs to the furniture repository.

'I'm not asking you to help me,' he said, provoked by her silence. 'I know where he is.'

'Nobody can help you. You know that.' She turned away from him, her face tight-lipped, angry, and walked towards the open windows.

He followed her. 'Uccello shot Nervi.'

He put a hand up to her shoulder to twist her round, but she shook herself free and went to the balcony rail and stood there, her back to him.

'It's a lie.'

'Why keep that up now?' He stood beside her. 'Uccello shot Nervi, and you know it's true.' He saw her hand go up, brushing across her forehead and then sweeping slowly over her hair and the movement was heavy with a weariness which, despite his own desperation, touched him. 'For God's sake let's be reasonable... I wouldn't be here unless it was the truth!'

Adriana turned towards him. His face was bone-white in the moonlight, his bitterness marked in taut lines giving it an ugly, pathetic quality, and against the stubborn loyalty in her for another man she felt the swift movement of pity and tenderness which this man so easily evoked in her. But she fought against it.

'I know him and I love him. He could never have shot Nervi.'

'You know me a little, too,' he said quietly. 'Do you think I could have shot Nervi?'

He leaned against the rail, his hand behind him hot against the cold metal, and he saw the stiff silhouettes of roofs and the pale pink and green upwash of lights from the Piazza San Marco, the great rust and gold pillar of the Campanile hard against the thin cloud wisps.

Her voice came to him, a whisper losing itself amongst the trailing greenery of the loggia: 'Yes, I know you did it... I know you've done this kind of thing before.'

He knew that she meant it, that she believed him an assassin. For a moment the anger in him almost drove him to reaching out for her, to shake her free of the falseness which surrounded her. But his impulse died before a sweep of sharp understanding and a curious relief. He had been wrong about her then. She hadn't known all that went on, even now the full truth about Uccello was hidden from her. The bitterness he had cherished against her was undeserved. She had been as much a victim as he. The evil he had suffered from her had never been hers...

'They fooled you,' he cried, 'just as they fooled me!'

The silhouette of her face was hard, unmoving against the light from the room behind them. Her hand went up to her neck and he knew that she was fingering the chain which lay against her warm skin, and he remembered the glitter of the little crucifix that day on the lagoon, remembered the freshness of her lace blouse, the clean, sweet delight of sky and sea.

'The moment you leave here, I am going to warn the police. Nervi was a good man. I hate you for what you've done.' Her voice was low, the uncertain whisper of a lost child. He looked down at his hands on the rail and the knuckles were white as he grasped the iron. They were both caught: only Uccello could release them. He saw the bright scores of scratch marks on the paint, heard the fret of the night wind against the leaves of the creeper and could smell the sweetness of her body as she stood by him like a statue. He raised his head and the geometric shadows of the roofs made a cold pattern before him. This was the moment, he thought, this now, when life closed in on one, its dirty walls narrowing.

'More than ever I want Uccello.' He said it suddenly, angrily. He dropped his cigarette over the rail and watched it slide down the slope until it jammed in the crack of a broken tile, and the red glow throbbed in the pale light.

The door of the flat burst open suddenly, slamming back against the wall. Mercer and Adriana turned, startled.

Spadoni, a revolver in his hand, came swiftly across the room to the window. Behind him were two policemen holding short rifles.

Spadoni stood in the window, his legs astraddle, his ruffled hair in untidy wings above his ears.

'Stand aside, signorina.' He made a brusque motion with the revolver, and Adriana moved away from Mercer.

Mercer and Spadoni faced one another.

'You were lucky, signore, that it was a carabiniere who recognised you on the street. Anyone else would have started a riot. You were unlucky not to realise that he had a plain clothes man with him. Just raise your hands above your head and keep them there.'

Mercer raised his arms. 'There's a revolver in my right-hand pocket,' he said dully.

Spadoni nodded to one of the policemen. The man searched him, stepping back with the revolver.

'You were wise not to try and use it,' Spadoni said curtly.

Mercer dropped his hands. 'It wasn't meant for you.'

'Good.' Spadoni stepped forward to the window. 'We'll go now. There's a gondola waiting opposite the house door. You've got three yards of open street to cross, signore. Try not to excite attention otherwise I cannot guarantee your safety.'

'Before we go,' Mercer was watching Adriana as he spoke, 'you remember that you promised me if I could put my hands on Uccello for you, you might believe my story and would take a chance on Boria?'

'I do, signore.'

'He's within twenty yards of us now. I can lead you to him.' He saw Adriana's hand go up to her breast and a spasm of alarm pass across her face and he knew he was right.

Spadoni hesitated, and Mercer drove home his advantage.

'If you don't do it now, you'll never get him. You can walk behind me with a gun at my back...'

Spadoni was silent for a moment, one hand raised to his mouth as he bit gently at a thumbnail. Then he nodded:

'*Bene*. But at the first sign of stupidity...' He raised the revolver significantly.

'Through that gable over there.' Mercer pointed along the roof and then began to climb the balcony rail. The two policemen covered him with their rifles as Spadoni clambered over, and then they followed.

Leaning on one hand Mercer went down

357

across the tiles, feeling the broken pieces slip under his feet. He waited in the gutter between the roofs and Spadoni came up behind him. Feeling the touch of the revolver against his back Mercer began to climb towards the gable. As he went upwards, hearing Spadoni breathing close to him, hearing the heavy scrape of the men's boots on the tiles, he was aware still of the face of Adriana as she had watched him when he had climbed over the balcony, a face white with misery...

The window of the gable was open and the room was dark within, except for a thin line of dim light from under a far door.

Spadoni put his hand on his shoulder, holding him back. A policeman took his arm and Spadoni climbed through first. Mercer followed.

They went silently across to the door, threading their way through piled up furniture and crates. Spadoni put his hand on the door and opened it quickly, his revolver raised. He stepped through and Mercer followed him.

It was a long room, cut on one side by three evenly spaced windows which looked out on the Piazza San Marco. The café lights and the flood lighting from the arcs which studded the balustraded cornice of the square struck through the small windows in a cold, ghostly pallor. The room smelt of dust and tobacco smoke. The walls were hung thickly with mirrors and pictures, some of them draped in white sheets. A pile of chairs stood pyramided in one corner and the floor space was crowded with tables, chests and other pieces of stored furniture. From the ceiling, like enormous bats, hung a row of cloth-swaddled chandeliers and close to the door stood a plaster cast of Perseus holding the head of Medusa.

At the far end of the room, near the window, a man lay on a canopied four-poster bed. A small reading-lamp threw a pool of red light over the bed and the brocaded folds of the cover were puddled with deep crimson shadows. As they entered and stood there, the man sat up, his body twisting towards them. The book he was reading slid to the floor and from the cigarette in his hand a rigid spine of smoke rose into the air. He wore a loose white shirt and dark trousers.

'Cassana...'

Mercer heard Spadoni's voice, knew that the man had turned from Cassana to look at him, but for the moment his surprise held him. Cassana ... so this was the man, and as surprise died slowly he began to understand so many things. Martellore, Paolo Cerva, Cassana, thief, genius, partisan, traitor, hero – and assassin. All this, and more – a laughing, attractive, quick-witted, mercurial nature which had nearly destroyed him and held Adriana bound. Yes, he could see now, this was a man who could hold a woman. He spun round on Spadoni quickly:

'This isn't Cassana. This is Uccello!'

Cassana slide to the edge of the bed and looked at them curiously. 'What is all this, chief?' There was no trace of alarm in his voice.

Spadoni moved his large body uneasily. 'What are you doing here, Cassana? I thought you were in Turin?'

Cassana shrugged his shoulders. 'I got back this evening. It was all a false alarm.'

'What's he doing here?' Mercer's voice was hard and as he spoke he went to a low table that stood at the foot of the bed. On it was a large suitcase.

Cassana stood up. 'That's the Englishman who killed Nervi? What is—'

Spadoni interrupted him with a wave of his hand. 'Never mind that. He says you are Gian Uccello. What are you doing here?'

'I know the caretaker of this place. I'm spending the evening with him. He's out getting some drink. Uccello?' He laughed and shook his head, puzzled.

'Yes, Uccello!' Mercer cried angrily. He had raised the lid of the suitcase. He saw the lips of Cassana tighten. 'Don't let him fool you, Spadoni. There's no caretaker to this place. He's here hiding up before he leaves the country. Look – a passport with his photograph but another name, a framed photograph of Adriana Medova, and a bunch of steamship tickets for the *Segovia* – she's lying off the Danielli now...' As he spoke he tossed the items from the case on to the bed.

'Let me see those.' Spadoni moved forward, his large body surprisingly alert, his voice harsh.

Mercer let the lid of the case drop. 'He's Uccello. He's the man who killed Nervi!' And as he spoke he saw from Cassana's face that the man realised he was caught.

'Look out!' One of the carabinieri shouted suddenly.

Uccello swung away from the bed and reached for the little table. Mercer was thrust sideways as Spadoni dropped the passport and moved forwards. The room echoed with the contained thunder of a shot as Uccello's hand came up and he fired. Spadoni's arm jerked and his own revolver dropped from his hand as Uccello's bullet grazed his wrist.

Uccello turned and with a swing of his arm sent the lamp crashing from the table. The flame of a rifle shot seared Mercer's face as a policeman fired. There was a crashing of glass as Uccello flung himself through the window.

Mercer picked up Spadoni's revolver from

the floor and raced forward. He was through the shattered window before the others and found himself standing in the wide parapeted way which ran around the great façade of the square. He saw the white movement of Uccello's shirt ahead of him and went after him.

Uccello reached the top corner of the runway and faced about. Mercer flung himself sideways and the hard stone of the parapet drove into his side. The bullet whined past him, hit the roof and ricochetted into the night. He pulled himself up and for a moment he saw the white stippling of faces far down below on the piazza, the hard gloss of coloured table tops and the great spread of coloured lights which seemed to fuse and swirl against his eyes. Then with a roar of wings the pigeons came up from the pavements, sweeping by him in sibilant vortex.

He heard the others shout behind him as he turned the far corner. Uccello was halfway along the top side of the square when he saw him trip over a ridge of leaded pipe. The man sprawled flat on the leads and the shock of his falling body came clearly to Mercer.

He followed him, careless of the stone projections that tore at him, hearing the hollow thud of his feet on the runway, conscious not only of the white-shirted figure that rose and fell before him, but aware, too, of the crowd down in the square which now stirred and shouted, releasing angry bursts of voices that swept up into the moon-pale night. The orchestra in Florian's played on, a thin, brittle jest of sound that seemed to mock the silent energy of his own lust to reach Uccello. He saw the man stop at a windowed pent and throw himself against the frame, seeking a way down from the roof. He kicked at the window until Mercer was only twenty yards from him and then swung away and ran on, lost for a while in the dark shadow of the great Campanile towering over the square.

Mercer plunged through the shadow and was out in the brilliance of lights that came back from the front of the Basilica of San Marco and the pale cream run of the Ducal Palace. Leaping the breaks in the runway where short walls swept down between the roofs, he saw beyond Uccello the black spread of the great lagoon and towering above it the white, light-spangled bulk of the liner anchored in the fairway, and he knew that there was no farther the man could go. They had come round the great sweep of the square and were now on the short leg that ended above the wide quayside. Cutting across the run of roofs rose a wall about eight feet high and beyond it a drop to the spread tables of a café. He saw

Uccello make a jump for the top of the wall and fall back. The man turned and stood waiting for him, and as Mercer came on Uccello raised his revolver and fired. Two shots.

The first drew sparks from the stone pediment of the roof. The second smashed into the tiles at Mercer's left hand and the splinters bit into his cheek and hand. He came on careless with anger as Uccello leaped on to the balustrade. Uccello turned sideways and fired. The bullet tore through the cloth of his shoulder and Mercer felt himself swung sideways.

Staggering, he flung himself forward and reached out for the man's legs. A foot smashed against his neck and he went backwards, pulling Uccello with him. They fell together in the wide gutter, and rolled there, panting, twisting, the frenzy of their struggle a dark confusion of striking arms and legs. A lean pair of hands clamped Mercer's throat and he felt the tortured heave of his lungs fighting for air. He struck at the shadowed face above him and a violent pain soared savagely through his wounded shoulder. The fingers about his throat tightened and he felt the laboured breath of Uccello hot across his face. Drawing strength from his agony, he jerked up his leg and drove his knee into the softness of the other's body.

Uccello rolled over, then rose, swaying, his hands pressed against the pain in his body. Mercer saw him struggle to the parapet, a black figure against the light-flooded sky. He saw the arms raised in a ragged, unsteady supplication as the man reached for the top of the wall. He rolled over, seeking to follow him, and as he pulled himself up he heard the thud of a bullet against bone and flesh and saw the man's arms swing in a wild balance for a moment. Then Uccello dropped away out of sight. A carabiniere raced past him, his rifle still half raised, and peered over the balustrade.

An age afterwards it seemed he was leaning over the wide stone parapet, looking down. A ring of carabinieri was holding back a crowd, a dozen café tables stood empty, red and yellow discs against the dark pavement, and one of them was crushed and twisted. By it, contorted in an ugly sprawl of limbs, lay the body of a man in a white shirt and dark trousers. A carabiniere rose from beside the body and stood undecided for a moment, then his eyes turned upwards. Spadoni at Mercer's side leaned out and, seeing him, the carabiniere moved his hand gently in a negative gesture over the body. A waiter came out from under the arcade and Mercer watched him drape a dark cloth about the still figure.

Mercer drew back and the movement

made him unsteady. Spadoni's hand held him, and the man said:

'We must get someone to look at your shoulder, signore.'

'There are a lot of other things to take care of, too.'

Spadoni nodded. 'They'll be done, signore. Thank God – there's time.'

Mercer turned away. Beyond Spadoni, her back to the parapet, Adriana was standing. He went slowly towards her. Her face was pale, immobile, and she looked straight ahead of her, her eyes still and shadowed with despair. He knew that in this moment there was nothing he could say or do which would give her life. He put out a hand and touched her. She moved like a sleep-walker, turning away from him and stepping over the stone ridges of the guttering with the care and abstraction of one passing down the dark corridors of a dream.

He followed her, the movement of his body pulling against the torn muscles of his shoulder, sending long fingers of pain through him. To his right the golden horses on the Basilica of San Marco reared towards the sky. The murmur of the crowds in the square was lighter now, relief and hope running through it. And, against his own pain, Mercer felt hope rising again in him.

This Large Print Book, for people
who cannot read normal print,
is published under the auspices of

## THE ULVERSCROFT FOUNDATION